Acquisition of Power

Erika Barr

PublishAmerica
Baltimore

© 2002 by Erika Barr.
All rights reserved. No part of this book may be reproduced in any form without written permission from the publishers, except by a reviewer who may quote brief passages in a review to be printed in a newspaper or magazine.

First printing

ISBN: 1-59129-307-3
PUBLISHED BY PUBLISHAMERICA BOOK PUBLISHERS
www.publishamerica.com
Baltimore

Printed in the United States of America

For Bryan

Acknowledgments

To my wonderful stepfather, Stephen Gottesman, thank you for making my dream a reality.

For this work of fiction, I had several factual questions. Thanks to Bryan Taylor for his invaluable assistance and further insight into how mergers play out. To Mariou Gottesman, for her ideas and skillfully-crafted Greek phonetics. To J. Kirby Taylor, for his answers to questions about monopolies and acquisition technicalities. Thanks to Paul J. Koskey for telecom input.

My thanks to the draft readers of this book for their support, suggestions, and encouragement: Christine Rowland, Elizabeth Oliver, Donna Rector, Desmond Bond, and Shannon Burleson.

Chapter One

1

"Greed is good." The sound from the television reverberated from the den, through the dark hallways of the Connecticut mansion.

James Atherton liked to watch Oliver Stone's *Wall Street* when he felt down. The character of Gordon Gekko amused him. Like Gekko, Atherton was wealthy—he as the result of his company, EPIK—but the comparisons stopped there. Atherton was kind and compassionate, something rarely seen in the corporate world. No wonder his employees revered him.

"I'm much better than you, Gordon Gekko," Atherton whispered to himself. "You're just a figment of someone's imagination…I'm the real thing."

A voice interrupted his musings. "I wouldn't be so sure of that."

Atherton cringed; he recognized the familiar, mocking voice. Only his father had the power and the privilege to reduce him into what he feared most—a loser, a dreamer, a nobody.

"I didn't hear you come in," replied Atherton. He refused to turn and face his father. There was no point. James Atherton Sr., or Senior, as he liked to be called, had an uncanny way of reading people. If his father saw his face, he would instantly sense his son's fear and anxiety. Don't give him that satisfaction, Atherton repeated to himself.

Senior darted towards the television. Anticipating his father's next move, Atherton switched off the movie with the remote control. Senior stood in front of the television. He appeared ghostlike; the television's remaining gray haze outlined his image. It was too dark for the men to see each other, but Atherton felt his father's knowing, steady gaze.

"Quite frankly, I'm surprised at you," started Senior. "You have a crisis on your hands, and what do you do? You sit there in the dark watching a video."

"It makes me feel good…you wouldn't understand it," countered Atherton. He paused momentarily, before continuing. He felt drawn into the familiar argument but resisted the urge to cease bantering. Something inside screamed to engage the old man, to let him have it this time.

"Care to join me for a drink, Senior?" asked Atherton. It was a rhetorical question, designed to annoy the old man; Atherton, Sr. despised alcohol.

Senior glared at him. "Nah, you go at it alone, boy. Besides, it couldn't make your predicament any worse."

Atherton refilled his tumbler, grimacing as Senior started his usual degradation process. He knew Senior derived pleasure from belittling him but was never quite prepared for the onslaught of abuse which came every time they got together. In one mighty gulp, Atherton emptied his glass; the cognac burned the back of his throat. Closing his eyes, Atherton reviewed the events of the last few months which had led to his reacquaintance with his nemesis, Dean MacNamara.

It had started when a technology analyst from the *Wall Street Journal* commented that EPIK's technology could lead to a great partnership with Anexa, MacNamara's telecommunications giant. Articles began to appear in the industry's respected journals and newspapers lending support to the partnership concept: two dynamic but complementary companies, both based in Manhattan's Silicon Alley, destined to unite. Rumors circulated for months within EPIK, but Atherton chose to remain quiet on the subject.

No one else had mastered U.S. wireless Internet communications like EPIK. Atherton lured scientists and executives away from Japan's NTT DoCoMo company to build his own version of the I-phone, equipped with cash cards ready for Internet commerce. The key to his success was not only EPIK's products and services, but the creativity of the employees to market it all. Easy-to-use phones, fast access to popular content sites such as stock quotes, sports, weather, soap operas, and news, combined with fast, built-in billing for e-commerce proved an instant success in the States.

The sound of Senior's cough broke Atherton's reverie.

"I see you're still here," said Atherton. Senior's unwanted, lingering presence usually coincided with a crisis. "You know, things are not as bad as you think. Did I tell you that EPIK has switched over eighty-five percent of PC-based Internet users to our own technology?"

Senior distorted his face. "Did I tell you that EPIK has switched over eighty-five percent of PC-based Internet users to our technology?" he ridiculed. "Don't insult me by throwing around your marketing statistics.

It's all that stuff that got you into trouble in the first place. I knew your success would be short-lived. It was only a matter of time before someone wanted a piece of your action."

Atherton's body stiffened. His father was right. At one time, even Goldman Sachs pronounced EPIK's vision as a technological revelation, a sure thing in the stock market. Now, they saw things differently. EPIK's continued dominance in the marketplace could only happen if partnered with a telecommunications company to penetrate more markets. Too bad the desired telecom partner was Anexa, MacNamara's Anexa. How Atherton and MacNamara had managed to stay clear of each other for so long was startling. Atherton knew it was only a matter of time before he had to face his rival.

Senior continued his cruel tirade. "Why bother with all the partnership crap? Let MacNamara take you over and save you the hassle." He paused, before adding, "And it wouldn't even be a challenge for him."

Atherton clenched his fists in anger. "Stop it," he cried out. "That's enough, Senior."

"Enough? I haven't even started yet," replied Senior coldly. "You're not smart enough to go up against a player like MacNamara. If you think a partnership will work, you're more stupid than I thought. MacNamara will finish you off and return you to the dismal life you started with. You're no Gordon Gekko. Face it, you were meant to fail."

Atherton's voice escalated. "I said, stop it Senior!"

His father ignored him. "Bye-bye pretty wife," he sang. "Bye-bye security, bye-bye power, bye-bye—"

Damn him, thought Atherton, slamming his fist on a nearby glass table. The tremendous force behind the blow shattered the heavy glass, scattering slivers across the marble floor. "I'll prove you're wrong! Know this. No one will tear my company apart."

2

Lucy Atherton had always been an early riser. She liked the peace of the morning, to sip her English tea in bed and to decide her plans for the day. Today, she watched her husband dress for an important meeting. He was a handsome man, who looked much younger than his fifty years, thanks to a healthy lifestyle of exercise and diet. His olive skin still held the tan from their recent trip to Tortola. As he groomed his jet-black hair, she noticed a few white strands; they enhanced his appearance giving him a distinguished yet alluring quality. Lucy watched the way women stared at her sexy husband

and instead of feeling proud, she found herself fuelled with insecurities. Atherton selected a tie and completed his dressing.

"God, that tie is so gauche. Perhaps, you could wear the striped Gieves and Hawks one I bought in London, last week?" asked Lucy.

Atherton looked at her with piercing blue eyes. He shook his head, wondering what went through his wife's mind. While he was mentally preparing for an important meeting, all she seemed to care about was the way he looked.

"It's not right for you."

Atherton ignored her protests and completed the Windsor knot on his Hermès tie. He liked this tie with its little animal characters. It had special significance, too. Gillian had presented it to him during their last rendezvous, around her neck, naked.

He walked over to his wife and gave her a peck on the cheek. "Lucy, you know I have an important meeting with Anexa's corporate team today. Don't give me any grief, okay?"

Lucy pursed her faded, lipstick-stained lips together. "I just want you to make a positive impression. You know, Bunny's husband is on their Board. You remember Barry Moore, don't you?"

"Yes, I remember him," he said, trying to remain as pleasant as possible. She was out of her mind to think Barry Moore was an ally, but now was not the time to debate it. It was impossible to predict what comment would set her off, and the last thing he wanted to do was to upset her. Today was an important day for EPIK. It was his responsibility to remain clearheaded and and focused.

"Tonight will be another late night so don't wait up for me," said Atherton.

"In that case, could you look at those fabric swatches on the dresser? They are for the new curtains in the living room. I want to give the room a richer feel," she added absently. *Greed is good.*

"Sure," he mumbled, wanting to leave as quickly as possible. He fingered through the brocade pieces and made his selection. "The gold one's fine," he said, holding it up for her inspection.

"Yes, I thought that, too."

"Let's hope that they last longer than the last set," he muttered, remembering she had redecorated the whole house only last year. Soon, he would have to put an end to her excessive spending. Even the wealthiest man on earth would struggle to keep up with her demands.

"Did you say something?" asked Lucy between her sips of tea.

"You have fun, dear."

"Love you, *dahling*." She waved at his exiting form. Lucy was too involved in her own world to catch his sarcasm. For her, today was just like any other day.

3

As her husband left, Lucy thought about her lunch date with Bunny. She flipped through her wardrobe, trying to decide which outfit to wear.

"Would you like some more Earl Grey, madam?" a voice interrupted her selection.

Lucy smiled. It was Carl, her new, young estate manager. He often surprised her by performing tasks not normally required. "Why don't you show mama how happy you are to see her this morning?" She reached out, unzipped his trousers, and grabbed his penis.

"Well," he said. "I would rather screw…than serve the tea." He removed his clothes and crawled into bed.

Lucy demanded the usual missionary position. After she felt satisfied, she pushed him away, turned her back, and dozed off. Carl kicked off the rumpled duvet cover and watched her body stir, twitching in a dream state. He sighed at the sight of his selfish, older lover.

4

James and Lucy Atherton grew up worlds apart.

Lucy's father, Sir Alexander, had accumulated a vast fortune, which allowed the family to own property in South Africa, a villa in Southern France's fashionable Cote d'Azur, a four-story house in London's Eaton Square, and a twenty-five-room, chateau-style mansion in Greenwich, Connecticut.

When in residence at any one of the properties, Sir Alexander employed a staff of housekeepers, nannies, cooks, gardeners, and his own house manager, to provide for the family's every whim. Twice a day, English tea was served. Cooks prepared freshly baked cakes and a selection of cucumber and salmon sandwiches. Another ritual, maintained from the colonial lifestyle, was the drinking of Sundowners. Sir Alexander would invite friends over to drink Martinis, or chilled Chablis, while watching the sunset. He spared no expense satisfying his every whim, or the whims of his spoiled daughter. Weekend trips to Bali, shopping trips to Paris, were common when Lucy was on break from Cheltenham Ladies College, her boarding school, in England.

Lucy grew up to think everyone lived as excessively as they did.

While Lucy led a privileged life, surrounded by wealth and all its trappings, Atherton struggled to overcome his humble, if not poor, beginnings. He fought his hardships by studying in school and setting his goals high. Atherton decided that he would be the first one in his family to make it big in the corporate world. When Harvard university offered him a full scholarship, he was on his way to fulfilling his dreams. Atherton spent several years consulting for Accenture, then Deloitte and Touche, before landing a partnership at the top-drawer consultancy firm of McKinsey. Lucy's father, Sir Alexander, one of McKinsey's most important clients, frequently requested Atherton for his projects. Atherton enjoyed this merger and acquisition work, and eventually accepted an offer to work for Sir Alexander.

"Son, I will be able to teach you so much more than you ever learned at university or in the consulting world. Join me and get ready to embrace the fast track," said Sir Alexander with shining eyes. "I will be your mentor. I will show you the intricacies of corporate politics. I will also introduce you to the finer things in life," he laughed, referring to their mutual interest in beautiful, *paid*, companions.

As Atherton secured his position with Sir Alexander's conglomerates, his father felt betrayed and abandoned. Instead of sharing in his son's success, he sought to degrade him and to remind him of his true roots.

"Hoity-toity, that's what they are!" exclaimed Senior, referring to Lucy and her wealthy father. "Boy, when are you going to stop dreaming? People like that will never truly accept you. You're out of your league."

Atherton laughed. "A little jealous today, aren't we? Just admit that you're happy for me."

Senior snickered. "Never."

"If you cannot bring yourself to congratulate me on my business success, at least, wish me well in my marriage," Atherton said in resignation.

"What marriage? Are you crazy? Don't tell me you would really marry that stuck-up bitch? You're only doing it to get your hands on her money."

Atherton sighed heavily. "Senior, her name is Lucy and I would prefer it if you remembered that. On second thought, I demand it."

"Demand all you want, but I will never do it. A whore, no matter how rich, deserves to be treated that way."

Atherton shuddered. Senior had gone too far.

"Father, if you can't accept my wife and treat her with respect, then I don't want to see you."

"Then, so be it," said Senior, smiling. "Mark my words, the prodigal son will be back."

5

Unlike Senior, Sir Alexander was thrilled to learn of Lucy's plans to marry his star executive. Insiders within the family said Sir Alexander wanted Lucy to produce a legitimate heir, so he could continue his legacy.

"Atherton, I don't have to tell you that my daughter is the most important thing in my life, outside of my companies. I assume you will do right by her," declared Sir Alexander.

"Sir, my intentions are honorable. We are in love and want to get married as soon as possible, before Lucy starts to sho—"

Sir Alexander interrupted him. "She's pregnant, isn't she?"

"Yes," confirmed Atherton. "Lucy and I want to name the baby after you if it's a boy," Atherton said proudly. Finally, he was going to be surrounded by a real family.

As a wedding present, Sir Alexander gave Lucy and Atherton the Greenwich mansion for their primary residence. Lucy set out to redecorate the property. She studied the design works of Paul Manno and Stephanie Boudin, who had decorated many of New England's finest homes including the one owned by the infamous Pamela Churchill Harriman. Sir Alexander had known Pamela's husband, Averell Harriman, the U.S. ambassador to Britain during World War II. Lucy relied heavily on Pamela for maternal friendship.

"You should tour my home, *Willow Oaks*," Pamela told Lucy. "My Louis XV and XVI pieces are exquisite."

Through Pamela's connections, Lucy created a magnificent house with European flair. Instead of solely relying on designers and their toady entourage, Lucy visited the decorator showrooms—to purchase antiques, fabrics, and paintings. At Sotheby's auction house, Lucy was known to bid, last minute, on Louis XV pieces; she had acquired a taste for them after visiting *Willow Oaks*.

For the formal rooms, she favored French Walnut Louis XVI pieces, antique mantels, dramatic silk curtains in bold colors, and even commissioned an artist from Paris to paint murals. One depicted Michelangelo's, *The Creation of Adam*. The dining room had an elaborate Baccarat crystal chandelier, boasting thirty-three lights, twenty-two candelabra arms, with three Cherubs each holding a wreath. Each bedroom was painted in pastel hues of green, rose, and taupe. In her bedroom she had a circa 1890 sleigh bed, in French Walnut, and a five-panel mirror. She was very proud of the Louis XVI mahogany gentleman's desk, with its black leather gilt-bordered top, which she displayed in Atherton's study. The only part of the house without immediate French influence was the living area. Here, the lady of the manor commissioned sofas and chairs overstuffed with down and covered with soft flowered chintz.

Lucy took pride in her excruciating attention to detail while the household staff found it impossible to keep up with her high standards and obsessive need to create the perfect house. All the sheets had to be hand laundered in soap from Paris and pressed with lavender water. Fresh flowers had to be displayed in every room, even ones no one occupied. Every morning, her personal maid brought her ice water and exotic selections of tea on a silver tray. Houseguests of the Atherton's were treated to Fortnum and Mason gift baskets upon their arrival. *Town & Country* magazine dubbed it the 'new' *Ma Maison*, a take-off on Napoleon's own home in France. Lucy loved this and sometimes, half jokingly, referred to herself as Josephine Bonaparte.

6

That James and Lucy remained happily married surprised most skeptics; they did not believe the whirlwind marriage would last. Together, James and Lucy braved two tragedies: losing their first child through a miscarriage and having their second child stillborn. It was Lucy's excessive drinking which emotionally separated the couple. Sir Alexander anticipated his daughter's behavioral problems becoming long term. He crafted his will accordingly, hoping to buy off his son-in-law. When Sir Alexander died of a fatal heart attack, Atherton learned he would assume control of half of the family's companies, on condition he did not divorce Lucy. Despite this twist, it had not crossed Atherton's mind to leave Lucy, despite frequent protests from his ever-present father.

"Leave the drunken cow," said Senior. "You've got what you wanted, so get out. You have money in your own right."

"Lucy is still my wife."

"If she's your dutiful wife, then why do you pay for that European piece of ass? Explain that to me!"

Atherton hated it when his father resorted to crass putdowns. "Look," he said firmly. "I'm not leaving her and that's final!"

"You mean you're not leaving the money or the power," said Senior. "Your pimp father-in-law knew exactly what he was doing when he changed his will. He knew how to keep you from bailing out of the marriage."

"Not true," said Atherton.

Senior laughed. "I know you better than you know yourself."

Chapter Two

1

Anexa's headquarters consisted of a series of towers. Building One was devoted to sales and marketing. The head of research and development led his team in Building Two. Finance, customer services, and other internal business services functioned in Tower Three. The latter housed Anexa's venture capital group which funded wireless Internet Communication start-up companies and acquired existing ones. This group had recommended EPIK as a target.

The existing Board of Directors could only be described as a dream team: celebrated *Business Week* entrepreneurs, wonder-boy MIT and Stanford graduates, razor-sharp attorneys, and opportunistic venture capitalists. Anexa's savvy CEO, Dean MacNamara, created a no-nonsense, high-performance culture, which rewarded its employees with stock options and high salaries. It was not unheard of to find a techie college dropout who had developed a new product, or an executive who had brought a desired pre-IPO company to the merger table, to be rewarded with millions worth of stock options. Anexa did not recruit employees in the traditional sense, by interviewing at top universities, or by placing job advertisements. Instead, an elite placement group hunted recruits then decided whether their potential was worthy of Anexa. One did not decide to work for Anexa; Anexa decided.

Talks with EPIK had been set up. MacNamara assembled his executive team in the main conference room: Barry Moore, Chief Legal Counsel, Priscilla Meyers, Anexa's Chief Strategist, and Cam Phillips, the VP of Global R&D.

Before the EPIK executives arrived, MacNamara had some words for his crew.

"Priscilla, I would like to thank you for positioning our analysts at Bank

Global. After the *Wall Street Journal* article appeared last month, I really liked our prompt reaction by having them tout EPIK's shares."

"I suspect Bank Global is betting on us to use them for future mergers," she said.

MacNamara looked at her and smiled. While her aggressive and forthright nature would have put off most people, MacNamara, on the other hand, was amused by it.

"Priscilla, you know, there hasn't been a formal merger announcement," MacNamara teased. "But if risk arbitragers start heavy buying of EPIK's stock and short selling our shares, it will give us the market's stamp of approval. As you all know, professional traders only do this when they think a merger will be successful."

Barry snickered. "It will be nice to see James Atherton's head on a platter, just like John the Baptist's."

"Don't make me go there, Barry. Everyone knows that Atherton and I have been rivals since Harvard days…this is not why we want EPIK, right Phillips?" asked MacNamara, making a subtle gesture by avoiding use of Phillips's first name. MacNamara hoped Phillips picked up on it.

Phillips did not seem to notice and continued to play with his Armani tie. It was odd to see the head of R&D so well-dressed. Usually, he was spotted wearing jeans or chinos with flip-flops in his daily routine with the techies. MacNamara disliked casual attire in the office, so much so that he venomously opposed any suggestion of Anexa following America's move toward business casual. The only reason Phillips and his team got away with it was because MacNamara needed them. Phillips's eccentric management style appealed to his engineers; they pledged sole allegiance to their leader. They placed Anexa on top of the U.S. telecommunications market. But MacNamara hated being placed in a subservient position, catering to Phillips's demands and his over-budget pet projects. Unfortunately, there was room for only one leader at Anexa.

Phillips proceeded slowly. "EPIK's Internet wireless technology is what everyone wants. I hate to admit this … even my group struggles with the complexities achieved by EPIK technology. Atherton has done an excellent job of mastering this niche area."

That's perfect, thought MacNamara. I have a legitimate excuse for eliminating him—poor performance and technical ability.

Priscilla elaborated on Phillips's assessment of Atherton. "He is also a risk taker. Just look at how he obtained market share. EPIK was first to market in the United States because they ignored wireless application protocol. They used existing available technology, namely the Web's open-standard, hypertext transfer protocol."

"Don't forget that brilliant marketing vision aimed at our culture's core. He embraced the philosophy of *information is power* and used it to save time and money," added Barry.

MacNamara looked pleased. His Board was coming to the same conclusion that he had reached months before.

"You have all hit upon the very reasons for which EPIK should not partner with Anexa. We should merge."

The excitement of the moment was interrupted; MacNamara's secretary announced the arrival of James Atherton and his group.

As they assembled around the oak table, MacNamara took Atherton aside and whispered in his ear. "How is Senior these days? Still talking to him behind closed doors?"

Atherton turned sharply to face MacNamara. Keep calm and focused, he told himself.

"MacNamara, you have done well for yourself. Just look at the views from these windows," said Atherton. "I am very impressed. I understand that you, too, derived your company's name from Greek?"

MacNamara's and Atherton's eyes locked briefly. "If my college Greek is still any good, EPIK is an abbreviation of the word communication, e*pikoinonia*," said MacNamara.

"Good, very good, Mac," said Atherton, continuing to patronize MacNamara. "And to think that you failed most of your college Greek courses. Obviously, you've improved since then."

MacNamara showed good sportsmanship by pretending to laugh along with his rival's bad jokes. Let's see who's laughing when you leave the meeting, thought MacNamara. Just thinking about what was coming up gave him great satisfaction.

As MacNamara and Atherton introduced the players, the meeting's agenda was distributed. Immediately, Atherton noted that the agenda had been titled: 'Merger.'

Atherton quietly whispered to his legal counsel. "No wonder MacNamara wanted me at this meeting. Everyone knows a CEO does not attend joint venture meetings. I believe I have unwittingly shown my support for his merger idea, just by being here."

His lawyer nodded, without speaking.

"MacNamara, before we begin, I would like to stress that we are not here to discuss a merger agreement in any form!"

MacNamara waved his hand dismissively. "Oh, my secretary must have made a mistake with the title. But what a good idea! Come on Atherton! Don't tell me that you have not considered a product extension merger. We are selling different but related products in the same marketplace."

Atherton should have known better than to have expected anything less from MacNamara. Damn him. The slightest mention of the word merger meant that he wanted to proceed with a takeover.

Avoiding eye contact with MacNamara, Atherton began, "Ladies and gentlemen, let's talk about a technology partnership. We have a proven business model which we would like to leverage into the Pan-European marketplace. EPIK believes that both companies can profit if we share the technology and customer base. It's the only way it can work. Our company cultures are too different even to consider a merger. Our corporate climate has never been better. Employee satisfaction is at an all-time high, R&D is producing incredible products, and sales are excellent.

Barry interrupted. "Have you forgotten about little Mr. Green? Surely you know, your Board and shareholders would make a pretty penny if this deal went through."

Greed is good. There it was again, thought Atherton.

"Barry's right, Atherton. You've gone soft on me. Tell me, how many employees do you have? Around a thousand worldwide? With that highly paid workforce, it's only a matter of time before your competition catches up and puts you in the red. My bet is that the competition will be able to produce your technology for less, with fewer people, and sell it for nothing."

"Cheap, cheap, cheap like a chicken," said Barry, eliciting chuckles from the Anexa team.

MacNamara stood up, put his hands into his trouser pockets, and casually walked over to the vast, west-facing window. The weak, winter sun had just disappeared below the horizon, leaving behind a peach-and-white-washed skyline. Light snow fell from the bleak sky, dusting the manicured grounds below. MacNamara spotted the tiny dot of a maintenance man distributing salt on the pavement, while a bundled employee hurried past him, no doubt coming back to work. He was fortunate people wanted to spend all their time at Anexa, not like other companies where employees waited desperately for five o'clock. He relished the serene view from this height, thinking this is how God must feel.

"Let me reinforce my position here," stated Atherton firmly. "First, streamlining my workforce is not an option and second, EPIK is not interested in a merger." He eyed the blank faces of the Anexa officers staring back at him—unconcerned and bored. Atherton rubbed his palms against his woolen trousers, surprised at how sweaty they had become, and waited for MacNamara's impending rebuttal.

MacNamara rubbed his temples to eliminate residual pressures. He took pleasure in feeling his powerful breath fill his lungs. It was time to make his move. Purposely keeping his back to the group, MacNamara spelt out the terms of his agenda. "Atherton, our courtship is over. It is my intention to orchestrate an arranged marriage. It's in the best interest for all parties involved. Anexa, EPIK, our shareholders, and our customers. I'm disappointed you can't see this."

Atherton was furious. "Hold on just a second! Maybe you're deaf, or something. EPIK's *not* for sale. The next thing I am going to hear is that this meeting is our due diligence meeting. I wouldn't put it past you to keep the security analysts and investors hidden from view, so they can obtain enough information to assess whether this merger is worthwhile. Where have you hidden them?"

"Your accusations are absurd. I suggest you take a five-minute recess to clear your mind," said MacNamara, hoping to further aggravate his opponent.

"Screw you! You snake, MacNamara! Do you hear me?" he yelled.

MacNamara closed his eyes. He smiled and thought about Sun Tzu's Chinese military essays, *The Art of War*, 'Agitate him and ascertain the pattern of his movements.' Atherton really had changed, MacNamara thought—so easy to manipulate. It was time to finish the kill.

"Tomorrow, we will send you our tender offer to start the process. I believe that you will find our combination offering of cash and securities too hard to resist. Let me leave you with this thought. No matter how many measures you put in place to discourage this merger, they will not work. I'm afraid such shark repellent has never worked on me. So try to be pleased Atherton. Your shareholders, a group which I believe includes your wife, will be thrilled to know that after months of speculation, there is a real buyer after all."

"MacNamara, forget your tender offer. You can take this Saturday night special and shove it up your ass," announced Atherton. He silently cursed himself for being blindsided. Surprise maneuvering was Mac's specialty.

MacNamara smiled. "For those of you who are interested. Anexa is derived from the Greek word for independence. This is something Mr. Atherton will not have for long."

2

Atherton was badly shaken by MacNamara's intentions to take over EPIK. If the merger proceeded, it was only a matter of time before Anexa destroyed everything he had built. Anexa's way of doing business included streamlining costs by reducing headcount, replacing top executives and scientists with its own breed, closing various facilities, and using outsourced personnel to replace permanent headcount. Inevitably, EPIK's creativity would vanish in Anexa's mammoth bureaucracy.

"What did you expect would happen? That MacNamara would agree to a partnership so you could access his marketplace? Don't say I didn't warn you!" Senior furthered Atherton's misery with his cutting remarks.

Atherton was not about to admit he had underestimated MacNamara, least of all to his own father. His ego was bruised. It was ludicrous to assume MacNamara might have acted differently.

"Fine, you made your point. Just leave, so I can think," said Atherton.

Senior pointed a finger at Atherton; any closer and he would have poked Atherton in the chest. "Just be grateful you can talk to me whenever you want."

3

Atherton called an emergency meeting with his team and the EPIK Board. He was not prepared to lose EPIK, especially to MacNamara. "You have probably all heard what happened at Anexa. We need to take some immediate action."

He knew he could trust, and count on, his people. They had all been with him since EPIK's formation. His colleagues were not just business advisors; they were friends, too. He and Lucy frequently invited them to *Ma Maison* for various holidays and functions. Atherton needed them, more than ever. He looked around the room and saw the concerned faces of his allies: Lord Richard Palerno, a famed venture capitalist, Jack Murray, Chief Legal Counsel, Michael Montgomery III, Harvard friend and financial advisor, and Yoshi Tachiwa, EPIK's head scientist and former DoCoMo employee.

Palerno was the first to speak. "James, we are all behind you. Perhaps it is your moral influence, but the team is ready to try to stop this nonsense."

"I wish Harvard had expelled MacNamara when they found out about his plagiarism," said Montgomery.

"Michael, I'm afraid he's still not over the humiliation that his best friend turned him in. We were not only roommates but close friends," said Atherton.

"So this is revenge?" asked Tachiwa. "Angry...betrayed by his best friend?"

"No, there's more to it. It's about two people who are too much alike. Isn't it true you and MacNamara spent your Friday nights memorizing quotes from *The Art of War* and fantasizing about corporate mergers?" wryly laughed Palerno.

"Come on guys. This is serious. We better talk about what we can do to fend off this attack. Let's talk about some shark repellent," said Murray. He was always the serious one in the group.

"Okay people, let's get our plan together," said Atherton. "I don't care if it takes all night."

Montgomery grunted. Atherton raised an eyebrow at his colleague's apathy. "Why don't we start with you, Montgomery?"

Montgomery scribbled into his Palm Pilot. "Hmmm. Let me look into our financial obligations. We could immediately accelerate any due debt should the merger happen. That way, Anexa would have to pay our bills up front."

"Good idea. The more deterrents we can think of to dissuade Anexa from merging with us, the better." Atherton turned to face Lord Palerno. "Richard, I want you to look into the possibility of EPIK combining with another telecom company, in order to fend off Anexa," said Atherton. "I would gladly merge with someone else rather than jumping into bed with MacNamara and his Hitler Youth movement."

Murray piped in. "Let me review any antitrust or regulatory laws which might create problems for them."

"Excellent. Another thing Jack, when that tender offer comes in, I want your legal team to put that offer under a microscope. Let's exploit anything and everything that would give us good PR exposure with the shareholders," said Atherton.

"Consider it done," confirmed Murray.

"Dare I mention selling off some of our product lines? It might deter Anexa," offered Tachiwa.

"Ouch. I don't want to consider that," said Atherton, rubbing his chin. He stood up. "Assuming Anexa makes their merger announcement, I want us to issue a press release stating that EPIK has reviewed the provisions of the deal and believes it would be in the best interests of the shareholders for EPIK to remain independent, blah, blah, blah...you know, the standard spiel."

"Shouldn't we see their offer first?" asked Montgomery.

"Shit, whose side are you on? You know what will happen to this company if MacNamara gets his hands on it," said Atherton sternly. Some of the things that Montgomery came out with were juvenile and idiotic. Did he not understand the importance of what Atherton had built up over the years? At times, Atherton regretted hiring his goodtime buddy.

Montgomery looked down in shame. Why did Atherton insist on treating him like an ignoramus? Surely, his position on the Board merited better treatment and respect.

"Another thing about the press release. I want us to announce a special warrant to current shareholders, effective immediately," said Atherton.

"Is this the extent of the poison pill?" asked Palerno.

"Yes, I think that's enough," said Atherton. "The shareholders will be able to buy discounted EPIK shares. Does anyone have anything else to add?"

"One thing," added Palerno. " …moral influence…causes the people to be in harmony with their leader, so that they will accompany them in life and unto death without fear of mortal peril.'"

Atherton smiled, recognizing the Sun Tzu quote. After thanking his team, he asked them to reconvene when the follow-up work was done. Unfortunately, in his haste to leave the meeting, Atherton had failed to notice the sarcasm of Palerno's final comment.

4

Gillian du Monde was one of few exceptional courtesans remaining in the world. As a former mistress of a European prince, Gillian had been introduced to Europe's wealthy, which secured her position both socially and financially. When she tired of the same social set, she relocated to the United States where she entertained the dot-com millionaires and other nouveau riche clients. She liked her new clientele. They were generous, fun, and typically easy to please—not like her European customers, who would complain about her buying sprees. Gillian only had two or three clients at one time. It was important to focus on each, as if he were the only one. She made mental notes of each man's favorite foods, clothes, hobbies, sports, books, and daily routines. She even went as far as securing each man's spouse's birth date, to remind him of the event, so he could reward his wife with a gift. Her motto was: keep the wives happy and secure more time with their errant husbands.

One of Gillian's most important skills was that she was an incredible listener. She would act as if what her client had to say was the most important thing in the whole world, injecting only enough to keep him talking. She knew how to cater to the fragile ego of the American businessman; behind his polished veneer was an insecure boy in need of coddling, reassurance, and distraction.

At thirty-five, or so she claimed to be when pressed about her age, she was young enough to choose selectively her clientele. But she was no fool. She knew her looks would not last forever. It was important to establish financial security through marriage, soon.

When Atherton had called Gillian, saying he was coming over, she knew from his tone that the meeting with Anexa had gone sour. Over the next hour, she prepared for his visit. Gillian chilled his favorite white wine, arranged a tray of fresh fruit, soft Bries and whole wheat crackers, selected the music, and lit some scented candles. For herself, she ran a hot bath, scenting it with a small amount of Lady Primrose bath gel—just enough to leave a subtle aroma on her smooth skin. Gillian delicately sponged her skin, inspecting every inch of her body for unexpected flaws but could not find any. After her bath, she applied a scent-free lotion all over her body, and sprayed Cartier perfume into her lush, crimson mane. Gillian touched up her makeup—not that she needed much on her creamy flawless skin—a touch of shimmery powder, a stroke of brown mascara, a hint of pink gloss. She added a little rouge to her décolletage and nipples.

Atherton arrived at Gillian's high-rise apartment in Manhattan's Midtown. He kissed his beautiful mistress, passionately. She drew him closer to her, teasing him.

"Hello, handsome," she said. "Welcome back. Why don't we have a drink out on the deck?"

She opened the sliding doors. James followed her closely, looking on approvingly at her perfect petite body showing through a transparent dress. He could see that she was wearing a La Perla G-string—she rarely wore any other brand of lingerie. Gillian turned on her stilettos, posed, and leaned against the balcony's rail—pert 36C breasts displayed hard nipples poking through silky fabric. *I am so lucky to have such a beautiful woman*, Atherton thought.

He had grown fond of Gillian. At first, he had viewed her only as his physical companion; now he relied on her as confidant, too. Atherton still loved Lucy but not like before. Her heavy reliance on alcohol and antidepressants disgusted him. Pills were for losers. With regular exercise and a positive attitude, he concluded, she could overcome any problems or obstacles in life. Instead, to his dismay, she preferred to do things her way, to seek the companionship of booze and pills. The intimacy he lacked with his wife was fully provided by Gillian.

"Gillian, I really could use a glass of wine," he said.

"How about a crisp Cloudy Bay?" she purred, pouring the hard-to-come-by New Zealand white wine into a glass and handing it to him. She smiled seductively at him and thought how good she was at her job. Soon, he would make her the next Mrs. Atherton.

Atherton took a large sip and put the glass down. He moved his hands over her torso, tracing the outline of her breasts. "You really look lovely this evening. Just the kind of distraction a man needs. The last thing I want to do is go home."

"So don't." Gillian moved his hands down her tiny waist and rested them on her full hips. She wanted to know what happened at the meeting—to find out if Atherton was still a player—to decide whether he was still worth the effort. "James…it's not like you to be rattled. MacNamara must have really surprised you."

He stiffened, moving his hands away from her body. "Jesus, Gillian. I was a fool. First, MacNamara set me up by having me attend his joint venture meeting. Then to make matters worse, he ignored our partnership idea and announced he was only interested in a merger."

"Interested in a merger," she repeated. "Hmmm."

"More like a takeover." His voice vibrated in aggravated tones. He clenched his fists. "Goddammit," he hissed, furrowing his brows intensely. "MacNamara will have to fight me to the end. There is no way, I will give EPIK over to *him*."

"Yes…right." She sipped at the chilled wine, savoring its smooth flavor. She patiently waited for him to continue before prompting, "Uh, huh."

"Well, he can try all he likes…my wife, Lucy, and I still own significant shares, which we would never sell."

Gillian stared at the red furrow between Atherton's eyebrows. *My wife, Lucy*, she repeated silently, as if *her* name was news. More disturbing to Gillian though, were the words, *we* would never sell. Had she miscalculated his feelings for the witch?

"Senior was right not to trust him," said Atherton.

Gillian looked at him strangely. She was confused. "Who?"

"Enough talk. Please take my mind off my problems," he said gruffly, leading her into the bedroom.

She took her dress off and moved on to the bed. "Why don't you have a closer look at my panties?"

He put his hand over her mound and immediately noticed something missing. He looked down and smiled. Gillian had treated herself to a Brazilian bikini wax.

"Very nice, sweetheart." He took off the minuscule material and admired her smooth skin. "Maybe my tongue could visit?" he teased.

Gillian moaned as he touched her. Between waves of pleasure, she wondered if MacNamara was capable of destroying Atherton.

5

One of the perks of holding Anexa's CEO position was that MacNamara had the company jet at his disposal. If he desired, he could spend weekends anywhere in the world. MacNamara frequently chose to spend his free time in California, enjoying solitude and fresh air on his Harley Davidson. It was a perfect way to wind down after a stressful week, or to calculate his moves on the next business venture. With the different microclimates around San Francisco, Palo Alto, and Napa Valley, it made sense for him to wear a leather jacket, T-shirt, and jeans; it could be warm and sunny one minute or cold and cloudy, the next.

He secretly liked the informalities the West coast had to offer. This fondness was probably a reaction to the structured and formal life he led back on the East coast. MacNamara's wife Tamara, one of New York's popular socialites, filled his calendar with society events, when she was not busy entertaining at *Windermere*, their estate in Westchester County, New York. He dreaded these events because it meant spending time with her.

"Going away dear?" asked Tamara. She already knew the answer but asked the question mechanically. Tamara did not care what he did on his own time, as long as it did not interfere with her busy social schedule.

"Yeah, I'm going to California. I'll be back late Sunday night. I have an early start on Monday." It was not unusual for him to work seventeen or eighteen-hour days. He had created an intense work ethic at Anexa, which he personally upheld.

"Don't forget the AIDS research dinner on Monday night at the Plaza Hotel. Wear the black-label Armani," she said, devoid of emotion. Tamara was on constant autopilot.

MacNamara averted his eyes towards the ceiling. "By the way, I've asked

Barry to join me this weekend. We need to talk some business."

"Sure, whatever Mac."

She glanced down at her French-manicured hands. It was commonly known that both Barry and MacNamara had roving eyes. Tamara did not mind it too much. She and MacNamara had not slept together in years. MacNamara did not push the issue; her bedroom skills were not worth the effort. It had been no surprise to him when she had suggested they keep separate bedrooms. Actually, he had welcomed the idea as it gave him freedom to come and go as he pleased.

Tamara continued with her lecture. "Just try to be discrete. I've worked very hard to get where I am today."

"Yeah, I hear you."

"Oh, and before I forget, have a nice trip," she said absently.

Pleasantries, thought MacNamara, summed up the extent of his banal marriage.

6

Barry was pleased when MacNamara had requested his presence for the weekend. MacNamara's invitations came infrequently; he rarely trusted anyone to accompany him on his biking pilgrimages. Indeed, a good sign, Barry thought. Maybe, MacNamara planned to promote him to Chief Operating Officer and wanted to discuss it with him.

MacNamara had other plans, though. He was still on a high after the meeting with Atherton, and wanted to have a post-mortem with Barry to review what had transpired. MacNamara replayed the meeting, over and over; he could not believe how Atherton had looked such a sucker. The way Atherton had walked right into his trap was simply delicious. Keep up the good work, MacNamara thought—it was essential to keep the momentum going.

As usual, the pilot landed on a private airstrip, just outside Palo Alto. Barry emerged from the jet looking like a cat that had just swallowed the canary.

"I hope you enjoyed your ride on the corporate jet. I don't let just anyone use it, you know," said MacNamara.

"What's not to like? Though, if I did have to complain, it would be about lack of air pussy on the flight."

MacNamara and Barry laughed together.

"I have the same bike for you that you had last time. Why don't we go to breakfast first, discuss some business, and then spend the afternoon cruising?

There are some things I need to talk to you about before we go riding."

"This is your show, man. I'm game for anything." Although, he was still on East coast time, Barry welcomed the chance to eat breakfast, again. "Any chance of getting some Douwe Egberts coffee out here?"

"Barry you're so nouveau riche, it kills me. Fucked if I know where to get that particular stuff," snorted MacNamara. "This is California where they live on great coffee, so I'm sure you can find something acceptable."

"If you don't ask, you don't receive," replied Barry.

"Actually, someone recommended a place where all the VCs hang out on weekends. I'm sure you can get a decent cup of coffee, there. Last time I went, the food was not spectacular, but the atmosphere was intoxicating. It's common to see VCs dressed in biker leathers, making dot-com or other tech deals, while eating greasy bacon and eggs. After business is done, it's Harley-cruising-time!"

"I can't imagine venture capitalists going to a place like that," said Barry. "Could you imagine posh whipping boy Palerno, hanging out there? What a laugh!"

MacNamara smiled. "You would be very surprised at who you might meet there. I'm sure even Palerno has been…"

Barry looked over at MacNamara. Despite being tired, he picked up the inference. "Mac, do you have a new boy at EPIK?" Maybe MacNamara had got to him? Palerno's English boarding school attendance made him a perfect target for MacNamara. If he had led a life of servitude in school, it would be easy for Mac to turn him into his fag. Men like Palerno, were waiting for a chance to replay their roles from schoolboy days.

"I knew it! You have, haven't you?" said Barry.

MacNamara smiled, furtively. "Time will tell."

7

When MacNamara and Barry arrived at the breakfast joint, they were forced to park their bikes at the back. All the front parking spots were taken up, Harley after Harley. This scene looked like a Harley Davidson convention, or something straight out of biker week at Daytona Beach, Florida.

"God Mac! Where on earth did you find this place?" Barry asked, removing his helmet.

"Pretty cool, isn't it?" I love to watch the VCs making big deals over breakfast, followed by their adolescent bike comparing out front," said

MacNamara.

"I suppose it's like being at the urinal, comparing your cock against the next guy's."

"Something like that."

Once inside, it was a cacophony of deal making and mobile phones ringing. They both decided to eat the Lumberjack's special, a breakfast consisting of pancakes, eggs, bacon, grits, toast, fruit, coffee, and orange juice.

"All I need to eat now is a bran muffin to make me shit for the rest of the day," said Barry.

"That's what I've always liked about you Barry. What you see is what you get. You're a man's man."

"Well, you've known me for too many years to expect anything else. How many goddamn mergers have we been through together? Ten? Fifteen?"

"Fun times. Speaking of which, what did you think about Atherton's hasty exit?"

"Pretty funny. You ran him right out of there." Barry knew how to play up to his boss. He prided himself on being an excellent ass-kisser.

"I enjoyed reading our press release yesterday, announcing our intention to merge with EPIK. I bet Reuters' followers had a field day! I assume the official packet was delivered to EPIK?" asked MacNamara.

"Yes, the tender offer was couriered over to EPIK, yesterday morning."

"I want us to prepare a follow-up to our press announcement. Let's hit hard at the benefits and synergies of this merger. Also, include in it something about my track record for running efficient companies. I want the shareholders to conclude we have offered a great deal—the best deal!"

Barry shifted in his seat. "Mac, your offer's generous. I certainly wouldn't have offered EPIK shareholders two Anexa shares per EPIK share, or assumed all the EPIK debt."

"That is why you are not CEO," said MacNamara smugly.

Barry pretended the remark did not faze him, though it did. MacNamara was the only one he allowed to get under his skin.

"Okay, Mr. CEO let's talk about getting some of the big block EPIK shareholders to buy into our plan."

"I like that. That would give us important leverage with anyone who was unsure about the deal. Obviously, we can't use Atherton's shares…maybe, we could get to his wife's, somehow?"

"Well, I was thinking more along the lines of securing the support of some hedge fund managers who own major blocks of EPIK stock," said

Barry. It was an excellent idea, and he knew it. He hoped Mac recognized it, too.

"We can do that, but I want you to figure out how to get Lucy Atherton's shares, just for the fun of it," said MacNamara.

Barry looked confused. For MacNamara not to get excited about good business advice was out of character. Did he really want to hurt Atherton that badly by attempting to drive a wedge between Atherton and his wife?

"Come on Mac, you can gain control of EPIK without getting personal."

MacNamara was silent.

Barry saw a flash of anger cross Mac's face.

MacNamara took a sip of the coffee and stared at Barry. Everything was personal. Barry should have known better than to utter such absurdities, thought MacNamara. He knew Mac's favorite line from *The Art of War*: 'All warfare is based on deception.'

"What did I say?" asked Barry.

MacNamara continued to stare.

"Oh, don't ask me to do that. We don't need her shares." Barry worried he would have to resort to shady dealings to acquire Lucy's shares. He had already gone to prison once and had vowed he would never return.

MacNamara's eyes darkened. He cleared his throat before speaking in a menacing tone. "Where do you come off acting like Barry the Righteous? As if you have some value system to uphold with your screwing around, drinking, and taking drugs."

"Hang on a minute—"

"Before me, there was no Barry. I made you!" MacNamara lowered his voice, when he realized other patrons were staring in their direction. "Do I have to remind you of your shithole existence in Detroit, where no one would touch you because of your record? Do you actually think that Bunny would have married you if you didn't have the lifestyle trappings I gave you?" he hissed. "Don't forget who brought you into Anexa."

Barry was stunned. "As your attorney, I—"

MacNamara interrupted him. "Let me make myself perfectly clear. You work for me! I want you to get Lucy's shares! Make this acquisition happen, at any cost!"

"Oh…uh…I see…well…" mumbled Barry.

MacNamara slapped his open hand on the table. "Lighten up Barry, you know how I like to kid around. Enough talk, let's go riding, my friend."

Barry knew MacNamara well enough to recognize he was not capable of cracking jokes about his business. He followed MacNamara outside and watched him talk to some VCs in the parking lot about their bikes. His attitude and countenance had changed, completely. There was no hint of the anger or malice, which Barry had witnessed, only moments earlier. Jesus, Barry thought, Jekyll and Hyde right before my eyes.

Chapter Three

1

Like her friend Lucy Atherton, Bunny Moore came from a privileged upbringing. Bunny had constantly rebelled against her environment, causing her blue-blooded parents much grief. At the age of six, following the family tradition, she had been sent off to boarding school.

Bunny excelled at her studies and sports but found herself unpopular with the school authority. She was expelled from several boarding schools for offenses such as smoking, drinking, and ignoring curfew regulations. Bunny's parents ignored most of her pranks, blaming her behavior on lack of maturity. Finally, they took notice when she was caught sleeping with a female student.

"Bunny, this is the new deal. Either you follow our rules and values, or face financial and emotional castration. It's as simple as that. Your mother and I have had enough of your wild ways," Bunny's father reprimanded her sternly.

Bunny was astute enough to know that her father meant business. He rarely raised his voice to her; this time, she knew she had pushed him too far. Better not upset the Puritans, she thought. If they fulfilled their threat, going without an inheritance was trouble. She quickly got her act together.

Her parents' patience paid off; Bunny was accepted to Hampton, the exclusive liberal arts college. During Bunny's junior year, her mother encouraged her to study abroad, just as she had done as a young woman.

"Darling, it's essential to complete your education with some sort of European stint. I just loved my days at the Sorbonne," said Bunny's mother, hoping Bunny would choose the same path.

"Mummy, if I do this, I want to escape the people I see everyday at Hampton College. What about a year abroad at the London School of

Economics?" asked Bunny. She hoped her parents would jump at the chance for her to attend the school—famous for its alumni as for its intensive programs. Bunny remembered reading somewhere that JFK had attended it, as well as Mick Jagger. If it was good enough for these party boys, it was good enough for her.

"That's a wonderful idea," said her father, a respected lawyer in the community. "I believe it has an excellent legal program, too. You might just find yourself an up-and-coming young lawyer to marry," he chuckled. "I was hesitant when your mother suggested this finishing school idea, but the more I think about it, the better it sounds." Handing over his problematic daughter to another man to deal with was extremely appealing. It could even save him some money.

Bunny had other ideas. She had no intention of ruining her party-going freedoms by marrying a boring lawyer. Besides, how could she tie herself down when she was not sure if she even liked men? Just tell the parental antiquities what they want to hear. "Papa, wouldn't it be so nice if I were to marry a lawyer?" she lied. "Hopefully, he would be just like you."

Bunny's mother could not have been more pleased her daughter had succumbed to her way of thinking. "Well, then it's settled. You can go to England, but on one condition."

Of course, the conditions. Bunny knew that the discussion had been going too smoothly.

"I don't want you to live in university housing," said her mother.

"But Mummy," she pleaded, realizing she would be cut off from the mass partying contingent.

Her father agreed. "No arguments, Bunny. We allowed you to live on campus at Hampton only because it was a private girls' school. It was bad enough that you lived practically like a servant in that shoebox they called an en-suite. Those English dormitories or halls of residence, as they like to call them, have unisex bathrooms. No daughter of mine will be subjected to those dreadful, backward conditions."

Unisex bathrooms were the furthest thing from her mind. "You two win. Where shall I live?"

Her father had thought up a solution. "One of my partners has a daughter who finished her studies in London. I think he told me she shared a flat in Chelsea with a girl named Tracy...no, maybe her name was Lucy."

"Papa, you decide what's best."

Bunny's parents were thrilled to learn that her prospective roommate was the daughter of Sir Alexander. They were not the only ones happy with the arrangement. Lucy instantly liked Bunny's vivacious, larger-than-life persona and welcomed the gregarious American.

"You're the chicky in all the society magazines," teased Bunny.

"Yes, just last month, I was on the cover of *Town & Country* and featured in Britain's *Tatler* magazine. I'm so pleased you noticed!" gushed Lucy.

"Well actually, my mother told me you were. I really don't care about gossip or, for that matter, parlor games," said Bunny.

Lucy laughed at Bunny's candor. "I can see that I have a lot to teach you. Something tells me, we're going to be great chums."

2

Bunny and Lucy remained close friends, over the years, sharing all aspects of their personal lives with each other. It was Lucy who suggested to Bunny that she move to Connecticut when her husband accepted a job at Anexa. Lucy found Bunny a beautiful Stanford White-designed home in New Canaan, just 30 minutes from *Ma Maison*.

Lucy introduced Bunny to her inner circle of friends. They encouraged Bunny to take up bridge, tennis, and golf. Bunny had no real interest in social events or hobbies, but she did them to please Lucy. It was not uncommon for Bunny and Lucy to see each other at least twice a week—for lunch in New York, for a charity event, or for a game of tennis.

Bunny and Lucy maintained their friendship, despite their husbands' frosty relationship. Since Barry worked for Atherton's chief rival, it was not possible for the men to form any type of friendship. When the merger of Anexa and EPIK was announced in the press, it threatened to complicate Bunny and Lucy's friendship.

"This whole merger idea is going to give my husband a heart attack," Lucy told Bunny over lunch.

"Come on Lucy, he's an athletic specimen! Just look at the way he works out. He runs ten miles every day."

"Even athletes suffer heart attacks," Lucy sighed, miserably. "Does Barry talk about *it*?"

"*Talk* about it? That's *all* he talks about—takeovers, mergers, whatever. It's like he's on a twenty-four hour high."

"James says that MacNamara planted the 'intention to merge announcement' in the press."

"Of course he did," Bunny snorted.

"Do you think Anexa will really take over EPIK?" asked Lucy. She was understandably worried. This merger would remove another link to the father she still worshipped. "I bet my father is rolling over in his grave."

"Don't be so morbid, love."

"Do you think maybe this merger thing would be good for both companies?" asked Lucy innocently. She knew little about business, leaving her husband to run the entire show. Somehow, she was beginning to think that her EPIK holdings might become important.

"Oh, I really haven't given it any thought. Listen, this is all too serious for me. Let's order a bottle of that snooty champagne you love and get sauced." It had been ages since they had got drunk together. Lucy loosened up after a few glasses of bubbly. Bunny often hoped they could repeat the time they both had had too much and ended up in bed. Lucy pretended not to remember anything while Bunny could not forget their intimate encounter.

"You've twisted my arm. How could I pass up drinking Cristal on such a beautiful afternoon?" Lucy rarely passed up an offer to drink.

As the waiter poured champagne into flutes, Lucy giggled and proposed a toast.

"To our friendship. May nothing come between us."

"Or man come between us," said Bunny.

Lucy blushed, took another large sip and felt the bubbles tickle her throat. "I have something to confess."

Bunny felt goosebumps. She had hoped for this moment for so long. "Do tell," said Bunny, refilling their glasses. It was going to be a fine afternoon.

"You remember my new estate manager?" asked Lucy.

Bunny was confused. What did the estate manager have to do with a confession? Surely, Lucy was planning to confess her love. What if she was wrong? Don't push things, if she's not ready, thought Bunny. Play along and find out what's up. "Sure, I remember your estate manager...Carl, right?"

Lucy giggled.

"Come on...out with it, girlfriend!" demanded Bunny. Bunny had already guessed the worst.

"We're sleeping together," she whispered.

Damn, thought Bunny. "Well no shit, Sherlock. You're fucking him. Maybe you could reintroduce us? That's, if you're willing to share." If it was the only way she could see Lucy, then so be it.

"Bunny, you naughty girl." Lucy felt lightheaded from the champagne. "Are you having lesbian flashbacks from your boarding schooldays?"

"Possibly. You went to an all-girls' school, too. Don't tell me you never compared tits and bush in the showers."

"Bunny, I never did."

"Tell the truth!"

"Well, maybe I sneaked a little peak," laughed Lucy. "But that doesn't mean I'm gay."

"In time, you'll come around."

"What did you say Bunny?"

"Nothing darling. Let's get the check. I'll take you home."

3

Carl was in the study when Bunny brought Lucy home. He heard the commotion in the main foyer and went to see what was going on. Lucy had an arm around Bunny's shoulders, and Bunny kept her upright by holding her around the waist. Another foolish outing with Bunny Moore, he thought. Lucy was paler than usual. She looked frail. Alcohol disagreed with her, especially in combination with her antidepressants. Bunny helped Lucy upstairs and put her to bed.

"Looks like you two had quite *the* lunch," he called out to Bunny, as she opened the front door to go home. "Oops, what I meant to say was, liquid lunch," he cackled.

Bunny froze, irritated by Carl's juvenile wisecracks. Why was he always lurking in the background? Bunny found it suspicious Carl would take a job as an estate manager for the Athertons. With an economics degree from Harvard, he seemed overqualified for the position. Besides, why would he waste his Ivy League qualification managing domestic staff and worrying about household tasks? Even if he was having an affair with Lucy, she was not reason enough to keep him at *Ma Maison*. Something, definitely, was up.

Bunny turned around and made her way back to the study. She paused in the doorway to study Carl, sprawled comfortably across Atherton's leather sofa. Stretched out, his athletic body was easily over six feet. He brushed his blond hair aside as it fell across his tanned face. Bunny noticed he wore his traditional outfit: a button-down shirt with the sleeves rolled up, a pair of khaki slacks, Gucci loafers without socks, and an English-style cravat. Carl was the poster boy for an Ivy League college. Bunny understood Lucy's attraction to him.

"I know you're…there," said Carl. "Watching me." He cocked his head to one side and met Bunny's gaze. "See, I knew you were there." Carl smiled broadly, flashing his perfect white teeth. He loved it when women looked him over.

Bunny crossed her arms. "Lucy and I go way back. It's good to get together and have some fun." She immediately regretted her words.

"So that's what you call fun, huh?"

"Just give her the rest of the afternoon to sleep it off," she said, annoyed. "Lucy will be fine by the time James gets home."

Carl nodded once and sat up. "It's my turn to…" He finished the sentence by mouthing the words, "check you out."

Bunny was slightly mousy but attractive in her own way. Her chestnut-colored hair, cut in a Louise Brooks-bob, framed her round face. She wore little makeup, from what he could see, except for sheer lipgloss, and a touch of mascara. What she lacked in model beauty, Bunny compensated for by dressing impeccably. She chose clean, simple-lined garments, to accentuate her tall, lean frame. She completed her outfit with subtle, gold jewelry.

"Stop gawking!" demanded Bunny. His stares made her feel uncomfortable—exactly what he wanted to accomplish. People hated the silent, aloof treatment he was so fond of providing.

Bunny watched Carl open up his monogrammed, silver cigarette case; he took out what appeared to be a hand-rolled cigarette. With elaborate movements, he lit the cigarette and inhaled. The rush hit him. He leaned back and uncrossed his legs.

"That's some cigarette you have there." She instantly recognized the aroma. "I bet the Athertons wouldn't like you smoking *that* in their house."

Carl held out the spliff and offered her a toke of the Thai weed. "I'm sure Mr. Atherton is too busy with his merger problem to care. As for Lucy, she's too straight to know any type of recreational smoke, legal or not. Besides, as you well know, she tends to favor the prescription and bottle form of pleasure. Lucy isn't a weed kind of gal."

Bunny sat down in an armchair, directly across from Carl. "Go on, give it to me."

Carl handed her the joint, and she inhaled quickly. "This is nothing," she boasted.

Carl smiled. "Try it slower."

Bunny repeated the exercise using his recommendation. Without warning, her body reacted. Her lungs burned, she coughed uncontrollably, and her throat caved-in as she gasped for clean air. This stuff was much stronger than the hashish she and Barry had smoked in college. Bunny passed the weed back to Carl.

"Careful, old dear. Don't overdue it."

Bunny felt an immediate rush. Instead of feeling mellow, she felt agitated and upset. "Don't *you* fucking old dear, me."

"Shhh...calm down. I'm just trying to look out for you."

"Yeah right. I wonder Carl, what is such a smart kid like you doing hanging around here? Surely, you could find a well-paid internship at one of the investment banks." She paused for a moment, trying to think of something else to say, but the drug made it difficult. "No, I got it wrong. Maybe a position as a walker in Palm Beach might be more suitable. I'm sure you could continue to swindle and to escort the ladies, there. You would get paid far more for your services."

"And leave my missus?" he questioned, pointing upstairs. "Not a chance." Carl took another hit. "Bunny, if I had to guess, I think you might be a tad jealous. There's no reason why we can't share her. In fact, I wouldn't mind watching your lipstick-lesbian action. I bet your influence could get her to change her conservative, boudoir ways."

Bunny didn't want to share Lucy. As for sleeping with Carl to be close to Lucy, Bunny decided it was out of the question. Carl was a smooth operator, a character not to be messed with. Her mind raced with the weed's stimulation. This impromptu session was too much for Bunny. She found herself losing control of her senses.

"You little shit, I'm going to keep my eye on you. Don't think you can fuck me over like poor Lucy. I've seen *your* kind before."

"Does that mean you're finished with the *Thai*?" he asked mockingly, handing her the weed.

Bunny greedily took one more hit and left.

4

After Bunny had gone, Carl finished the weed. He decided he was in the mood for some of Atherton's Scotch. After reviewing the liquor cabinet's selection, he decided on Glenmorangie's ten-year-old Ardbeg and poured it into a goblet. Carl liked to treat himself to fine things. Early on, he had decided he would live life to the fullest, experience everything, even at the expense of someone else.

Carl retired to another leather couch, this one near the large bay window. He positioned himself so that he could view both the foyer entrance, in case someone important looked for him, and the spectacular rose gardens outside. The effect of the drug and Scotch combination kicked in. He felt relaxed, comfortable, and warm. His tastebuds relished sweet liquorice, espresso and chicory notes. Life could not get any better than this. It was a far cry from his humble beginnings in the Midwest.

During his youth, Carl and his mother, Martha, lived in a state-subsidized house, sharing it with three other families. By American standards, they lived well below the poverty level. The bathroom frequently flooded sewage into the rest of the house. The house was infested with rats, mice, and roaches. Because they did not have money, the inside of the house was practically bare.

Cardboard boxes, containing old clothes, lay here and there. One of the families had a picnic table; everyone shared it to eat meals. The only piece of furniture that Martha and Carl owned was a second-hand couch, which doubled as Martha's bed. Carl did not have a bed; he slept on a cushion of blankets thrown across the concrete floor. At one time, drug dealers probably occupied the house; both the front and back doors showed evidence of repeated forced entries. Each family took turn at securing the house at night: the picnic table was moved across the back door, and several catches secured the front door.

To support them, Martha worked three housecleaning jobs. Unfortunately, there was seldom enough money for anything other than basic essentials—food, water, and electricity. Other children his age celebrated birthdays with presents and parties; Carl learned not to ask for anything.

"Hey retard, you're wearing the same pants you had on yesterday," taunted children from his school. "Your pants are so high that we should call them high-waters," they laughed.

Although he lived in a bad neighborhood, Carl was eligible to attend a magnet school for gifted children. He excelled at his studies and knew if he did well, it was his ticket out of this living hell.

"Momma, I'm going to get us out of here. Just you watch! I'm going to make you proud."

"Son, I'm proud of you just the way you are." Martha pulled out a plastic bag and gave it to Carl.

Carl saw through the bag. He recognized the set of collector comic books he had been admiring for months.

"But how did you know? We can't afford it."

"Carl, I started a new cleaning job. It's about time I got you a little something. Besides, the owner pays his janitorial staff quite well."

"What's his name? I want to thank him personally." Carl was so excited he jumped up and down.

"Son, his name is James Atherton. I'm sure you can thank him, sometime. Just remember to say an extra prayer tonight."

Carl forgot the name of James Atherton until several years later; he saw it in black-and-white, amongst his mother's important papers. Carl was stunned as he read who was the real father of Carl's stillborn baby sister. He was old enough to know that Mr. Atherton had a wife and concluded that his mother's employer had tricked his mother into sleeping with him. Containing his anger, Carl could not bring himself to ask his mother the truth. Instead, he built up intense hatred for Atherton. Carl was reminded of this tragedy every year, on the dead baby's birthday, when his mother's tears would mark her loss.

"Carl, have you said your prayers today?" asked Martha. "You know why it's an important day for me." She turned her head, so he could not see her tear-stained face.

"Mama, don't cry. Baby Alice is in heaven. She wouldn't want you so sad." He put his arms around her, trying to comfort her. "I said my prayers three times today," he lied. Carl had stopped saying his prayers the day his mother had lost her baby.

5

When Carl came to, he was aware of someone sitting next to him. His eyes refocused on the male figure and, to his horror, he saw James Atherton staring at him. He must have drifted off. Damn that Bunny Moore for goading him on! He would not have smoked so much had she not been there.

Atherton spoke first. "You discovered my Scotch. At least, you don't drink the cheap stuff. Next time, mix the Ardbeg with water. It's ninety-two proof, you know." Surprisingly, he did not appear to be angry.

"Well sir...you caught me." It was the only thing he could think of saying. "I must have slipped off after reviewing the household budgets."

Atherton chuckled at the absurdity of Carl's lie. He had guessed what had transpired after reviewing the remains of Carl's solo party. Atherton stared at the young man. He had something familiar about him; he was ambitious, he looked sad, he dressed to impress, he wanted the good life. *Greed is good.*

"Throw him out!" scolded Senior. "He's partying on your dime!"

"Quiet," hushed Atherton in defense of Carl. "He's just a boy. Leave him alone."

"Are you okay?" asked Carl, scanning the room for another person. He did not see anyone else. The hash must have been stronger than he thought.

Atherton understood Carl's confusion and, quickly, got rid of Senior. "Yes, I'm fine. I was just imagining what my father would have said if he had seen you lounging about like that."

"Oh yeah. I see your point." Carl shifted uncomfortably. "Sir, it won't happen…"

Atherton changed the topic. He was curious about Carl and wanted to find out more about him. "Did you go to college?"

Carl looked surprised. Atherton caught Carl off guard, as he did not expect him to be so personable. Carl had kept his distance from Atherton to avoid contact.

"Mr. Atherton, I studied economics at Harvard."

"Well, how about that. I went there. Merit or money?"

"Pardon?"

"Rich daddy or poor daddy?"

"Oh, I won a scholarship."

Atherton looked pleased. "Me too. You should be working for my company," he announced unexpectedly. "Even my wife says I have a knack for hiring good people."

"Maybe I could consider it, after your company fends off the attack," said Carl, referring to the merger announcements he had read in the press.

"How about that? An estate manager who reads the trade journals? I like you even better." He rested his hand on Carl's shoulder. "Do you know where I can find my wife?"

Carl felt his body stiffen. He did not like it when men touched him.

"Bunny left her upstairs."

Atherton frowned, looking up in the direction of the master bedroom. His tone turned serious as he responded curtly, "Carl, it was a pleasure talking to you. We'll talk more later."

Carl politely waved goodbye, then cursed under his breath. How could he have been so unprepared for that encounter? He would have to be more careful in the future.

Chapter Four

1

Barry and MacNamara's weekend trip to California proved to be successful. Not only did they devise a strategy to fulfill their bid for EPIK, but they also fitted in some free time in Las Vegas. It was Barry's idea to burn off some steam playing in the casinos and partying with hookers.

"Come on Mac, let's get some girls and have a private party. It is the least you can do for me after I agreed to ride those damn motorcycles, all weekend long. To tell you the truth, I would be surprised if the guy downstairs ever works again," said Barry, pointing to his manhood.

"How about this instead. I will pay for you to play out your wicked ways. You know I have no interest in sleazy hookers or cheap booze. Do what you have to do, and I'll see you in the casino."

MacNamara could not resist playing blackjack. It was his only real weakness.

"Just remember that I want to leave on the jet at midnight."

2

As soon as MacNamara and Barry had landed on the East coast, Barry telephoned Priscilla.

"Miss Meyers, I need to see you before you leave for work."

Priscilla had expected his call and invited him to come on over. He made excellent time and arrived in less than twenty minutes. Priscilla had given him his own key to her Central Park West townhouse but, on this occasion, he did not have a chance to use it. She had anticipated his arrival and surprised him. She greeted him at the door, wearing a revealing negligee.

"I like this kind of hello," he said, admiring her shapely body. Thanks to the fine work of her plastic surgeon, she passed for someone in her mid-thirties. Priscilla fiercely guarded her true age; Barry suspected it was around fifty. Her looks and body were sculpted to perfection. Her full breasts had been youthfully boosted by a lift, providing relief from heavy, ugly, brasseries. Priscilla showed off her ample assets by favoring sheer blouses without wearing undergarments. She repeatedly had her tiny waist liposuctioned, to accentuate her womanly hips. Knowing one of her best features was her slender, tanned, racehorse legs; she vigorously exercised them, performing strenuous weight and cycling routines. She wore open-toe stiletto heels, without pantyhose, to emphasize her toned legs and used a self-tanning cream to hide ugly varicose veins.

"How was your male bonding session with MacNamara? Let me guess. You dressed up in biker leathers and rode Harleys."

"Don't be a bitch, Priscilla."

"I suspect Mac must have read Jim Rogers's book, *The Investment Biker*, one too many times, and it went to his head. I can just imagine you two riding around California in your biker gear, trying to experience all that life has to give you. Are you facing a midlife crisis?" She giggled and went into the kitchen to fix coffee.

"Believe whatever you want," he shouted after her. Barry made himself comfortable, collapsing on to one of her custom-designed suede couches. He put his feet up on the coffee table and waited for her to return.

"Okay, give me the low down on what you guys are planning." She emerged from the kitchen, holding two coffee mugs. She poured a couple shots of Baileys crème in her mug and a few whiskey shots in Barry's cup.

"Mac doesn't want anything to interfere with the merger. He's so desperate for it to succeed that I don't think he's acting rationally."

"What do you mean?"

"Well, for example, he wants control of Lucy Atherton's shares. I told him it wasn't necessary, since we could get public statements from a few hedge fund managers to support the merger."

"And?"

"He absolutely freaked out. I have never seen him act that way, before."

"That's weird. How much does Lucy own anyway?"

"Five percent."

Priscilla raised both eyebrows. "Significant…" She paused to sip her coffee. "But not a deal breaker."

"Yup."

Priscilla smirked. "Mac must have a personal agenda."

"Yeah, I suspect so. Listen, you're good at dealing with these sticky situations. Do you want to try to handle this? I will be busy enough trying to locate the hedge fund managers owning blocks of EPIK stock," said Barry, trying to pass the buck.

"Gee thanks, the easy one for me." She clasped her hands around the warm mug. How could they get close enough to Atherton to get to his wife? She needed—an insider, a spy—someone Atherton would find irresistible. "Barry, let's hire someone to get close to Atherton, a fresh face with business smarts. She could persuade him the merger is a good deal, even go as far as blackmail him to gain control of his shares."

"What about his existing mistress?"

"Gillian du Monde is no businesswoman. That's why we need a newcomer."

"Hmmm. Priscilla, I like your idea. Mac will think it is straight out of his Sun Tzu bible, '...there are five sorts of secret agents to be employed...native, inside, double, living and—'"

"'Expendable'," she interrupted. I will contact Elite Placement to secure our person as soon as I get to the office.

"Great, then it's a done deal. Maybe Mac will want to investigate Atherton's mistress himself, just in case something comes of it. Speaking of which, do we have time for a little something?"

"Sure, let's adjourn this meeting my way." Priscilla winked, removing her nightgown.

"I'm all yours." Barry threw his hands up into the air and chuckled.

Priscilla put on a David Sanborn CD and danced sexily around him.

"More, more," said Barry, removing his own clothes.

"Are you going to be able to take what I have in store for you next?" she purred, eyeing his erection.

"Try me."

Priscilla straddled him and started to gyrate slowly.

"Can't you go any faster?" he pleaded.

"No. Put your hands around my neck and squeeze gently. I want to feel light-headed."

Barry did as he was told. In his many conquests, he had not been with anyone else who had wanted asphyxiation during sex. Barry had heard this forbidden pleasure was extremely dangerous to the recipient—suffocation, if choked too long.

Priscilla ignored the dangers and started to ride him faster. "Squeeze my neck harder," she rasped. "I'm going to come." After a few moments, she removed herself from him and looked down at his flaccid penis. "What's happened to you?"

In his efforts to prevent strangling her, Barry had lost his hard-on. "Priscilla, I think you're really sick. How do you expect me to enjoy myself? All I can think about is accidentally choking you to death and ending up back in prison!"

"Don't be so melodramatic," Priscilla hissed. She picked up her nightgown, muttering insults about his manhood. "If you can't get it up, I'm off to take a shower."

She could be such a selfish lover. Barry called after her, feeling used and abandoned. "Hey, what about me?"

"Do me a favor and don't ruin my upholstery when you *do* yourself," she called back. "It's fun to turn the tables on *you* for a change."

"Stupid cunt," he grunted, collecting his clothes.

3

Just when Barry thought he would have to search for hedge fund managers owning significant blocks of EPIK shares, MacNamara surprised him by giving him a list of contacts.

"I assumed you were not interested in my idea," said Barry, remembering MacNamara's outburst in California.

"Barry, it's an excellent idea. I wouldn't expect anything less than this from my number one," said MacNamara, trying to win him over. "I believe you will find these names useful."

Barry knew MacNamara well enough to know he would still want the Lucy project done. Barry placed calls to the hedge fund managers on the list. He found all three willing to hear MacNamara's position on the merger. All expressed concern about the whereabouts of the meeting. They wanted Anexa to ensure a clandestine location.

To maintain the strict secrecy desired, the meeting was held on a private yacht, moored just off Cumberland Island, Georgia. Before the meeting started, Barry caught up with MacNamara on deck. "You never fail to amaze me with your connections. How did you know that each of these guys had a five percent block of EPIK?"

"Stick with me Barry boy, and you'll do just fine."

Barry shivered beneath his navy cashmere overcoat, amazed at his boss's tolerance to the cold wind. "You know, you look like you're ready to go sailing…in the summer…not sit through a meeting."

ACQUISITION OF POWER

MacNamara dressed the part of a preppy yachtsman. He wore a crisp, white shirt tucked into chino pants. For effect, he had draped a navy blue sweater over his shoulders. His attire would have been perfect had it not been wintertime.

"Whose boat is this anyway?" asked Barry.

"Remind me to tell you after the meeting's over," replied MacNamara casually, heading down into the cabin to begin the meeting.

MacNamara started, immediately. "Gentlemen, thank you for your time. I'll get right to the point. The merger of Anexa and EPIK is a no-brainer. As our *Wall Street* announcement indicated, not only are we offering a lucrative deal for the shareholder, but we also have a vision to create an even more profitable company."

One of the hedge fund managers spoke up. "I wanted to say that your press release describing the potential synergies between Anexa and EPIK was excellent. I'm anxious to hear about your vision of the future."

This was the positive opening response MacNamara needed. "The German market is a must-have for any mobile phone company with Pan-European aspirations. You see, it's the largest mobile market in Europe."

"What would stop EPIK from partnering with Deutsche Telekom? DT already owns that telecommunication market," said another manager.

"Asia," stated MacNamara, smiling. "There's another deal brewing. Anexa and DT have entered into a deal which details a partnership between our Asian operations and their European operations. This deal is conditional, though. It will only go through if the Anexa/EPIK merger is successful."

"So, DT wants a piece of the Asian market, and you presumably want to profit from EPIK's Internet phone usage in Europe. That's clever," said the senior hedge fund manager.

Barry added some statistics. "Remember when analysts projected Asia would have one hundred and forty million wireless subscribers, with twenty percent of them being active Internet browsers? They were off by a factor of two. Of one point two billion wireless subscribers, Anexa owns sixty percent of the global market, thanks in part to Asia."

MacNamara continued. "Our global telecommunication infrastructure is in place to take advantage of EPIK's technology."

The hedge fund managers were impressed. "What do you need from us?" one asked.

"It's quite simple. I would like you all to support the merger between Anexa and EPIK, publicly."

"Done," they said in unison.

The senior manager stood up and extended his hand to MacNamara. "You have our support."

MacNamara pressed his lips tightly and nodded. "Thank you."

As a precaution, Barry and MacNamara let their guests leave first. When they were alone, Barry asked MacNamara about the yacht's ownership.

"It belongs to Lord Palerno."

4

While Barry and MacNamara finished their meeting with the hedge fund managers, Priscilla met Anexa's head talent recruiter. Using her EPIK-built mobile to contact Anexa's head recruiter, she had sent through detailed criteria describing the perfect corporate spy, capable of seducing Atherton.

"You put together quite a composite, Priscilla. I especially liked the digital photos you sent so I could find an appearance match," said the head recruiter. " Let me tell you about the candidate I have for you. She's a recent NYU graduate. Beautiful, intelligent, and savvy."

"Harry, I don't want an inexperienced recent graduate."

"Just take a look at her resume, photograph, and our background report. I think you'll change your mind."

Priscilla was struck by the girl's beauty. She had not seen such vivid, green eyes, before. The girl had thick red hair, dewy skin, and full bow lips. Priscilla glanced over the girl's resume. She took her time to read Anexa's background report. Priscilla was impressed. The report detailed the recruit's outstanding academics, her Phi Beta Kappa standing, internship at EPIK, lavish spending habits, and rejection of an offer from the C.I.A. Although the girl came from a modest background, Priscilla could see that, with her brains and beauty, the girl could easily live out her wildest dreams. More important, though, was Priscilla's instinct that the girl could be molded to fit into her plans.

"You were right. It looks as though Diana Roberts has definite possibilities. You outdid yourself on this one. Well done."

Harry was pleased. Priscilla infrequently thanked anyone. "Something else you might want to know. Our records show that she called Anexa last month asking for a job interview. Some coincidence, huh?"

"Set-up the date but let me handle the interview process. I have specific ideas on how to run it."

5

The Roberts family held on to their upper-middle-class standing by a thread. Diana's parents struggled to keep up with the moneyed lifestyle of their neighborhood. Her father was a college engineering professor, her mother a homemaker.

Early on, her father had tried to instill a tough work ethic. "Diana, it's important to focus all your energies on your career. We can't afford to put you through college if all you think about is dating and getting married. Don't waste your time with men."

Her mother, meanwhile, had filled her head with dreams of glamour and money. "Don't end up like me, a frumpy housewife. You should be one of those executives—wearing a suit, carrying a leather briefcase, and driving a fancy car."

While in college, Diana lived beyond her means. She replaced emotional companionship with material spending. She amassed several pre-approved credit cards, which she used to treat herself to designer clothes. With her monthly allowance from her parents and income from her part-time job as a research student, she was able to make the minimum monthly payments. Her parents were oblivious to her lavish possessions. When she went home for visits, which were infrequent, she made sure she left behind evidence of her spending—leaving the designer wardrobe back at her Upper East Side apartment.

To economize like other college students did not occur to Diana. Her dream was to live glamorously, and she was not willing to wait. Once, someone had told her she could manipulate anyone because of her incredible beauty. Diana did not forget it. She frequently used her beauty to her advantage.

Problems surfaced, close to graduation time. As she had increased her number of cards, she struggled to make the minimum payments, and missed several months worth. Creditors phoned incessantly and threatened to contact her parents.

One afternoon, while taking a break from pursuing lucrative job opportunities, she decided to have a coffee at Sammy's café. Using a whole table, she spread out her latest job offers to compare each package's compensation offering. Each promised a modest salary but did not appeal to Diana's yearning to become a highly paid, glamorous executive.

"Is this seat taken?" said a man's voice. What a ridiculous question. Anyone could see that she and her company letters fully occupied the table.

Diana looked up and saw a tall, handsome young man. She smiled at him but hesitated as she looked back at her papers.

"If you feel uncomfortable, I could sit somewhere else," he responded, running his hands through his thick blond hair.

Diana knew this guy could mean trouble. The last thing she wanted to do was to divert energy from her career plans by becoming involved with a man. There was something about him that caught her attention, though. He was too gorgeous to turn away.

"Please do sit down and join me."

He sat opposite her and extended his hand. "Carl Swan."

"Hello, I'm Diana. Diana Roberts. I've not seen you here, and I'm Sammy's best customer." He flashed a smile, remaining mum. Carl had been using his day off, to wander around Greenwich Village, when he had passed the coffee shop and spotted the beauty sitting alone.

Carl ordered another coffee for Diana and hot tea for himself.

"How very English, Carl," she teased, feeling her cheeks flush.

"Yes, it's something I picked up when I was in England."

Diana was impressed. While all her friends had taken exclusive holidays to Europe and the Caribbean, Diana had not left the U.S. "Were you there on business or pleasure?"

"Neither. I studied abroad for a year while an undergraduate at Harvard." He made it sound as though he came from family money. He had struggled to earn enough money for that year away. Between his studies, he had worked two jobs to save money. Carl collected his thoughts. He scanned her array of job offers. "It looks like your schooling is about to pay off."

"I'm not an Ivy Leaguer, by any means, but a state school gal with grand ideas."

He laughed. She had a winsome quality, and he liked it. Carl pointed to her pile of papers. "Any good offers in there?"

"Tons, but I'm holding out to hear from the company I really want to work for."

He was intrigued. "I bet they don't know how lucky they are. May I ask who it is?"

"Anexa, the telecommunications company. Have you heard of them?"

"Who hasn't?"

Diana was unable to tell if he was mocking or congratulating her.

"I've been offered a job at EPIK," he said indifferently. Carl neglected to tell her he already worked for the Athertons but in a different capacity. He had no need to advertise it. They were just two strangers.

"Well, make sure they give you stock options. If the proposed merger goes through, you'll be rich," she advised seriously.

He smiled, pleased by her consideration. "Would you see me if I told you I was already rich?"

What the heck, she thought, a nice Harvard boy couldn't do any harm. She grabbed a paper napkin and wrote down her number. "Here."

6

Priscilla received word from Harry that he had arranged a date for Diana's interview. What Diana did not know was Priscilla already wanted to hire her. Using the pretense of an interview, Priscilla planned to dazzle Diana by appealing to her monetary desires. With military-style planning, she organized an unforgettable day out in New York. Priscilla would spare no expense in gaining Diana's approval. She even planned how she would dress. Typically, Priscilla wore Prada or Gucci but knew she would have to knock Diana out. She opted for a couture Chanel suit, paired with strappy Manolo Blahnik stilettos, and a Hermès Kelly bag.

On the day before the interview, Priscilla couriered an EPIK phone over to Diana. When Diana turned it on, she found her itinerary.

7:00 a.m.	Chauffeur pick-up at home
8:00 a.m.	Helicopter ride over NYC
11:00 a.m.	Lunch at Le Cirque

Diana had expected a limousine to pick her up but was impressed when a chauffeur-driven Bentley pulled up outside her apartment. Once in the car, Priscilla called on the phone.

"I'm looking forward to meeting you, Diana. Are you ready to have some fun?"

"Yes, I am," said Diana. She knew of several investment banks, which lured recruits into employment by spending outrageous amounts of money on ski trips, dinners at top restaurants, even offering high-end BMWs as perks. She decided that if Anexa wanted her enough, they would have to pull out all the stops to impress her.

Diana's driver pulled into a private airport and drove up to a helicopter pad where Priscilla was waiting. To protect her freshly lacquered hair, Priscilla had covered her head with a Hermès scarf. Black sunglasses masked her eyes; she used the advantage to inspect Diana without being obvious. To

Diana, she looked like a model out of *Vogue* magazine. This is how I want to live, thought Diana—the Bentley, the clothes, the helicopter. *Greed is good.*

On board Anexa's private helicopter, Priscilla opened a bottle of Dom Pérignon and poured the champagne generously into glasses. Priscilla sensed Diana's exhilaration, which the young girl was trying hard to hide. It pleased Priscilla to know she had Diana just where she wanted. I have your number missy, contemplated Priscilla.

"To a successful interview, and to a special lady," proposed Priscilla. They clinked glasses and sipped their drinks.

"Do you always entertain like this?" Diana felt overwhelmed; the champagne went straight to her head and her adrenaline was pumping.

"Only people important to Anexa get this treatment. We like to reward achievers and dynamic executives working for us, as well as our top customers. But enough chatter, let's finish off this fantastic champers and get up in the air." Priscilla wanted Diana to feel comfortable enough to relax to let her hair down.

Diana had set her own agenda, too: keep focused, hold out for the best offer, and limit the booze. At least, she was on track on two out of the three goals.

After the spectacular ride, Priscilla whisked them off to lunch at Le Cirque. She had made sure they would have the best table and had persuaded the chef to include Diana's favorite foods on the list of specials.

Diana immediately spotted grilled sea bass with steamed vegetables on the menu. Normally, she avoided ordering this favorite dish because of the cost. With Anexa picking up the tab, she ordered it, happily.

When the moment seemed right, Priscilla made her move. "Diana, we want you to come work for us at Anexa."

The time had come to discuss the deal. Diana rested both hands in her lap and twisted her napkin. She took a deep breath and met Priscilla's gaze just as she had been instructed to do at college in the interviewing skills class.

"I have several offers on the table," Diana replied confidently. "What would persuade me to go to Anexa versus another company?"

"A smart girl like you has already done her homework. You know exactly where you want to go. Otherwise, you would have returned to EPIK, where you did your internship."

Diana reached for her iced water.

"Am I right?" pressed Priscilla.

Regain control, Diana commanded herself, find out what numbers they're willing to offer.

"Miss Meyers, it would be foolish of me to make a decision without considering all my options carefully," said Diana. Was she pushing too hard?

Priscilla diverted her attention away from Diana and signaled the waiter. "Yes, ma'am."

Priscilla pointed to her gold watch. "I'm afraid we're on a bit of a timetable. Could you please bring out our lunch?"

I've blown it, thought Diana. I've put her off. She watched Priscilla scan the room for familiar faces, purposely avoiding eye contact with her.

Priscilla was irritated by Diana's aggressive behavior. What was it about recent graduates who thought that the world owed them something? Diana was just another pretty, spoilt face, who needed someone to put her back in her place. Perhaps, a nice spot in the mailroom, considered Priscilla. That would cure the cocky attitude! But this was not the time, or the place, for that. She needed this girl to bring down Atherton. Just wait patiently, thought Priscilla, there will be a time to watch her grovel.

The food arrived and was placed accordingly.

Priscilla broke her silence. "How many other companies will make you an executive straight off, then give you European marketing responsibilities?" lied Priscilla. "If that's not reason enough, then the salary and stock options will more than take care of the lifestyle you already lead."

Diana's eyes widened. Her heart raced in anticipation. Was that an offer? Good negotiating skills!

"Before you eat—" Priscilla handed Diana an envelope, containing a slip of paper. "Read it. It will help you digest easier."

Diana read the two figures written on the offer. Never accept the first offer, her inner voice told her. *Greed is good*. Diana calmly focused herself and said, "I want fifty percent more stock options and a twenty percent increase in salary." There, she did it.

The little, grabby, conniving bitch! Better let her have what she wants, thought Priscilla. The end results will pay off. MacNamara will be pleased and promote her even higher. She extended her manicured hand to Diana. "Welcome to Anexa."

7

Barry and Bunny were having afternoon drinks when the phone rang. It was Priscilla wanting to fill Barry in on her day with Diana Roberts. Barry took the portable phone and his drink and headed for the privacy of his study.

"I wanted to let you know that our girl is in place. She has accepted our offer and begins on Monday."

"That's great. By the way, you owe me from the other day." Barry hated having to pleasure himself, especially when he had a capable woman who could do it for him.

"Get it from your wife," snapped Priscilla and clicked off.

Barry went back into the lounge and grabbed Bunny from behind.

"Christ, you scared me!" shouted Bunny. "What are you trying to do?"

Barry maintained his stance and whispered into her ear. "Maybe I could tie you up, just like the old days?"

"Barry, stop it! Don't be such an animal. I'm not in the mood. Besides, I want to finish my drink."

"Fine," said Barry. "You used to be a great lay."

Chapter Five

1

Just before Christmas, Tamara MacNamara hosted a holiday extravaganza at *Windermere*. At the beginning of each year, old and new money lobbied Tamara for the chance to see and be seen at her party. Approximately three hundred guests received invitations to this highly sought-after affair. Tamara's guest list was as spectacular as the party itself. What made her parties legendary was the eclectic mix of people she brought together. Tamara played hostess to politicians, minor royals, dot-com millionaires, artists, socialites, even pop stars. Guests expected parties with unusual themes from Tamara, who reflected the themes through the music, decorations, and food.

"Tell me, you haven't invited the Athertons?" MacNamara asked Tamara, knowing that Lucy recently had joined Tamara's bridge group.

She fidgeted with her diamond-faceted Cartier watch. "Actually, yes I have. Lucy and I have become rather close friends."

"We've not invited the Athertons before, why start? You couldn't have picked a worse time given Anexa's move on Atherton's company."

"Maybe instead of scolding me, you should consider thanking me," said Tamara, arching a perfectly plucked eyebrow.

"Do what?"

"I have given this some thought, you know. As you're planning a takeover, I have chosen a masquerade ball for this year's theme. This way, it'll be fun for you to watch your opponent, while hidden behind your mask. Besides, didn't you always tell me one should keep one's enemies close?" She knew she was right. Tamara looked pleased with herself.

"I didn't think you had it in you." Tamara brought up some valid points; perhaps this charade was not such a bad idea; perhaps Atherton would bring along Senior.

2

Lucy was excited to receive an invitation to the MacNamaras' Christmas party. She knew that all her socialite friends would attend, including her best friend Bunny. Maybe, she and Bunny would have time to fly to Paris to have something made, especially for the party.

Unfortunately, her husband was not keen to attend a MacNamara-sponsored party.

"You know, I hardly ask anything of you," she pleaded with Atherton, "but I really do want to attend this party."

"You understand what these people represent to us and to our company," he said firmly. "Lucy, we can *not* socialize with the people who are threatening to take over EPIK. It's insane!"

"I've become friendly with Tamara MacNamara. She's not the one who is after us. Besides, she's trying to extend an olive branch."

"They're playing games. I will not be a part of it. Besides, did you know that my whole Board has received invitations? It's out of the question. I won't go."

"Well I'm going, with or without you! My best friend in the whole world will be there, and I want to go," she added childishly.

"Suit yourself. I'll get Lord Palerno to escort you. I believe he's going, too."

"You see? If a rational man like Palerno's going, so can you."

"I said no, Lucy!"

"Find someone else to go with Palerno. I'm taking Carl with me."

"Suit yourself," he said, folding his arms across his chest. There was no winning her over.

3

Lucy made a special effort to prepare for the party. She spent an entire day in a New York City day spa, relaxing and pampering herself. She emerged, looking positively radiant. Lucy chauffeured her hairdresser to *Ma Maison*, so he could cut, color, and style her hair for the big night. She had him create a hairstyle adorned with crystal beads. Lucy opted not to buy a European dress. Instead, she had Badgley Mischka create a stunning, red strapless ball gown, shimmering with thousands of beads.

Lucy looked in the mirror and held up her antique gold mask.

"You look beautiful tonight," said Atherton, watching his wife get ready for the party. Part of him still loved the Lucy he had known years ago. He hoped she would, eventually, return.

Lucy put her mask down. "It's not too late for you to get ready, you know."

"Let's not get into all that…" Atherton delicately hugged his wife for several moments. He released his hold and put his hand under her chin.

"I have something for you to wear to your prom. Close you eyes." Atherton opened a black velvet box from Charles Krypell. He placed the spectacular necklace around her neck and, gently, clipped on the earrings.

"Look in the mirror."

Lucy opened her eyes. Atherton had selected an eighteen-carat, yellow gold, twist necklace, embedded with rubies and diamonds. The earrings were twisted and jeweled to match the main piece. She touched the necklace, then the spectacular earrings.

"Oh my goodness. They're wonderful. This is such a surprise." His timing could not have been worse, given Lucy's new feelings for her young paramour.

"Lucy, I know things have not been right between us for some time. I hope when this Anexa thing clears, we can start to put things back together. You could go into a rehab program to cleanse your body of those awful antidepressants. The doctors could help you combat the alcohol."

"You think our failed marriage is all my fault?" She placed her hands on her hips and glared at him. "I *need* to take antidepressants. It's medically proven some people have a chemical imbalance…I am one of them."

"I believe you're strong enough to overcome your issues."

She rolled her eyes and shook her head. "You're not listening to me!" Lucy turned her back to him and went into her closet in search of her evening shoes. "Why do I even bother?" she muttered.

"Fine, forget I mentioned the antidepressants," he shouted. "You could still use some drying out. The Lucy I married wasn't a drunk."

Lucy returned, holding a pair of diamante-strappy sandals. "Don't be ridiculous! I'm not a drunk."

"Oh God, just take a close look at your skin and hair! The alcohol has damaged you."

"A few minutes ago, you were telling me just how beautiful I look."

He nodded. "I know what I said but—"

"Stop your lecturing! I've heard enough for tonight."

Before he could respond, there was a knock at the door. Carl had been listening to their argument and decided it was time to save Lucy.

"What is it?" Atherton's voice rose in irritation.

"Sorry, it's Carl. I can come back if you wish."

"Just a minute," Lucy called out, "I'll be right out." She turned to face her husband. "Looks like my date is here."

Atherton grabbed his wife's arm. "Wait a min—"

Lucy pulled her arm away. "Don't touch me," she hissed, opening the door and walking into the hallway.

Carl noticed Lucy's necklace and matching earrings. He guessed the ensemble was probably worth around forty thousand dollars. Some people were born lucky, he thought.

"Why Mrs. Atherton, you do look especially lovely, this evening."

Lucy smiled, and Carl took her arm. It was nice someone noticed, she thought.

"Hey, don't be so forward with my wife," said Atherton.

"Oh, for heaven's sake, it's just my arm," said Lucy. She winked at Carl. "If he only knew," she whispered to Carl.

Atherton followed them outside to the waiting, chauffeured car. He turned to Carl.

"I want you to take special care of my wife. Leave the party by eleven-thirty and I want her home sober."

As he watched them leave, his gut instinct told him something was not quite right. Hope I don't regret not going with her, he thought.

4

When Lucy and Carl arrived at *Windermere*, they felt the electric atmosphere. Glamorous couples exited their limousines and walked on a red carpet towards the main entrance. Paparazzi screamed celebrity names and snapped picture after picture.

"Just like the Oscars," said Carl. It was his first black tie affair.

As Carl did not own a tuxedo, he decided Atherton owned too many tuxedos to notice one missing. Carl raided Atherton's closet and selected a tux that fit the best. After admiring himself in his newly acquired Calvin Klein tuxedo, Carl searched for appropriate dress shoes. Unfortunately, Atherton wore shoes two sizes larger than Carl. It was going to be hard to keep those shoes on, he thought. With luck, Lucy would not want to dance.

"Carl you look wonderful, tonight." Lucy nuzzled up to him and took in his aftershave. "You smell great."

Carl hoped no one was watching this overt display of affection. "Lucy, be careful. Let's not cause suspicion." The last thing he wanted was to upset

Atherton so soon. Carl still needed time to plan out his revenge and did not want to risk ruining the picture by having him find out about the affair.

"Don't you just love the way Tamara decorated her house?" asked Lucy.

Tamara spared no expense in creating a magical aura for her festivities. Outside, the house seemed covered with white lights; they reflected across the snowy lawns creating an endless white, cashmere blanket around the property. Burning torches, decorated with huge white bows lined the main drive. Hidden misters added fog to enhance the mysticism.

"Lucy, darling, I'm pleased you're here." Tamara greeted her friend at the entrance. "James couldn't join you this evening?" she asked, air-kissing Lucy on both cheeks.

"Something came up. Tamara let me introduce you to Carl, our estate manager." Carl bowed his head and moved her hand up to his lips, lightly kissing it.

Tamara blushed. "I'm so pleased to meet you Carl." She faced them and recited her party rules. "My parties are so exclusive no one, outside the revelers, knows what goes on within these walls. Two rules for tonight; first, you must keep your mask on at all times; and second, do not reveal what went on here this evening."

"But I've read all about your parties in the past," said Lucy. "I'm confused."

"That's what we send out and authorize the press to print. You won't find the media *in* here tonight. Let me advise you, the private party on the top floor is for the open-minded," she warned. "Please, go and enjoy yourselves." Tamara disappeared into a crowd of well-wishers.

Carl turned to Lucy. "Don't you think that was strange? Open-minded? Very curious."

"Maybe we should have a peak upstairs first? I know I'm a little curious."

Lucy and Carl journeyed to the top floor to find what Tamara had referred to as the 'private party.' To their surprise, they found what looked like a series of opium dens, designed to look straight out of the last century. Velvet curtains partitioned several rooms. Large silk cushions, trimmed with beads, were tossed on the floors. Real fires burned in each room, as did incense, which masked the smell of the pipes. Seated musicians played exotic tunes on tribal drums and horns. It was a modern day Bacchanalia.

"Would you look at that?" Carl pointed to masked attendants, with silver serving trays. From the waist up, each Adonis was bare, except for the scant cloth which covered the groin area. Their sole function was to hold out serving trays, offering guests a selection of hashish and marijuana.

"I thought your friend was pretty straight. I would not have guessed she was into all this."

"Frankly, it doesn't surprise me at all. Parties get harder to plan every year. You see, your guests expect you to outdo the last soiree," said Lucy, eyeing one of the robust attendants.

Carl caught her looking at the young man and quickly tried to distract her. He did not want her seeking amusement elsewhere.

"Hey Lucy, this is not my scene," he lied. "Let's go downstairs and find your friend, Bunny. Do you know what she'll be wearing?"

"I know exactly what her dress looks like, so we'll be able to find her. She told me to meet her in the main ballroom."

Lucy and her escort searched the ballroom for Bunny; MacNamara watched from behind his black demonic mask. He looked down at his watch. It was about time she showed up. He had been waiting for the Athertons. As he moved closer to the couple, he realized that Lucy's escort was not her husband. This was going to be better than he had imagined. MacNamara knew if he could have just a few moments alone with her, he could convince her to join up with the other side—Anexa's winning side. He made a mental note to reward Tamara for contriving this setup.

MacNamara timed his introduction perfectly, stepping out in front of Lucy and startling her.

"Lucy Atherton, I presume."

Lucy reached out for Carl's arm.

"Do I know you, sir?" Lucy did not recognize the mellifluous voice possessed by the tall, dark figure. The stranger's eyes seemed to dance, almost seductively, as he focused on her. She felt a strange sensation run through her body.

"Indirectly, of course," he played on, "but that's no reason why we shouldn't become acquainted immediately."

Carl spoke up on her behalf. "Look pal, Mrs. Atherton is not interested in playing your game, whatever that might be."

"And who might this be? Surely you're not James Atherton?" mocked MacNamara. "Hmmm...but I see you have the same taste in clothes." He noted the ill-fitting tuxedo and concluded this young man had made himself very comfortable in the Atherton household.

Carl squirmed at the scrutiny.

Lucy looked at the stranger closely. "You must be Tamara's husband, Dean MacNamara."

"When beauty is mixed with intelligence, it can be a lethal combination. Yes, I'm Dean MacNamara, but I ask my friends to call me Mac." He motioned for a huddled group standing in the corner of the room to join him. Ignoring Carl, MacNamara introduced Lucy to his entourage.

"Lucy Atherton, I would like to introduce you to friends, new and old. Please meet Priscilla Meyers, Cam Phillips, and Diana Roberts. Of course, you already know Barry Moore and Lord Palerno."

Phillips fumbled, first fidgeting with his enormous bird-like mask, before successfully extending his hand. "Pleased to meet you Mrs. Atherton."

"Me too," chimed in Priscilla.

Diana nodded and waved. Carl recognized her green eyes through her sequined mask. He moved away from the group, so he could sneak around, and surprise her. Since MacNamara had failed to introduce him, no one noticed as he slipped away.

"Lucy, you must be very confused about the merger announcements. I want to assure you this move is in your best interests. Your father, certainly, would have approved of it," said MacNamara.

Lucy looked over at Lord Palerno, wondering what he was doing with this group. "I'm not sure I should be discussing any of this without my husband."

MacNamara appealed to her ego. "Surely, a woman of your intellect understands the importance. I want to talk to *you* Lucy, not your husband. Do you not own five percent of EPIK?"

"Well, yes, but—"

"Let me tell you why Anexa is your future," he interrupted.

Lucy panicked and turned to Carl for his advice, but he was gone. She remembered that Lord Palerno was in the group, so addressed him.

"Lord Palerno, you're my friend. Perhaps you can assist me here."

Lord Palerno was pleased to oblige…to assist his real corporate master.

"I suggest we retreat somewhere where we can take off these ridiculous masks and have a proper chat. Besides, we are all in need of refreshment," said Palerno.

"Excellent thinking my friend." MacNamara slapped Palerno on the back. He looked at Lucy. "Coming?"

"Well, I suppose I can spare a few minutes. My escort seems to have disappeared."

"You are among new friends, now," said MacNamara.

5

Not believing his luck, Carl walked around Diana several times to experience her beauty. When he had spotted her weeks before, at Sammy's coffee shop, he had thought she was beautiful. Tonight, all dressed up, she was stunning. From behind, he whispered into her ear.

"Hello, my friend from the coffee shop. Lose your friends and meet me in the next room."

She turned and caught sight of Carl's blond hair. Despite her shock, she discreetly followed him to where they could be alone.

"What a fabulous dress you're wearing. It looks like a couture creation."

"It's something from Paris. I think of it as part of my signing bonus," she giggled, remembering the day she had outwitted Priscilla and secured herself a generous salary.

"Must have been *some* signing bonus."

"Forget about that. What are *you* doing here? This is such a surprise! Did you accept the offer from EPIK? How do you know Lucy Atherton? Do you have a date tonight?" What she really wanted to know was why he had not telephoned her.

"Too many questions." Carl did not want to let on he was Lucy's escort for the evening. "The only date I have tonight, is you. Care to explore this hedonistic party with me?"

"Yes, please."

6

Just as MacNamara finished explaining his points of view on the Anexa/EPIK merger to Lucy, Bunny and Tamara burst into the room.

"Oh, there you are!" cried Bunny.

MacNamara was furious at his wife's timing. Couldn't she have waited until later? Tamara was always playing the society hostess and couldn't bear to think someone wasn't enjoying her party. "Tamara, if you don't mind, we would like to be left alone."

"Oh, what nonsense. I'm sure you've finished your business. Everyone, I do hope my husband has not been boring you." Tamara ignored the deadly look MacNamara shot her. "Please put your masks back on and join the fun."

The only ones who looked relieved at Tamara's interruption were Lucy and Barry. Barry was desperate to try out the smoking dens, so Tamara's timing was perfect. No point in wasting a perfectly good party rehashing details of a deal that was inevitable, Barry told himself. He noticed his wife's countenance. Bunny looked like someone having a great time.

"Tamara's been giving me a complete house tour, Lucy. Come join us," said Bunny, trying to rescue her friend.

"Sounds like fun. I'm coming too," said Barry, seeking his escape.

"Sorry Barry, girls only," said Bunny.

Barry looked wounded, but Priscilla managed to perk him up. "Your stupid wife doesn't know what she's missing. Her loss is my gain. I'll help you have the time of your life," Priscilla whispered to Barry.

MacNamara shook his head in disapproval as his wife left the room. "Bunch of druggies. I can't believe in this age of AIDS and drug problems that she condones this behavior. I'm just *so proud* of my wife's fine accomplishments—socialite, hostess, and chief drug dealer. On that positive note, Barry, why don't you and Priscilla join the party? We're virtually done here."

MacNamara's sarcastic comments went to waste. "Thanks boss," said Barry, thrilled with his freedom. "You should try some grass. It would help soothe your lingering headaches."

"I'll pass, thank you very much."

As Barry and Priscilla left, MacNamara and Lord Palerno edged closer to Phillips.

"That went very well, Mac. I believe Lucy understood your points. It was smart to explain everything in layman terms," said Palerno.

"How do you think it went, Phillips?" asked MacNamara.

Phillips swayed slightly. To combat his nerves, he had been drinking non-stop since his arrival, hours ago. Parties made him uncomfortable; he felt out of place wearing fancy clothes. Phillips was so intoxicated; he was in no position to comment on anything.

"Layman terms or not, Lucy Atherton knows shit about business. I think you seduced her, like some cheap swami. It was an unethical thing to do."

His outburst took MacNamara by surprise. "Come on, she's a grown woman. I bet she has only heard Atherton's one-sided opinions on the merger. She has the right to know her options."

"Phillips, you don't care about Lucy. You're upset about something else," eased Palerno.

Phillips was silent for a moment. His mind raced with incoherent thoughts stimulated by the alcohol. He was not sure if he had heard MacNamara tell Lucy that EPIK's research and development team were the future of the new organization. If this were the case, he was too young to retire but too old to be looking for another vice president position. He had four kids to put through college, plus a hefty mortgage on his brand new house. Phillips knew he needed the Anexa job to maintain his lifestyle.

"Sorry guys. I guess I got a little flustered when you started talking about EPIK's research and development team. For a moment, I thought you might replace my team with theirs." He looked down, suddenly feeling ashamed.

Palerno put his arm over Phillips's shoulders. "This is a good, honest deal Phillips. All parties will emerge financially set for life. Deep down, I believe you agree with that, too."

"You've done great things for Anexa," said MacNamara. "You read too much into what I told the Atherton lady."

Drunk or not, Phillips knew he was on the way out.

7

Tamara had no intention of continuing the house tour for Bunny, for Lucy, or for anyone else. She hoped to spend time enjoying her own party. Before they parted, Bunny thanked Tamara for rescuing Lucy from the Anexa mob.

Lucy was still thinking about her impromptu meeting with MacNamara. "Bunny, you really missed quite a discussion back there. MacNamara sounded pretty convincing to me, explaining the benefits of the Anexa merger. I can't understand why James is so adamant that we have to fight this opportunity."

"Don't start to become one of MacNamara's sycophants. Before you know it, you'll be singing the Anexa company song, like Barry. Lucy, make up your own mind on this."

"Of course, I just needed your advice."

"Maybe you should get your business advice from James. I gather he didn't come with you tonight."

"No, he didn't. I came with Carl."

Bunny grimaced thinking about her last encounter with the little prick. "What's *that* look for?"

"You should that know I saw him downstairs with a very young girl. They looked rather cozy," she paused, "if you know what I mean."

Lucy turned pale. "I'd better sit down. I'm feeling a little faint."

Bunny helped her over to a sofa. Lucy sat down and started to cry. She had really fallen for Carl. Unfortunately, she had mistaken his attentiveness as a sign of commitment to her.

"I suppose I'm not as young and beautiful as I used to be. I can't seem to get it right. I lost my husband's attention years ago, and I've grown into a pathetic, alcoholic housewife. I'm just a dupe. How could I have been so stupid as to misread Carl's feelings?" sobbed Lucy.

"Boy, you're wrong if you think sleeping with a man is a sign he loves or respects you."

Lucy took a tissue from her Fendi clutch bag and dabbed her tears. "You're going to have to cheer me up."

"You got it sweetie. Let's go and drool over those studs Tamara hired to stand all night long to serve us mind-altering substances."

As luck would have it, Bunny found one of the upstairs rooms unoccupied. While Lucy busily arranged pillows and throws to create a comfortable sitting area for them, Bunny subtly locked the door.

"This is just like college, huh?" On her way in, Bunny had selected a small piece of hashish and some rice paper from the waiter's tray. When she unwrapped the gold foil, the drug released a sweet aroma. Bunny expertly crumbled the resin mixing it with tobacco from one of her Dunhill cigarettes. She rolled it into a thin joint and handed it to Lucy.

"My treat. You light first."

Lucy lit her present and inhaled. Straight away, her senses felt alive. For a moment, she thought the crimson velvet curtains were on fire and that the musicians floated above her.

"You're right. It's just like college." Lucy reclined, resting her head on a plush pillow. "This is living." Her eyes shone.

Bunny smiled. She knew this was just what Lucy needed. The effects of the drug would reduce her stress, mellow her out.

As Bunny smoked, she watched hundreds of lights surround Lucy. She looked as though she was the sole focus of spotlights.

"Lucy, you are so beautiful."

Lucy sat up and stared at her best friend. Bunny, always, was there to support her. She was Lucy's rock in life. No one understood her like Bunny did. If anything happened to Bunny…

She became emotional. Tears ran down her cheeks.

"Lucy?"

Lucy closed her eyes. She raised a finger to her lips to silence Bunny. Lucy unzipped the back of her red gown and took it off. Bunny thought she was seeing things. As the drug took over, her brain played out two events. One eye, followed a fox running through the desert, vivid fluorescent colors flying everywhere. The other saw Lucy crawl over to her, naked. Bunny felt the room spin. She felt human warmth surround her. Bunny closed her eyes and dreamed. Lucy was making love to her.

    Bunny spoke to the mirage. "I love you Lucy."

    Lucy stroked Bunny's hair and caressed her breasts. "I love you, too."

    It was as if no one else existed. No one else mattered. Unknown to the lovers, security cameras filmed their every move.

Chapter Six

1

Lucy was reluctant to continue her affair with Carl after Bunny's report of his rendezvous with the mystery woman. Although her body desired him, her mind gave contradictory warning. The negative attitude became mutual; he grew tired of her constant, petty demands. Carl had no intention of becoming Lucy's househusband. Instead, he decided to stop wasting his time with Lucy, rather to focus on a plan to wound Atherton, to pay back the suffering caused to his mother. Carl decided to accept Atherton's job offering at EPIK, which would place him in a stronger position to strike when the time was right.

One morning Carl said, "Lucy, I'm considering taking up your husband's proposal to work for him at EPIK."

She raised her hands in protest. "What about the position you have here? Haven't I told you what a splendid job you do? All my friends are envious. What am I going to do?"

As usual, she thought only about herself. She was a typical example of a privileged 'only child' who always got her own way.

"I'm very flattered to think that you value me so highly. This opportunity will allow me to utilize my college degree. Try to be happy for me."

"But I found you first. I know I'm being selfish. I just can't help it. Can't you stay with me, just for a little while longer," she pleaded.

"Sorry Lucy. This is something I need to do."

She raised her voice.

"I'm quite aware that you disappear when it suits you! At the Christmas party, you were supposed to be my date, not that floozy's."

"I was your escort, not date."

"Whatever. It was your duty to stay by my side, not abscond with some bimbo. Your true upbringing was clearly illustrated by your unforgivable behavior."

Carl restrained himself from saying something he might regret later. He knew better. Diana was not a bimbo.

Carl moved closer to her. "Lucy, you are a special woman. You are too good for me, and I think you know it. Let me be the one to beg. I want to hold you one last time, to feel your silky skin next to mine, to smell your beautiful hair, to—"

"Yes," she interrupted. "I would like that very much, but you're right Carl. I am too good for you. Another time, another place, another world."

2

Without wasting time, Carl contacted Atherton's office. Atherton was not available to take his call, so he left a message with Candice, Atherton's secretary.

"Candice, I want to make sure my message reads correctly. Do you mind reading it back to me?"

"Not at all sir. The message reads as follows: Mr. Atherton, after witnessing the shenanigans of Lord Palerno at the MacNamara Christmas party, it looks like you need all the trustworthy colleagues you can get. Now would seem a good time to take up your offer of employment. Regards, Carl Swan."

"That's perfect. Thank you Candice."

When she gave Atherton the telephone message, he was intrigued. Atherton thought back to the night of the party. Lucy had not mentioned anything strange when she returned that evening. If anything, she had said her hosts provided her with an unforgettable evening. He had concluded she had had a good time. When he had asked her about Lord Palerno, Lucy had told him they had exchanged pleasantries, nothing further. Atherton had received a similar story from Palerno, talking with him the day after the party.

"James, it was the typical, boring, society function I absolutely abhor. Quite a waste of one's evening, if you know what I mean," said Palerno in his upper-class English accent. His cavalier attitude had made it easy for Atherton to dismiss any suspicions he might have held.

Atherton had almost forgotten about the party until he read Carl's message. His gut instinct told him something was up.

Not wanting to feel left out, Senior arrived, just in time to add his comments.

"Carl wants something. His whole demeanor is suspicious."

Atherton agreed silently.

"Hey, boy," said Senior. "Cat got your tongue?" You know you agree with me."

"Okay, okay I agree with you, but there's something more to Carl's behavior. I just feel it," replied Atherton.

"It's not what you feel but what you *know*," said Senior smugly.

"What do you mean?" asked Atherton.

"You *know*. You know—about them."

Atherton guessed Lucy was carrying on an affair with Carl but dismissed her attachment to him as a passing phase. Carl would end up like all her other lovers, used and discarded. He could hardly condemn her for her extramarital activities, especially when he was carrying on with Gillian.

Candice buzzed in on the intercom. "Mr. Atherton, do you want me to follow up with Mr. Swan?"

"Yes, clear my calendar for the rest of the day. Organize a meeting with him, immediately."

"Yes, sir. I'll get right on it," she responded loyally. "Will there be anything else? Would you like lunch?"

Atherton motioned to Senior if he wanted to eat. It was a ridiculous gesture and, deep down, he knew it.

"I can't remember the last time we shared a meal together," said the old man, licking his lips in anticipation. "A nice lean corned beef on rye would suit me fine."

Atherton addressed Candice. "Please get me two corned beef sandwiches on rye, one with mustard, one without."

"My pleasure," she said. "You sure are hungry today."

3

Carl was pleased when Candice called him back to ask if he could come to EPIK for an urgent meeting with Atherton. He knew his message would do the trick and intrigue Atherton. It was important for him to remain cool, calm, and collected, when they met. Don't come unglued like the last time, he advised himself.

He dressed in a dark blue suit, accompanying it with a nondescript tie. As he looked in the mirror adjusting it, he remembered a useful piece of advice from his mother. He smiled as he thought of the image her words conjured up.

"Always picture your interviewer sitting on the toilet, naked," said Martha.

"Disarm the interviewer, even if it is only in your mind. It's the best trick for a bad case of nerves."

When Carl arrived at EPIK, Candice ushered him straight into Atherton's office. Atherton was engaged in a telephone conversation and motioned to Carl to sit down. To Carl's relief, Atherton's casual body language set the tone for an informal meeting. Atherton stretched his hands behind his head and put his feet up on his desk. It was impossible not to notice the Gucci imprint on the bottoms of Atherton's shoes. Atherton continued to talk on the phone; he flicked his yellow-and-blue diamond patterned tie, revealing a Hermès label. It contrasted nicely against his crisp, blue, double-cuffed shirt. Nice ensemble, thought Carl—undoubtedly Lucy's touch.

"Sorry about the wait. Do you mind giving me five more minutes?" asked Atherton, covering the telephone's mouthpiece.

Carl nodded. This delay gave him time to observe his immediate surroundings. Atherton's office was tastefully decorated. Instead of possessing a typical steel and black leather feel, the room's decor reflected a comfortable elegance. Carl could see Atherton's desk, bookcases, and meeting table were made from walnut. They were designed to look antique, with gilt borders and exquisite carvings. A finely-woven, cream carpet covered the floor, further emphasizing the walnut. Potted trees and ivy plants occupied spaces.

Carl stood up and walked over to examine the watercolor paintings. The artist had used vibrant colors to express heat and sunlight. Each scene showed the striking contrast of lush flora against whitewashed walls of Mediterranean architecture.

"Which is your favorite painting?" asked Atherton, as he hung up the telephone.

"Hard to say. I do like this one, though." Carl pointed to a painting, showing a white Italian villa overlooking a blue ocean. Brightly colored red geraniums stood on the steps of the villa.

"Yes, I like that one too. It is called *Cappucini Convento*. Have you heard of the artist, Ilana Richardson?"

"No, I haven't."

"Lucy introduced her paintings to me a few years ago. They met through a mutual friend in London. Anyway, when I asked Lucy to decorate my office, she suggested using Ilana's paintings. It's a great idea, because they make me feel relaxed. Maybe, I'll get a chance to go to one of her open houses, someday, if I get a break from all this work."

"Speaking of which, where do you find time to read so much?" Carl pointed to the hundreds of leather bound books on the bookcase. He had perused some of the titles and was surprised by the diversity. This unique selection boasted everything from *Barron's Finance and Investment Handbook*, *PADI Open Water Diver Manual*, to a biography on mathematician John Nash, the schizophrenic Nobel Prize winner. "Quite a wide variety."

Atherton laughed. "Do you think I read only business material? Everyone's entitled to some brain candy. Keeps the mind fresh."

"I'll remember that."

Atherton moved over to the meeting table.

"I appreciate you coming here to meet me at such short notice. Please, let's have a seat."

Atherton buzzed his secretary on the intercom. "Could you please bring in some water?"

Atherton's secretary brought in the water and poured it into two glass tumblers.

"I'm sorry. I didn't even ask if you liked sparkling water. Can I get you something else, or is this okay?

Carl was not sure if he was being tested. Interviewers pulled stunts like this one, to test interviewees' reactions. He thought about his mother's advice and smiled. "Sparkling is just fine," he said.

Atherton bounded on. "The message you left alluded to something about Lord Palerno. Tell me something I don't already know."

"I thought it odd that the Anexa mob virtually kidnapped your wife at the party."

Atherton wrinkled his forehead. He did not like hearing anything suspicious about his wife. Her problems with consumption of alcohol left her vulnerable to manipulation.

"How could they kidnap Lucy, if you were supposed to be her escort?" Atherton was not amused she had been left alone with anyone from Anexa, even for a moment. Lucy had conveniently forgotten to tell him about this happening.

"MacNamara arranged to get Lucy on her own without me. Palerno was part of the group, suggesting she listen to MacNamara's offering." Carl left out details about his own rendezvous with Diana Roberts, making it appear MacNamara had given him the slip.

Atherton's steely eyes focused in on Carl. "Are you absolutely sure about this?"

"Yes. There is something else you should know. On the way home from the party, Lucy told me all about the merits of Anexa. She spoke as if she had been brainwashed."

"That two-timing pommy bastard," swore Atherton, thinking of Palerno's sinister involvement. He stared out of the window for a several minutes, before he closed his eyes, then rubbed his fingers across his furrowed brows.

It was apparent to Carl that Atherton was hearing it all for the first time. He wondered what he should do next. "Sir, can I get you some more water, or something?"

Atherton shook his head. "I've heard enough. Let's move on to another topic. As you are aware, this Anexa merger consumes most of my time. I have a limited amount of free time. Tell me, why do you think I cleared my schedule to see you?"

"Well, I did wonder."

"So we don't waste time with guessing games, I'll tell you why. First, I want to address the issue of you screwing my wife," he said coldly.

Taken by surprise, Carl felt his stomach tighten. He held back his nausea as the color drained from his face. Carl hoped Atherton would welcome him as an ally. Instead, his high hopes for a positive meeting were shattered.

Sensing Carl's fear and discomfort, Atherton decided to soften his approach. It was not the boy's fault, entirely. Lucy had, obviously, agreed to participate in the affair. It was easy to understand how the affair had transpired. She needed emotional contact, which he could not fully provide. The more he worked, the more she drank, until both of them were plagued by bitter and lonely lives.

"Look Swan, I'm not going after you solely. I know it takes two to tango. You're not entirely to blame. When I first suspected it, I thought about ringing your cocky neck. After reflecting on the matter, I can see that you have put a sparkle back into her world. Before you were on the scene, it was booze and anger. Now, at least it's booze and glee. I can thank you for that much."

"Mr. Atherton, I—"

"Don't interrupt me. I'm not finished. I want your word—your affair with my wife is over. You've taken advantage of a very sick woman. She desperately needs professional help, not a lover."

If he were to permit the affair to continue, there was the risk of Lucy leaving him for Carl. No telling what Lucy might do if she thought she was in love. There was no way that he was going to let this young stud interfere and threaten his marriage. He had much to lose, especially if he broke the conditions outlined in Sir Alexander's will. Senior would have a field day with him if he failed to keep the company intact. Marriage to Lucy was going to be to the bitter end.

"Yes, yes you have my word," stuttered Carl, trying to meet Atherton's penetrating looks. He was truly ashamed; he felt childlike in Atherton's presence.

"Good. For the next topic, the job offer."

Carl was stunned. It was the last thing he expected to hear.

"I didn't expect to get a second chance," said Carl.

"That makes two of us," announced Senior, joining the meeting, uninvited.

Atherton ignored the intrusion and continued talking to Carl. "Everyone needs a break." Focusing his full attention towards his father, he added, "I am a believer in second chances."

"I don't understand," said Carl. "Why are you doing this?"

"That's easy. How universal is your last name? When I saw the name Swan on our house payroll, I ran a background check. Can you imagine my delight when I found out you were Martha's son? Why you never said anything, is beyond me. Your mother is an honorable woman. Not many people have morals like her. She is someone I greatly admire. God knows how many times I had tried to convince her to leave her cleaning jobs and work for EPIK."

"There are more surprises at every turn," said Senior. "This is better than a soap opera if you ask me. You plan to keep an eye on Lucy's Romeo by offering him a job."

"It's called kindness and obligation. I owe Martha," replied Atherton.

Carl winced at the mention of his mother; as he suspected, Atherton owed her because he felt guilty about baby Alice.

Atherton repeated himself. "I owe Martha…"

"You owe nobody!" screamed Senior. "Don't trust the kid!"

Atherton heard Carl mumble through Senior's tirade. "The last thing I wanted to do was use connections."

"Nonsense. You knew he would find out sooner or later," Senior shot back.

"Connections, nepotism, or whatever you want to call it. Those were the things that saved your ass after I caught you playing in my family boudoir," said Atherton simply, following his father's lead.

Senior grunted his approval.

Carl locked eyes with Atherton. "I thought we were off that topic."

Atherton closed his eyes realizing how his father influenced his every move. I can't continue like this, he thought. I have to break free and use my own judgment.

Carl spoke, "Mr. Atherton, are you going to give me a second chance, or not?"

"No, of course he's not," snapped Senior.

"Yes, I am," said Atherton, challenging his father's authority. "Did you bring your university transcripts with you?"

"This is crazy!" shouted Senior. "I'm leaving, before you do more damage. I can't stand to watch this."

Atherton was relieved when Senior disappeared as quickly as he had appeared.

4

Carl produced a copy of his Harvard transcript and passed it to Atherton. He was pleased that he had remembered to bring it.

"Although my major was in economics, I took several courses from the Business School."

Atherton pretended to review the transcript. He remembered it from the background report. Carl had been an exceptional student. Maintaining an A grade point average at a top-ranked university was not an easy feat.

"This is all excellent. I like your choice in coursework. Tell me about your mergers and acquisition classes?"

Carl detailed his knowledge of accounting rules, SEC regulations, even displayed understanding of back-end information system processing.

"I'm impressed," said Atherton. "I would like you to consider an internship position to work alongside me as a business analyst. I expect prompt, detailed position reports on all issues affecting this merger. I want to keep abreast of everything, from every angle. You will attend all meetings with me. Be prepared to eat, sleep, and drink this Anexa nightmare. If you prove yourself, I will consider dropping the intern title and discussing a more permanent role. My legal team will update you on what's been going on. I will call a Board meeting in two days, to find out where we stand on blocking the merger, so be prepared."

This was better than Carl had hoped for. He had thought he might get a position in one of the departments, such as accounting or information technology; that he would get to work alongside Atherton had not occurred to him. This was the break he had been looking for!

"Mr. Atherton, I would be honored to work alongside you, to learn."

"Then that's settled. You will receive a written offer confirming our arrangement. Martha spoke very highly of you, so I hope you live up to her words."

Carl swallowed hard. There was no going back.

5

Atherton put in extra hours at the office to keep abreast of the merger situation. He telephoned Lucy to let her know that he would be home late. Her private line rang continuously, so he concluded she was out for the evening. He left a message on her answering machine, telling her she should not expect him home before midnight. His next call was to Gillian, but she appeared to be out, too.

As he hung up feeling disappointed, his computer beeped, informing him he had urgent email. Atherton recognized the sender's name.

To: JAtherton@EPIK.com
From: CPhillips@Anexa.com
Subject: Blank
I'm unclear about Anexa's future technical direction under Dean MacNamara. Along these lines, I would like to propose a meeting to discuss mutually benefitting opportunities. Please keep this confidential.
CP.

Atherton was dumbfounded. Why did Anexa's top technical scientist want out of the company? It was strange. Perhaps, he had had disagreements with MacNamara. Atherton called his legal counsel to seek input on Phillips's email message.

"Glad to find you're working late," said Atherton.

"I'll be lucky if my new marriage survives, given the hours I work around here," replied Murray. "Anyway, you didn't call to ask about my love life. What can I do for you this evening?"

"Jack, I just received an email from Cam Phillips. He says he wants to meet to discuss *opportunities*. What do you make of it?"

"Did the email come from Anexa or his personal ISP account?"

"It originated from Anexa."

"Hmmm. Either he's genuine and stupid, or part of one of MacNamara's elaborate games. Whatever you do, do not meet him without me."

"Agreed. Do me a favor. Run a background check on him. See what you can dig up. I don't want to go into this meeting unprepared, as I did with MacNamara."

"Give me a few days. I'll get back to you."

"There's something else. I want you to execute the golden handshake for my so-called *friend* Lord Palerno. I want him out of my company before the next Board meeting. That man's double-dealing days are over."

Good move, thought Jack. Palerno had quietly approached him trying to sell him on the benefits of the Anexa merger. Inevitably, Palerno must have approached the other Board members, too.

"Consider it done. I'll draw up the papers immediately."

Just as Atherton hung up the phone, Gillian walked into his office, clad in a beautiful mink coat. She closed his door, locking it behind her.

"I'm going to have to take away your security badge," joked Atherton, "Coming in here, whenever you like."

"Oh, you wouldn't do that," she purred.

"Never. You're just what the doctor ordered…perfect timing. Actually, I called you about an hour ago, too."

Gillian grinned. "You should buy me one of those pagers."

"Far too crude for you. Maybe you should utilize the EPIK phone I gave you."

"And be a slave to technology? No way. How are things going?"

"Not too good. If this merger was only about money, I would be jumping for joy, but it is not. I know MacNamara will tear my company apart. That's his way. Acquire. Streamline. Sell. Move on."

"I suppose he will fire good people," she mused.

"Yes, exactly. What's terrible though, is that he uses people. He will convince them to stay on for the sake of the company, obtain their knowledge, then, when he has no more use for them—bang."

"Bang?"

"He'll give them two weeks notice and fire them without severance. Did I tell you that the Svengali invited my whole Board to his, so-called, legendary Christmas party?"

"I hope no one went."

"Try Lord Palerno…and my wife."

"You're kidding."

"No, I'm not. That Palerno showed support by going could be the death of me at the next Board meeting. If they support this merger, I will not have a leg to stand on. Which is why Lucy's shares are so important to me."

"No doubt you have a plan to secure her shares. Hopefully, it will include jewelry and a romantic trip."

"As a matter of fact, you are right on both accounts."

"She's a lucky lady."

Atherton walked over to the window and closed the blinds. "If she's lucky, then what does that make me?" he asked, eyeing her long legs.

"Luckier." Gillian took off her coat, dropped it to the floor, and smiled.

"Jesus! You came all the way here with no clothes on?"

"Does red lipstick and Chanel No. 5 count?" She perched herself on his desk and spread her legs. "I'm a little chilly. Come warm me up."

6

When Atherton returned home, he was surprised to find Lucy still awake. She pretended not to notice his arrival by continuing to watch the television. From the look on her face, Atherton assessed she was in a foul mood.

"Sorry I'm so late. I didn't expect you to wait up for me."

"What makes you think I did?" Lucy's eyes remained focused on the television.

"Look, I've had a hard day. If there's something bothering you, just say it." His patience was thinning. She had a life of leisure and luxury. Most people only dreamed about the life she led. Why was she always so miserable?

"Frankly, I'm surprised you give a damn...thought you only reserved your soft spot for your mistress."

Atherton spun around and stared.

"Oh?" she asked playfully. "Did I say something that struck a nerve?"

He spotted the empty bottle of gin, lying next to her bed. "You're drunk."

"I'm sick of being treated like a doormat!" she exploded. "Not only do you do as you please, but you feel the need to control everything I do. Things were just fine when you had your mistress, and I had—"

"The houseboy?" he fired back. "I'm surprised you lowered your standards by sleeping with the help."

"*You* were the hired help at one stage. My father thought you were irreplaceable...I'm not him."

"Don't try me Lucy."

"You don't scare me. You're nothing. Just look at the way you're mishandling this merger."

"My socialite wife thinks she knows how to run a company," he spat.

"This little socialite owns five percent. Some people respect that."

"Like Dean MacNamara?"

She folded her arms and smiled, smugly.

"He's using you!"

"At least he treats me with respect, which is more than I can say about my husband."

"Why are you so mad at me all the time? Can't we ever have a happy moment?"

"You must live in a fantasy world. Find me a household which doesn't have problems!"

"Fantasy? *Your* whole life has been a dream. Who're you trying to fool?"

"Sure, thanks to my father, we're wealthy, but I'm empty inside. Did you know I'm lonely? You've done so many things to alienate me and—"

"Like what?" he interrupted.

"If you let me finish, you'll find out," she said flatly.

"Sorry, please continue."

"James, what kind of a husband turns his back on his wife the day their baby dies? You've never let me get close to you since then. The absurd thing is I found someone to fill that void, and you had to take him away. You're continually punishing me. I've had enough and I want out. I want a divorce."

"Let's talk later, when you're sober enough to comprehend what you mean. You don't have a clue as to what you're saying." There was no point talking to her in this boozed state. Likely, she would forget this incident had even taken place after she slept it off.

"Don't patronize me! I know exactly what I'm saying. I'm filing for divorce."

Divorce was out of the question. The last time Atherton spoke to his attorney about the possibility, he was sorely reminded of the financial consequences it would have on EPIK—and on him. Damn Lucy's father for controlling their lives from the grave! There had to be some way to appease, to placate, her. The answer was not forthcoming, until Senior helped out.

"Tell her to divorce you," insisted Senior. "Say it!"

"If that's what you really want, then fine, so be it," said Atherton.

"Hah, you're trying to trick me. MacNamara warned me you would pull a stunt like that. I am not about to fall for your devious plan."

What now?

"Don't panic. Keep following my lead," soothed Senior. "Tell her she was responsible for the stillborn baby."

"Oh no! I can't stoop *that* low," said Atherton.

"Hey, who else is here?" asked Lucy.

"Do it!" commanded Senior.

"Lucy, you mentioned the loss of our baby, and how I didn't respond to you. Did you ever think about the impact your drinking had on your pregnancy, or our marriage? You killed our baby." So there it was, Atherton had said it after thinking it for so long.

"The doctors explained that her being stillborn had nothing to do with me," she said.

Senior quickly added more commands for Atherton to follow. "Give more specific information. Keep it going! This will work, trust me."

Atherton followed the orders.

"Pregnant mothers are supposed to monitor their baby's kicking every hour or so. If no movement is felt, something could be wrong with the baby. But you wouldn't have known anything was wrong, would you? You were too out of it to have noticed anything out of the ordinary. It was a wonder the baby didn't have the umbilical cord wrapped around her neck any sooner."

"How can you be so cruel?" Lucy buried her reddened face in her hands and wept. "You're horrible! I hate you!"

"That's my boy!" said Senior. "Sock it to her!"

"You can hate me all you want but you can't run from the truth. You have no one to blame your life on except yourself. If you file for divorce, it's your decision, not mine. You will have to live with that consequence for the rest of your life," said Atherton.

Lucy's head was spinning. He was talking so fast that she had a hard time keeping up with him. Perhaps, she was rushing things. "Maybe, we should separate to see how things would be."

"No way," said Senior. "Accept no compromises."

"Forget it, you might as well go for the divorce. I will not wait around for you while you make fleeting decisions."

She felt so confused. What they needed was a holiday together, just like ones they used to take when they were first married. Yes, that was a splendid idea, she thought. "James, perhaps you're right. I am rushing into things without thinking clearly. Why don't we spend some time together? We could have a break, away from all the madness."

"What? Right now? I can't leave EPIK with MacNamara all over my ass." Her conception of the world bewildered him; Lucy lived in a fishbowl, only thinking about herself.

"Either you agree to go away with me, or I file for divorce."

"No compromises," repeated Senior.

If that's what it took to secure his financial future, then so be it, thought Atherton.

"No!" cried Senior. "Don't think like that!"

"Lucy, get some rest. You have some planning to do," said Atherton.

She looked at him trying to comprehend what he had just said. Did that mean planning for a divorce, or for a trip?

He sensed her confusion. "Lucy, go ahead, plan a nice trip."

7

The prospect of getting back together with her husband exhilarated Lucy. She could not remember all the details from the night before, but she knew her husband did not want a divorce. At the first sign of daylight, she telephoned Bunny to ask her to come over.

"Hello?" Bunny mumbled, half asleep.

"Boy, do I have news for you!" blurted Lucy excitedly. "You're not going to believe what happened last night,"

"Darling, what time is it?"

"Never mind. This is so important. James and I are getting back together."

Bunny sat up. "Maybe you should fill me in."

"Come over! Have a champagne breakfast with me!"

"Lucy, you can't leave me hanging on for one more second. I refuse to wait until breakfast." Food was the last thing on Bunny's mind. She felt sick thinking about Lucy's annoucement.

"We had a huge argument when he came home last night. After I threatened to divorce him, he basically repented."

"That's a strange way to put it. Don't tell me you bought his act. I bet he's up to something." Everything seemed to be going so well between them: she could not face losing Lucy.

"No, he was sincere. We talked about the baby's death, and I think we sorted some issues out."

Bunny laughed cruelly. "How can you forgive him so quickly? Have you lost your mind? Did it occur to you he's trying to secure your loyalty so you won't sell your EPIK shares?"

Lucy was quiet, hurt by her friend's comments.

"Are you still there?" said Bunny.

"Yes, I am."

"Maybe you should know this. Barry told me Atherton's position at EPIK is unstable. Even his own Board is questioning his motives for blocking the merger."

"Well…more reason why I should stand by my husband. I hoped you would be happy for me."

"Why can't you see that other people love you? I wish your choice of partner was someone else."

"Bunny, I'm sorry. I didn't mean to mislead you…we're still friends."

"Friends," she repeated. "Is that what you think we are?"

"Well, yes…the best of friends."

"Lucy," Bunny sighed. "If you can't see or face what has happened between us, then I don't want to be your friend anymore. We are *not* being the kind of friends I would like us to be."

"Oh." Lucy did not know what to say.

Bunny knew Lucy would not openly love her. "Do me a favor."

"Yes, of course! What?"

"I'm going to need some time alone. You've hurt me—used me."

"I did not mean to hurt you," said Lucy sadly. She heard Bunny's line click and go dead. Lucy felt numb.

Chapter Seven

1

Jack Murray decided to deliver Lord Palerno's severance package in person. He wanted the satisfaction of seeing Palerno's reaction.

As he drove through the impressive stone gates, up the long winding drive, he marveled how Palerno lived in this fifty-room, ten-acre Long Island estate all by himself. Palerno often boasted to his acquaintances his house was a mini replica of *Blenheim Palace*, on the ancestral Marlborough-Churchill estate near Oxford, England. Murray had to agree with Palerno's braggadocio as he viewed the splendid property. The architects and landscape designers had done an excellent job copying *Blenheim's* baroque architectural style, while creating aesthetically pleasing gardens.

"We built a bridge to connect two natural lakes. Trees and hills have been moved to soften the landscape," Palerno bragged when complimented on his breathtaking property.

As Murray approached the elaborate, carved front door, his eyes were drawn to the sculptures guarding the entrance. Two wolves displayed their sharp teeth through partially open mouths, simulating growling. Typical Palerno, thought Murray. Pets were often said to resemble their masters; in this case, the concept was correct.

Before he had a chance to knock, Palerno surprised Murray by opening the door himself. More startling was Palerno's state of dress. The Lord wore a bright purple velour bathrobe with matching gold-crested slippers. A chunky gold cross dangled from a heavy-link chain and nestled in his thick chest hair.

"Interesting ensemble," said Murray, watching Palerno slowly tighten the belt around his gaudy robe. "No butler today?"

"I thought it would be more appropriate to answer it myself. I suppose you are in possession of my golden handshake?" he asked rhetorically, pointing to Murray's paperwork.

What an ass, thought Murray. Even right to the end, he has to be clever. "Yes, Lord Palerno. You'll find your severance package in accordance with your contract." Murray handed Palerno the packet. "Not that you need the money."

Palerno laughed. "It was nice doing business with you, Jack Murray." He twisted his neck, looking eagerly over his shoulder.

"May I ask you something? Why did it take you so long to sell us out? You were with EPIK ten years."

Lord Palerno paused, his stubby fingers groped at the cross. "Oh, that's an easy one. You were a nice investment, which happened to mature technically, at ten years. As one might say, EPIK was ripe for the pickin'," he mocked, using a southern accent.

"You fucker."

"Charming." He grinned, pleased he had elicited such a reaction. "Have a nice day and remember, *Greed is good*." A high-pitched male voice giggled from within the mansion. Palerno smirked and firmly shut his door.

2

Atherton frowned as he thought about his predicament. He hated how Lucy had gained the upper hand by forcing him on this vacation. He should have listened to Senior and resisted her demands. When she had announced they were going off to Europe in less than two weeks, he confided to Murray he was trying to repair his broken marriage. How else could he explain his sudden departure? The last thing he wanted to do was admit his wife controlled the purse strings.

"I want to let you know you're doing an admirable thing," said Murray. "Not many men would take personal leave during a crisis like this."

"Between you and me, marriage is far more important than running any business. It's not that I don't care about what's going on with this merger, but I need to refocus some of my priorities."

"I can keep things running for the week you're away. We'll need you back soon to keep the team focused in the right direction," said Jack, worried about Palerno's lingering influence on the Board. "While you're away, you might want to consider removal of more deadweight," Murray added.

"Meaning what, exactly?" said Atherton, raising an eyebrow. Throughout his career, Atherton had prided himself on having a loyal and supportive team behind him. If there were more traitors in the company, it would come as a surprise.

"Before we removed Palerno, he approached me on several occasions trying to muster support to have you ousted. He claimed he had the votes of several Board members, who thought you were foolish not to support the merger."

"So what?"

"Come on friend. You know what a shaky position we are in. You read our analyst's report this morning, didn't you?"

Atherton sighed. "No, I haven't read it yet. Too much going on."

"Look, maybe this trip will benefit you. I think you need a timeout to relax and to refocus."

"You've roused my curiosity. What's in the report?"

"Basically, he found out our top hedge fund managers are backing the Anexa merger. They are preparing to go public with their statement, tomorrow."

"Palerno was behind this?"

"Yes, in collaboration with MacNamara."

"I should have seen this coming. Let's get our group together today, for a Board meeting. I want to hear what they have to say. Let's find out who are my friends…"

"Okay."

"Just tell me one thing. I need to know that I have your complete trust."

"Yes," he said unwaveringly, meeting Atherton's eyes.

3

As the Board members assembled into EPIK's main conference room, Atherton noticed very few looked directly at him. Murray must have been right. This meeting had trouble written across it. Most of the Board members sat as far from Atherton and Murray as possible.

"The body language already says it all." Atherton spoke out, trying to disarm his group. "Let's put our personal feelings aside and focus on the business at hand."

Michael Montgomery chuckled.

Atherton glanced in his direction. "Something to say?"

Montgomery shook his head and then remained quiet.

Yoshi Tachiwa raised his hand. "Where's Palerno? I heard a rumor he was asked to leave the company."

"Yes, that's correct. I pride myself on having a loyal team. Palerno was playing for both sides. In the end, he sided with Anexa."

"He was not fired for disagreeing with you?" asked Tachiwa humbly.

"Is that what you thought?"

Montgomery spoke up before Tachiwa could answer. "Speaking on behalf of the group, we don't know what to think. You fired Palerno without our input. You hired your estate manager as your assistant. And I understand you will take a vacation with your wife right in the middle of the merger situation."

Carl squirmed in his chair at the unfavorable mention of his name. He knew his presence made the Board members uncomfortable.

"Let me address each point. Lord Palerno was a traitor. He was not a team player. He was only interested in what was good for him financially, not what was good for the company. Yes, I have hired Carl Swan as an intern. He has excellent skill sets and academics, which will benefit EPIK. Do I have to remind you, I hired each and every one of you? As for my one-week break, EPIK has always maintained a policy that family comes first. This is a personal leave of absence, which I ask you to respect. While I'm on leave, the company's day-to-day decisions will be handled by Murray, who will keep me abreast of all urgent issues."

Montgomery was not buying into Atherton's reasoning. "Your words of 'what's good for the company' don't exactly measure up to your current practices. After careful consideration, we want you to know that we support this merger. Financially, the deal makes sense and we cannot ignore it. The shareholders profit, EPIK profits, our debt gets cleared, EPIK leverages synergies and expands its customer base. If these are not compelling reasons for us to merge, please tell us what are? It is our responsibility to our shareholders to do what is best, and the merger with Anexa is that. James, let's go forward with this, before our stock price gets too high and Anexa gets cold feet."

"Look Montgomery, let's say, for argument's sake, that we did merge. This new company would violate free trade practices and fair competition. In essence, we would have created a monopoly. Think about it, if someone asked us for a list of competitors, could we really provide one? The answer is no!" declared Murray.

"What's your point?" asked Montgomery, agitated by Murray's comeback. Obviously, Murray was trying to suck up to Atherton.

"The point is, I believe the government will get involved and break apart what has been merged," replied Murray.

"Pure speculation," rebuked Montgomery

Atherton spoke up. "Oh? And say the government did avoid involvement…do you honestly think MacNamara would keep our culture, employees, and products intact? Hell no! Think about it. He would sell off and streamline EPIK as fast as he merged with it."

"Is that all you have to add? Surely, you have more compelling reasons to be against this merger?" Montgomery scanned the faces of the other Board members, to make sure he still had their support. Most of them nodded as he sought their response.

Atherton was no fool. He knew what Montgomery was up to. He was trying to make himself look clever. The problem was Montgomery was out of his league, talking about issues without experience to back him up. The Board swayed towards agreeing with Montgomery's position because, on the surface, the merger looked good from its financial perspective. The Board had to be reminded of why Anexa and EPIK could not mesh.

"Let me leave you with this thought—Daimler Chrysler. Remember when the two automotive giants merged? Within the first year, high expectations of shareholders, management, and employees were crushed. Cultural differences between German and U.S. employees could not be resolved, eventually leading to interference in business operations. Needless to say, the stock dropped. I believe the same would happen to us."

Montgomery ignored him. "I think we've heard enough. Why don't we take a vote? Our company by-laws state a Board majority is needed to approve a merger before we inform the shareholders."

Atherton tried to regain control of the meeting. "Don't forget my wife and I, jointly, own ten percent?" he warned.

"So what? Anexa has the support of several hedge fund managers, who make up much more than that. I move for a vote."

"Fine, then let's see who supports this merger. I want to see your faces. All in favor of this merger please raise your hand."

He watched six of the ten Board members vote in favor of the merger. Atherton shook his head in disbelief. "Let the record show that I think this is terrible mistake. A costly lesson for all of us."

"Inform the shareholders of the decision and send out proxy ballots," said Murray.

"If we have any luck, the shareholders will vote against the merger," Carl whispered to Atherton.

"Highly improbable. You've just witnessed the death of EPIK," he said somberly. Carl was too inexperienced to understand what had just transpired.

As the meeting broke up, Montgomery came over to Atherton and extended his hand. "Nothing personal, James. I hope you understand."

Atherton refused to give him his hand. "Just remember this, as the merger plays out. Our credo at EPIK is our commitment to our employees and their families. Everything else comes second."

"Whatever," said Montgomery.

"James, let's go and get a drink," said Murray. "I could use one."

"Sounds good," said Montgomery.

Murray glared at him. "Piss off, Judas. You're not invited."

Chapter Eight

1

Carl arranged to meet Diana at Sammy's coffee shop. Since their chance encounter at the Christmas party, he could not get her out of his mind. She was funny, charming, beautiful, and smart. Diana possessed everything he could possibly want in a woman.

Diana walked into the shop, spotted Carl, and waved.

"Hi there," she said. "I'm so glad you called." Diana removed her cashmere coat, carefully folding it over the back of an unoccupied chair. She was casually dressed in a white turtleneck sweater, tucked into woolen, mocha-colored trousers. Her brown boots were simple, yet elegant with a slight heel. Diana's red locks were pulled back into a ponytail and clipped in place with a pearl barrette.

"You look great. Actually, you *always* look wonderful."

She smiled, pleased by his reaction.

"New boots and coat?" he asked.

"Yup." Diana was impressed he had noticed her purchases. Not many men paid enough attention to notice details.

"I suspect EPIK isn't paying me enough." He pulled at his shirt, making a funny face.

"I negotiated a fair deal at Anexa. You should have let me help you prepare for your negotiations."

"You're probably right. I missed out. Looks like you'll have to buy this round of coffees," he joked. "Can I get you the same thing you had last time, café au lait using a Columbian blend?"

"Mmmm…lovely." She was excited to see him. His company made her feel nervous, but in a good way. Everything was going so well—her career at Anexa, the possibilities with Carl.

Carl returned with the coffees. "Here you go. Your café au lait, just the way you like it. One-third coffee, the rest steamed milk," he said, faking a French accent.

"You do a very good Parisian accent. Very BCBG, *bon chic bon genre.*"

"Is that a good acronym?"

"Yes, very cool," she confirmed. "Very upper class."

My God she was beautiful, he thought. Maybe he was out of his league. What did she see in him?

"When are you off to the continent? Your new job involves European marketing, *n'est-ce pas?*" he teased.

"That's right. You're looking at Anexa's European Marketing Director for the big-three countries. I have responsibility for the British, French, and German markets. As a matter of fact, tomorrow, I have a meeting with my new boss, Priscilla Meyers, to go over my job specifics."

"Hopefully, you can be based here in the States and commute. I really would miss you if you became one of those high-flying expatriates living abroad." Carl noticed Diana's glow when she talked about her career. He hated to spoil her mood but wanted to let her know how he felt.

"Carl, we only just met," she said. "Let's not rush into anything."

"Look Diana. I like you, and I think you like me. We're both mature enough not to have to play games. I'm not asking you to put your career on hold or anything. I'm asking you not to make decisions which would affect our relationship."

"Our relationship," she repeated, carefully.

"Yes, our budding relationship." Carl put his hand over hers. "Help me out here. Don't make me look like a lovesick schoolboy."

She chuckled. "Fawn over me! A woman could get used to this treatment."

2

Every Tuesday, Gillian received her delivery of fresh flowers to decorate her apartment. When her doorman called to say that she had a visitor, she expected to see her usual delivery person with her lily arrangements. When she opened her door, Dean MacNamara barged into her apartment, pushing her aside, and locking the door behind him.

She was shocked at the unexpected arrival of this unwanted visitor. "What in the hell do you think you are doing here? You better get out before I call the police."

MacNamara let out an evil snigger. "I wouldn't do that if I were you.

Don't you know who I am?"

"Yes, I do. Please leave my home." Atherton had pointed him out to her many times. She knew the face of his nemesis quite well.

"Don't be ridiculous Gillian. I just got here." He sat down in one of her overstuffed chintz sofas. He looked around and nodded his approval. "Nice pad. I especially like your Fabergé egg display. Are they real?" he taunted.

"Get out," she hissed.

"Not before we discuss some business. Be a love and fix me a gin and tonic. Make one for yourself. It will calm you down." MacNamara evaluated her looks and decided that she was quite pretty. No wonder Atherton used her services, he thought.

"I'm afraid we have nothing to discuss. I'm not looking for new clients."

"Oh, I think you'll have one more opening after you hear what I have to say. Does the name Gualberto Benicini ring a bell?"

She shivered as she remembered her Italian lover. That fateful night, twelve years ago, seemed like yesterday. Gualberto had arrived to see her, after drinking most of the night. He had accused her of having an affair with one of his friends. When she had denied it, he had gone over to her desk and taken out her pistol.

"Confess! Tell me you are sleeping with him," slurred Gualberto, pointing the gun at her.

"My darling this is so untrue. You know that I love you. Give me the gun," she said vehemently.

"I have seen you with him. If I cannot have you all to myself, then we both shall die," he sobbed. Gualberto started to fire the gun, randomly. Gillian screamed and fled to the bedroom. The next thing she remembered was another gunshot, then screams from people in the plaza, below—scenes straight out of a B-movie.

"Hey babe, snap out of it. Don't make me ask for that drink again," said MacNamara.

His tone made it quite clear he was not going anywhere. She obeyed him. She went over to her drinks cabinet and mixed him the drink.

Gillian handed him the gin and tonic. "That matter is in the past."

"I don't believe it is. My sources, which are very reliable I might add, have told me the Italian police still have the case open. Apparently, the murder of a prominent government official is not easily forgotten."

"He shot himself, then fell." Why was she defending herself to him?

"Whatever you say, Gillian. It's their word against yours. *Yours*...the word of a whore."

"Please tell me what you want, then be on your way."

"And I thought we were just beginning to have some fun, together. Perhaps, this little secret would be very useful to the Immigration and Naturalization Service. I would think the body trail would be very interesting to them."

Gillian had heard stories about the INS deporting resident aliens in legal trouble in the U.S., no matter how minor the incident. "I'm listening."

"Of course you are," he said smugly. "The deal is this. You will report personal information to me about James Atherton. I want to know anything he is doing which might affect my takeover plans. For your efforts, I'll make sure your secret remains confidential."

Gillian wished she had not answered the door. She closed her eyes. "Fine, I'll do it."

"Good girl," he said, patting her on the back. "Let's seal this deal, properly."

"What? I just agreed to your pathetical blackmail. Get out."

"Not before I experience some of your infamous skills." MacNamara pointed to his crotch. "Go on, get busy."

In all her years as a courtesan, she never felt so used, so cheap. Gillian unzipped his trousers and performed what she was told to do. After a few minutes, he roughly pushed her head aside.

"I honestly don't know what all the fuss is about. I could get better head from my dog." MacNamara stood up, zipped his trousers, and left the apartment.

Gillian remained seated on the floor. In MacNamara, she had met her match.

3

Diana was on a high. Life could not have become any better for her. Her glamorous and well-paid position at Anexa afforded her new pleasures. At the Chanel boutique, they knew her by name; she was one of their best customers. Only last week, she had completed her Fall wardrobe by picking out a few more couture suits. The boutique staff had complimented her on her new car, even remarking that the shade matched the color of the Chanel's Fall line. Diana was pleased with her gray 911 Porsche; it reflected her new status.

After spending two weeks attending Anexa's rigorous orientation program, Diana was relieved when Priscilla scheduled a meeting to discuss her responsibilities.

"What do you think so far?" asked Priscilla, eyeing Diana's new designer suit.

"I just love it. The people are so nice," gushed Diana.

"That's good to hear."

"I'm quite anxious to go over to Europe to start my responsibilities."

"I'm glad you brought that up. There has been a change in plans."

"Pardon?" Diana looked confused.

"There's a situation here which needs your immediate attention."

"What about Europe?"

"Europe will have to wait. We have to do what's best for Anexa. Things change quickly around here."

"Well, I'm sorry about your situation, but I didn't join Anexa expecting to be jerked around."

"You're acting like a child," scolded Priscilla. "Besides, beggars can't be choosers." Priscilla handed her a report. *Greed is good.* "Should I remind you of your present situation?"

Diana opened the report and looked through the pile of documents, detailing her existing credit obligations. "You have a copy of my credit card statements?"

"Of course we do. Anexa keeps an eye on its employees. Looks to me like you're spending as if you were the president of the company. I've got to hand it to you. At least, you have good taste in clothes and cars ... not that you need a car in Manhattan."

Diana's mouth dropped. She was stuck. With her overwhelming financial troubles and the high expectations of her parents, she had to remain at Anexa. "Tell me about this temporary position?" she mumbled. "It's temporary, right?"

Priscilla outlined Diana's new role. "This merger is very important to MacNamara. He wants you to move into the EPIK headquarters ASAP and act as his eyes and ears. You will be a junior executive within the integration team."

"That's ridiculous. When was I demoted to junior executive?"

"You were not an executive to begin with." Priscilla happily corrected her.

"You're making it sound like a corporate spy position. I don't have those qualifications!"

"*Au contraire, mon amie.* On the contrary, my friend." Priscilla mocked

Diana in French. "With your brains and body, I think you'll do just fine."

"This is harassment," said Diana, raising her voice. No one had duped her like this. "You never had any intentions of sending me to Europe."

"Ah, now you're living in the real world."

"You tricked me."

"Wipe that ugly scowl off your face. Act like a team player. The sooner you do, the better it will be for everyone." Priscilla had her right where she wanted.

Chapter Nine

1

It did not take long for the good news to hit the corridors at Anexa. Barry and MacNamara thrilled staff by going around the building, confirming the rumors. Anexa would take over EPIK.

Cam Phillips heard what had happened at Anexa's Board meeting from Barry. "You look pretty happy," said Phillips, as Barry bounced into his office, beaming. "Is there something going on?"

"Today is a great day for Anexa. We are going to be the leader in both telecommunications and wireless," said Barry. "Nothing is going to stop us."

MacNamara stepped into Phillips's office and joined them. "Is Barry filling you in on the good news?"

"Hi, Mac. Actually, he just started. You must be thrilled."

"I'm *thrilled*. Tell me what you think."

Ever since the MacNamaras' party, Phillips had purposely kept a low profile, avoiding his boss. He knew his drunken ranting about the way MacNamara had handled the conversation with Lucy Atherton would not be forgotten easily. Too bad he could not meet with James Atherton sooner, to try to secure a position within the new organization.

"Well, I think this announcement is great news," lied Phillips.

"You do?" asked MacNamara, raising his eyebrow.

Phillips decided he had nothing to lose, at this point. "Do you have an idea of what the new R&D structure will look like? Maybe I could make some suggestions."

Barry and MacNamara exchange looks.

"Let's close the door. We'll need some privacy if we're to discuss those details," said MacNamara.

When Barry closed the door and shut the blinds, the room felt smaller.

Barry scanned the debris of telecom parts scattered around the room. "I had not realized our vice president had such a small, dark, dingy office space. How do you find anything in this pit?"

"Well, it is small," Phillips agreed, misinterpreting Barry's sarcasm for sympathy. It was about time someone noticed that he camped out in such small quarters. He breathed, drank, and ate Anexa; the least they could do was to repay him.

"Mac, you'll have to make it up to him."

"It's small but not as tiny and cramped as a prison cell would be," said MacNamara.

Phillips looked at MacNamara. What on Earth was he talking about? He felt his throat tighten, and his mouth dry up. "Excuse me?"

"Barry, do you want to do the honors or should I?"

Barry shrugged his shoulders. "Sure, boss. I just love doing your dirty work," bantered Barry.

"Would someone please tell me *what's going on*?"

"Well, for heading up R&D, you're a bit of a dolt," said Barry.

"That's an understatement," added MacNamara. "Did you really think we wouldn't find out about your secret correspondence with James Atherton? You were pretty stupid to use the company's email. You know that we regularly inspect the server's message log?"

"I wasn't aware we invaded our employees' privacy," mumbled Phillips.

"That's the beauty of the private sector. We can do whatever the fuck we want," said Barry.

"What do you want from me?"

"That's easy. You will resign immediately from Anexa, stating you will pursue another opportunity. Traitors are not welcome here," said MacNamara.

"I'm not doing or signing anything until I talk to my attorney. Anexa owes me after fifteen years of service."

"Anexa doesn't owe you squat. Either you write your resignation letter, or I turn over your correspondence to the SEC for insider trading," said Barry.

"That's ridiculous. I never discussed anything of the sort," said Phillips, alarmed.

"Yes, you did and we have emails from your company account to prove it," said MacNamara.

"You set me up! You bastards!" Phillips realized Anexa had the capability to doctor emails from him and would use them against him.

"Stop wasting our time. Just write the goddamn letter," growled

ACQUISITION OF POWER

MacNamara. "Barry, make sure Security escorts him out of the building. I want everyone to see what happens to traitors."

2

Atherton listened to his final voicemail message of the day and was surprised to hear it was from a distraught Cam Phillips.

"I wanted you to know I've been fired from Anexa. I'm afraid I'm no longer useful to you given the recent turn of events. I had hoped we could've worked something out, but this doesn't seem to be the case. My apologies."

Atherton called Murray to find out if anything had come back on Phillips's background report.

"I'm afraid the report has not been completed, yet. If anything important does surface, I'll fax you while you're in Europe."

"I have a feeling about this guy. He's an honest man. Call me, if something interesting surfaces."

"You got it! How are you holding up? You must still be pretty upset after our Board meeting."

"That's an understatement. You were right about me needing some time to regroup. I'm going to use this time off to reflect and to think about a lot of things. Thanks for asking."

"Sure, no problem. Well then, have a safe trip."

3

Phillips drove to his home in White Plains, just outside New York City; he felt defeated. He dreaded the conversation he would have to have with his wife. It was bad enough facing the humiliation of getting fired but not receiving any compensation posed a serious threat to their finances. Overcoming redundancy at this point in his career was going to be tricky. Where was he going to find another VP job, one which paid well, when the job market offered younger, less expensive, personnel?

"Lisa, I have some bad news," he announced, returning home. "I've been fired," he blurted out. Phillips may have been an excellent engineer but was a lousy communicator.

His wife was smart enough to have guessed this might happen. The news still came as a shock to her. "There must be something for you to do at Anexa. Couldn't you talk to Mac?"

"No, he was the one who instigated it. I'm out and that's it."

"What about that other CEO you were trying to meet with?" she asked, hoping for some good news.

"I did not get a chance to meet with him before this happened. Anyway, I left him a phone message on my way home tonight. I doubt anything will come of it, though. Without my job at Anexa, I'm of no value to anyone."

Lisa gave her husband a hug and tried to reassure him. "Listen, things don't always go as we plan, but they do happen for a reason. We'll survive."

He pulled away. "Have you seen our mortgage payments and bills? What about the kids' college funds?"

"Look, I'm not saying this will be easy. Maybe we can get a loan to help us through. I can go back to work."

"You haven't worked since the kids were born. What kind of job will you find which will cover our bills?"

She remained calm and focused. "Cam Phillips, you listen to me. That job was killing you. Your management rarely thanked you for all the ridiculous overtime you put in. You spent more time worrying about Anexa than your own family. As far as I am concerned, this news is a blessing in disguise. You need to refocus your priorities so you can spend more time with your family. It'll all work out in the end, you'll see."

"I don't know Lisa. All I can see are bills and more bills."

"Honey, I understand, I really do. What's done is done. You need to unwind. I'll go run a hot bath for you. When you're done, you can join us for supper. The kids will be over the moon to see you home early, for a change."

He looked at his wife and saw the look of concern on her face. She really loved him. "I love you, Lisa. Thank you for being so supportive."

4

While Phillips was at home receiving consolation from his wife, Atherton was finishing some last minute details, so he could head out of the office and begin his time off. He read Carl's latest report, returned phone calls, and decided it was time to call Gillian. She had left several messages for him, so was pleased when he called back. She had her own reasons for wanting to talk to him, given the recent ultimatum from MacNamara.

"Hi darling, where have you been hiding?" she said.

"You know what it's like around here."

"If you're working late, I can come around and cheer you up. Remember the last time I surprised you? I bet you don't look at your desk quite the same," she laughed. It was not like Gillian to be so forward. Atherton was too distracted to notice.

"I want to talk to you about something."

"Oh?" she inquired.

"Lucy trapped me into going with her to Europe."

"That's what you wanted, right? To do some damage control on your marriage, so she wouldn't run off with her lover boy."

"My problem is that she wants to leave right in the middle of my troubles with Anexa."

"I see."

"The other thing is, I don't know if I'm capable of spending an entire week with her. How will I fake my emotions?"

"Well, if she's toasted on fine European wine, then it won't really matter. She won't notice."

"But for one week?" Atherton sounded desperate.

"What if you had a stowaway tag along to distract you?"

"You're kidding. You would go with me? I mean, follow us?"

"Sure! I'll even help you sort out details to keep Lucy happy and tipsy enough that we can spend some time alone, enjoying ourselves."

"Gillian, you're wicked!"

5

Gillian decided to retire to bed early for the evening. Her head hurt from a pounding migraine, not alleviated by analgesics. In the early hours of the morning, MacNamara telephoned, waking her up. She recognized his number on her caller identification and hesitated before answering his call. He was the last person she wanted to talk to but understood the ramifications if she did not pick up.

"What do you want at this time of night?" The sound of her voice caused her head to hurt, even more.

"For a paid whore, I'm surprised by your grouchy demeanor. How about a nice, 'Mac, how are you?'"

She was in no mood for his games. "Like I said, what do you want?"

"How about some information, pretty please. What's my old pal up to?"

"We spoke yesterday. He's going to Europe with his wife to take some time off. I think he said something about securing her loyalty by rekindling the romance in their marriage."

"Oh really. Tell me more."

"Well, before the EPIK Board approved the merger, he talked about taking Lucy away, so he could romance her."

"So he could keep control of her shares by securing her affections."

"Something to that effect."

"Hmmm. I don't know why that would be so important…with the merger going through," mused MacNamara. "Something else must be tying him to her."

"Ponder that one without me. I wouldn't mind going back to sleep."

"Well, excuse me. We wouldn't want you to lose your looks and wind up on the filthy and disgusting Rue St. Denis, in Paris. Isn't that where all deadbeat European prostitutes end up? I can just picture you, standing in a decrepit doorway, wearing cheap, black nylon lingerie. Your body hasn't been washed since the last client but you're still looking for some *l'amour sur scène*."

"At least give me credit to work in Pigalle, or Montmartre," she retorted. "My professional status is higher." She was not going to give him the satisfaction of bullying her. It was bad enough he was blackmailing her.

"My mistake, please forgive me. A whore with taste deserves to live where Delacroix, Degas, and Van Gogh once painted."

"Don't forget Toulouse-Lautrec. He drank himself to death in Pigalle. Maybe you would like a similar fate for me?"

Gillian heard his faint chuckle. "I would love to stay online and chit-chat with you more but—"

"Please don't let me keep you up, Mr. MacNamara."

"Goodnight then, my sweet *femme de la nuit*."

Chapter Ten

1

Lucy mapped out the perfect getaway trip for Atherton and herself. She booked accommodations at hotels where they had stayed during their honeymoon. Instead of flying on the Concorde, she chartered a private jet to take them to London, Paris, and Greece. She was extremely pleased with her decisions and could not wait to share them with Atherton.

She found him sitting alone in their den. Before entering the room, she paused to watch him. He remained perfectly still, staring into the darkness of the night.

"James, are you all right?" she asked softly.

He was deep in thought and looked up, startled. "Oh, I didn't hear you come in. I was just thinking about work." The truth was he was thinking about Gillian, fantasizing about their upcoming escapades.

She positioned herself next to him on the couch and put her arms around his neck. She nuzzled up against him, smelling his Creed aftershave. "I'm glad you're home and can enjoy a break." For once, she did not smell of alcohol.

"Me too," he sighed. "I feel like I have aged in these past few months, with all the pressures from work."

"You certainly don't look as though you have. Do you want to hear about our plans?"

"Darling, I'm sorry. Of course I do," he lied. "Tell me about our adventure." The more details he knew, the better; he and Gillian could conjure up distractions, so they could be alone.

"Our driver will pick us up and take us to the airport. We fly to London, staying two days, then on to Paris. I've booked the Ritz, and then I thought we might go to Versailles." *Greed is good.*

"I would love to stay at the *Trianon Palace* in Versailles for one night, so I could eat at their seafood café."

"Let me guess, you will want crab, lobster, chilled Pinot Blanc, and all the chocolate mousse you can eat." She surprised him by recounting the details of his favorite meal from their last trip.

"Remember when I asked for more chocolate mousse and—"

"They brought out the whole dessert plate from the kitchen—with a big spoon!"

They laughed together. It felt good.

"Do you think that we'll have time to go to the south of France? I would love to cycle around Porquerolle." Atherton was fond of the French 'Golden Islands,' accessible only by ferry, where cars were forbidden.

"You read my mind!" said Lucy. Her voice bubbled with excitement. "Cycle trip complete with picnic…it's on the agenda."

"Wonderful. What else?"

"I thought we might spend the rest of the time relaxing in Greece. The islands, Skiathos or Skopelos—deep blue sea, white sands, olive groves, white-washed villages."

"Ouzo and Retsina," he teased, remembering his visits to the local tavernas.

"I remember how you became so involved in the local backgammon game that I almost thought that I was a widow," she teased back.

His eyes twinkled. "Don't tell me you forgot about our escapades on the nude beach. Who would have thought Sir Alexander's daughter was capable of such antics?"

"You were the naughty one. You goaded me into running around topless."

"Those were good times Lucy. It feels so long ago."

She winked at him. "We can make those times continue."

Not under the present circumstances, he thought. Lucy's condition made it impossible. Besides, his relationship with Gillian was perfect. He had all the pleasures—a woman without the nagging responsibilities.

Lucy grabbed his hand and tugged at it. "Let's go upstairs and start our second honeymoon."

Atherton followed her in silence. He couldn't remember the last time they had made love. Just think about Gillian, he told himself.

2

Atherton arranged some special surprises for Lucy during the trip, thanks to Gillian. He desperately wanted this vacation to be memorable for Lucy, in the hope she would fall back in love with him and call off the divorce threat. For the flight to London, he catered Lucy's favorite foods and drinks. At breakfast, they feasted on mangoes, strawberries, and kiwis, while drinking vintage champagne. Lunch consisted of grilled tuna with steamed vegetables. When her crème brûlé dessert was brought out, Lucy discovered a turquoise box next to her crystal dessert bowl. She unwrapped the white ribbon, surrounding the Tiffany box, opened the black velvet box, and let out a squeal of delight.

"They're exquisite!" Lucy examined the three-carat, emerald-cut diamond earrings. "I'm going to put them on."

"I'm glad you like them." Gillian had thought of everything. "A token of thanks for arranging this trip."

"Thank you, darling. Everything has been so wonderful. I think I've eaten enough for the whole trip." She refilled her glass with wine.

"I've reservations for us at the *Portman House* when we land."

"But, I couldn't possibly eat another bite," she groaned.

"Oh yes. Beluga caviar, beef Wellington, chocolate profiteroles, and Penfolds Shiraz—"

"Stop it, I can't."

"Then, we'll have to check into the hotel for some you know what...."

Lucy giggled. "I don't know if I can do that either. I'm still sore from this morning, last night, and the night before."

"I promise to be extra gentle." Atherton surprised himself by finding just how easy it was to make love to her without getting emotionally involved.

"I'm glad we did this. I really love you, James."

Everything was working to plan! It was easier than he imagined. He stroked the outline of her face and ran his hands through her hair. "Sweetheart, I have always loved you."

"I'm dreaming," she said before passing out in his arms.

3

The *Trianon Palace Hotel* was about forty-five minutes from France's Orly airport. It was an elegant white hotel, discreetly located behind Versailles palace. When they drove up the gravel drive and passed through the wrought iron gates, the taxi driver was caught off guard by the beauty of the majestic hotel.

"Ooh-la-la," he said. "*Très chère.*" If these rich Americans could afford to stay here, he hoped they would give him a generous tip.

When the couple checked in, Atherton continued to hold Lucy's hand and stole quick kisses, just as Gillian had instructed him to. Lucy was pleased that his affectionate behavior caused the check-in staff to inquire if they were newlyweds.

"*Nous avons réservé une chambre au nom d'Atherton,*" Lucy told the clerk trying out her French.

"You speak French well very," said the clerk. "Yes, I have your reservations here, Mrs. Atherton. Welcome to the *Trianon Palace Hotel.*"

A brochure from the hotel's Givency spa caught Atherton's attention. He asked about treatment availability. If Lucy were occupied, he could catch up on EPIK business, then meet Gillian who had checked in the day before.

"Darling, this time is supposed to be for us," she resisted.

"I think a little pampering won't hurt," he said, scanning the spa's brochure. "It says here, they do therapeutic massage, peppermint body scrubs, and seaweed wraps. Doesn't that sound good?"

"Well, it does! Are you sure?"

"Just enjoy yourself," he said, bidding her goodbye.

"*Monsieur, vous avez un message des États-Unis,*" said the concierge.

"*Je suis désolé, c'est ma femme qui parle bien le français.* Sorry, it's my wife who can speak French," replied Atherton. It was the only thing he could say in French other than hello, goodbye, and thank you. Atherton knew the importance of attempting French, as anything else was deemed rude. "Could you please repeat what you just said?"

The concierge smiled at Atherton's efforts. "You have a message from the United States." He handed him a message from Jack Murray.

"*Merci,*" said Atherton.

"*Monsieur,* please…" The concierge waited until Atherton's wife was out of earshot. *Madame du Monde est dans sa chambre.* Ah, excuse me, Madame du Monde is in her room, room number ten-twenty."

"Ten-twenty," repeated Atherton.

"*Oui.*" The concierge winked at him, understanding his arrangement. After all, mistresses were part of the French culture.

Atherton removed some Euros from his wallet and handed them over to his accomplice. "Could you see to it that my wife is fully occupied at the spa for the rest of the afternoon?"

"*Absolument,*" said the concierge. "Absolutely. No problem." He discreetly took the money and put it in his pocket. "*Amusez-vous bien!*"

4

Atherton called EPIK and got through immediately.

"Hey, James! You sound like you're next door," said Murray.

"You can thank Minitel. The French know how to run an excellent telecom service."

"So, enjoying your trip?"

"As a matter fact I am…I mean, we are. What's up? I received your message."

I wanted you to know the background report came back on Cam Phillips. What's interesting is, before he worked for Anexa, he worked for the government."

"In what capacity?"

"He did a stint at the OIA, the Office of International Affairs within the National Telecommunications and Information Administration. Not only that, but he was instrumental in defining some of the FCC's regulation on foreign participation in U.S. telecommunications companies. He should have some good contacts, which could come in handy."

"Do you think he will return to the public sector?"

"I doubt it. I bet he's used to a private sector salary. Why don't we contract him as a consultant, to work with the integration team?"

"Yeah, I like that. Talk to him. See if he's interested." Atherton loved the thought of MacNamara finding out Phillips was back on the payroll. "How's everything else going? What's the general mood like?"

"Better than expected. We're getting mixed reactions from the employees. Some are excited about the merger. Others are worried. We'll have to manage some expectations."

"What about our friends from Anexa?"

"They've sent over a junior executive to be included in the integration team. Her name's Diana Roberts."

"Keep her at bay until I return. I suspect MacNamara will use her as his eyes and ears."

"That's what I thought."

"Anything else?"

"Nothing I can't handle. Just enjoy the rest of your trip."

"Thanks, I will," said Atherton. He hung up the phone, got undressed, and headed to the shower to get cleaned up. His next stop would be Gillian's room.

5

"*Qui est là?* Who is it?" asked Gillian.

"Room service," said Atherton.

She recognized his voice and opened her door. "*Bonjour, mon cheri.*"

Atherton went in and closed the door. Gillian kissed him on both cheeks. She nibbled at his lower lip.

Atherton grabbed her derriere and pressed her against him. He kissed her plump lips, ferociously.

"I need you. It's been too long," she whispered hoarsely.

He picked her up and sat her upright on the bed. "Undress," he commanded. As she disrobed, her nipples hardened in anticipation.

Atherton knelt down. "Open your legs," he ordered. He kissed her mound, blowing softly at her clitoris. Using his fingers, he gently opened her delicate lips to examine her. Her pink skin glistened with moisture.

"Tell me what I'm doing to you," he said. Atherton liked to play this game.

She moaned. "You're examining me," she responded. She felt his nose go between her folds and take in her aroma. It was too much for her. She squirmed and moved her hips forward, thrusting herself on to his face. He understood her need and began to expertly circle her opening with his tongue.

"More," she cried. " I need you to—"

Atherton stopped, stood up, and pushed her back on to the bed. He grasped her legs and put them over his shoulders. He felt her grab his hard penis and guide it inside her. Gillian gasped as his entire length went into her in one stroke. He felt harder and longer than usual. She closed her eyes and placed a finger in her mouth, greedily sucking on it. Atherton shifted his weight back and forth quickly. Gillian moaned in ecstasy.

"Harder, harder," she cried out. "Make it hurt."

He shuddered, taking one last movement, before collapsing on top of her.

"God, that was good," he sighed.

6

Jack Murray paid an impromptu visit to the Phillips' home after his conversation with Atherton. Lisa Phillips opened the door, and Murray was greeted with a cacophony of children's voices in the background.

"I'm afraid I caught you at a bad time," said Murray, wishing he had called first. "No, it's always like this, she said patiently. "Can I help you?"

Murray noticed that despite her plain looks, there was something attractive about her. Maybe, it was her calm demeanor. "My name is Jack Murray. I was hoping to speak to your husband. I'm from—"

"EPIK," said Cam Phillips, appearing behind his wife. "Like I told your boss, I'm no help to anyone."

Lisa ignored her husband. "Come in Mr. Murray. I hope you don't mind the mess."

"Organized chaos," said Murray, stepping over baby and toddler toys. "I bet the kids know exactly where every toy is."

"Except the toy boxes," said Phillips.

"Can we offer you a drink?" asked Lisa.

"A glass of water would be nice."

"Coming right up." Murray watched her go into the kitchen. She was too good for Phillips.

"What brings you here?" Phillips interrupted Murray's thoughts.

"James Atherton asked me to come and talk to you, on his behalf. He's detained, at the moment."

"You know I no longer work for Anexa?" asked Phillips glumly.

"Yes, we know that. Did they make you sign a non-compete disclosure?"

"No. Why would that matter to you since the merger is underway, and I've been fired. I'm not part of the new organization."

Lisa returned, handed Murray his drink, and sat down to join the conversation. "Anexa did not recognize my husband's value."

"Their loss is our gain."

"How do you figure?" asked Phillips.

"Mr. Atherton understands the importance of your extensive telecom knowledge. Our scientists could use your input and experience. Would you consider working for EPIK as an independent contractor?

Lisa answered for her husband. "Do you know how much Cam was making at Anexa?"

"I think if your husband chose to work for Atherton, his financial woes would be insignificant."

"I still don't fully understand my role or my function," said Phillips.

"Atherton wants to keep good people around. He knows you would be a valuable asset, given your experience and government contacts. In the short term, you would work in the integration team. After that, the sky's the limit."

"I'm still not sure about all this. I can't afford to be dumped after the short-term period expires," said Phillips.

You can't afford not to take this offer, thought Murray. Why was he playing hard to get? "When Atherton returns, you can talk to him in person. I just wanted you to know he didn't forget you. Please keep this offer confidential, so we can go around MacNamara and put you back on the payroll."

"I didn't say yes, yet."

Lisa nudged her husband. "Mr. Murray, we'll talk it over and get back to you."

"Okay," said Murray. He shook hands with the couple and left.

Chapter Eleven

1

MacNamara's head of security at *Windermere* was a fairly new employee. Only months before, he had been a contractor for a Los Angeles company, which specialized in security for the Hollywood set. Ronnie Harvey had met Dean MacNamara when they literally bumped into each other at the LAX airport; Harvey had been rushing to catch a flight to Vegas, while MacNamara had been intently searching for some tablets to relieve his pounding headache.

"Hey, man. Sorry…you okay?" said Harvey, realizing he had almost knocked the business-attired man over.

MacNamara grimaced, as he continued to search for the pills. His face had turned white and his hands trembled. When would the pain stop?

Harvey thought the guy was having a heart attack. Maybe he had triggered it with the collision? "Sir!" said Harvey loudly. "Can I call you a doctor?"

The voice jolted MacNamara's concentration. The pain—it had disappeared. MacNamara examined the stranger, whose words of concern had eliminated the pain.

"Listen man, you gotta sit down for a while. You don't look so hot."

Harvey decided to postpone his rush—he could pick up another plane later—and sit with this guy until he sought medical help. Don't need this to turn into a bigger problem, he thought.

After establishing rapport, MacNamara was interested in Harvey's profession and offered him a chance to head up *Windermere's* security. If you're ever interesting in switching to private security work, please give me a call," said MacNamara, handing him a business card.

Harvey did not think about moving to the East coast—until he ran into financial trouble. Harvey remembered meeting the charismatic CEO and called him up to see if his offer was still valid.

"Changed your mind?" asked MacNamara. "You must have a good reason to want to leave the sunny weather."

"Nah, I'm just in need of a change of pace."

"When can you get here?"

"Actually, I'm calling from the LAX. My bags are packed and I'm on the next flight out."

MacNamara laughed. "Fine! I'll have our driver pick you up and bring you to *Windermere*. My wife, Tamara, can get you settled until I get home. We can talk about your duties, then."

2

One of Harvey's responsibilities was to periodically review *Windermere's* security tapes. One particular night, he could not believe his luck; he encountered an unexpectedly saucy screening. The tape showed Bunny Moore making love to a blonde whom he did not recognize. Although the tape posed no security threat to the MacNamara household, Harvey was clever enough to understand its importance. He toyed with the idea of using it for personal gain—Mrs. Moore would pay handsomely to eliminate this evidence—but decided it would be in his best interest to give it to MacNamara.

"Has anyone else seen it?" MacNamara asked, after reviewing the tape.

"Nope. Just me."

"Let's keep it confidential. I appreciate your loyalty in bringing it to my attention. As a thank you, you'll receive more in your next paycheck."

"That's very generous of you, boss, but I was just doing my job," he lied, knowing he could use the money. Harvey was satisfied he had done the right thing, delivering the tape to MacNamara. MacNamara had an uncanny ability to read people's thoughts, and Harvey guessed MacNamara would, eventually, have found out about the lovers. It was important to remain on MacNamara's good side.

MacNamara looked at him oddly. Most people would not turn down extra cash. "Just take the money."

"Thank you, sir. If you don't need anything else, I'll be on my way."

This tape was just the thing to seal Lucy Atherton's fate. She was such a stupid, emotional woman. Didn't she know all rich people had surveillance equipment installed in their homes?

3

MacNamara reached Barry on his cell phone and asked him to drive over to *Windermere*. Priscilla was already *en route*. They arrived at the same time and were led to the entertainment room, where MacNamara waited patiently.

"What's she doing here?" MacNamara pointed to Diana. "This is a closed meeting."

"She was with me when you called," said Priscilla. "Don't worry, she has signed a confidentiality agreement." She turned to Diana. "Good girls don't blab, do they?"

"No, Priscilla. I understand the consequences of violating corporate secrecy agreements," said Diana.

Priscilla looked at MacNamara.

"Fine, this might be good for her work education. Diana, thank you for joining us."

Diana smiled politely at MacNamara. He was handsome and well-mannered. Too bad she reported to Priscilla.

"So what's going on?" asked Barry, joining the group. He finished zipping up his trousers; openly displaying he had just finished using the bathroom.

"Hello, Baz boy. Get comfortable. We're going to watch a movie. Might as well leave your pants down for this broadcast."

Priscilla groaned. "You brought me all the way out here just to watch a dirty movie?"

"Patience, my dear. Everyone, please take a seat," said MacNamara. He dimmed the lights and started the tape.

As soon as Barry recognized Bunny, he cried out. "What the fuck is this? Turn it off!" Barry walked over to switch the power off.

MacNamara had anticipated his movement. He grabbed Barry from behind, holding him in a bear hug. "Sit back down. Keep quiet. You're spoiling it for the rest of us."

"Come on Mac. Please stop it," pleaded Barry.

"No! Shush! It only gets better."

The tape played out the passionate love scene between Lucy and Bunny. MacNamara watched the expressions of his audience; he enjoyed watching their faces as much as he enjoyed watching the tape. True to form, Priscilla showed elements of amusement. Barry, on the other hand, looked horrified. Diana stopped watching the tape after realizing its smutty content, and stared at the ground, waiting for the end.

When the tape finished, Priscilla was the first to speak. "I had no idea Bunny had it in her—lusty."

"There's nothing *in* her. That's the problem," said Barry. He was disgusted by his wife's actions. "Stupid bitch, wait till I get my hands on her."

"Now, now Barry. Calm down. I should be thanking you for this. What Bunny has accomplished here is beyond words," said MacNamara.

"I'll say," said Priscilla. "She's practically tongue-tied."

"That's not funny," said Barry. "Mac, why did we all have to watch this?"

"Because I wanted to share it with all of you. This tape will ensure I get Lucy Atherton's shares."

"What are you talking about?" asked Barry. "You don't need her shares. The merger's going through."

"Don't be an idiot. I want personal satisfaction."

"I still don't get it. What does the tape have to do with her shares?"

Diana spoke. "Blackmail, I assume." She was still looking down at her feet as she spoke. Her long, wavy hair covered her shamed-colored face. Her liking for MacNamara as a distinguished, gentlemanly figure dissipated as quickly as it had developed. He was just like Priscilla, cold and calculating.

MacNamara was pleased with Diana's answer. She was stunning and smart, a lethal combination. "Your perception is correct, blackmail it is."

"Blackmail? You have got to be fucking kidding me!" said Barry. His hands trembled as he nervously lit a cigarette.

"After she sees her tryst on tape, I think she will be persuaded to sell her shares in exchange for the tape's destruction."

Priscilla looked at Barry, then MacNamara. "That will never work," she said.

"That's why you are not CEO of Anexa," he shot back at her. "Of course it will."

"Mac, the Security and Exchange Commission will never allow such a transaction," pleaded Barry.

"That is why I hired all of you—to make it happen! Disguise the sale—cover it under a pyramid of offshore accounts, or something. I don't care how you do it. I just want the end result."

"Not a wise move," muttered Priscilla.

MacNamara was annoyed and disappointed by his team's apparent lack of support. "Why do you all care so much about Atherton, anyway?" he snapped. "He's unfit to run EPIK, or any company, for that matter."

Everyone in the room was staring at MacNamara.

"Any guy who talks to his dead father—is a lunatic."

"What?" asked Barry.

"It's true. His old man died during our sophomore year. I caught him, on several occasions, in our dorm room, carrying on heated conversations with dead daddio. Of course, he denied it every time I asked him why he contacted the dead."

"I could use a drink," said Barry.

MacNamara patted Barry on the back. They would listen to him and see Atherton for what he really was—a sick psychotic. MacNamara carefully selected a bottle of champagne and passed it to Barry.

Barry proceeded to open it. The cork flew out nearly hitting Priscilla in her backside. She glared at Barry while MacNamara doubled over, shrieking with laughter.

Barry gulped down two glasses.

"Hey, take it easy. You're drinking a prime vintage like a barbarian. Savor the flavor," said MacNamara. *Greed is good.*

Barry was right about MacNamara, thought Priscilla. He was acting more outrageously than ever before. She needed to talk to Barry in private. "It's been a long day Mac. We really should be heading out," said Priscilla. "Come on Barry, you need to go home."

"Always the den mother," said MacNamara. He walked over to Diana and put his arms around her. "You all leave if you wish. But Diana is staying here with me, to help finish this lovely bottle." He squeezed her, tightly.

Diana looked to Priscilla for help, but Priscilla ignored her silent plea. "I really should go too," Diana protested, trying to break free.

"Nonsense," replied MacNamara. "My driver can drop you off, later. I want to hear all about you."

4

"I told you he was screwed up," moaned Barry. "Remember the stuff about California? One minute he acted normal, the next he was a raving loon."

"Shut up. Let me think," said Priscilla, pacing. "He's going to get us all put in jail if we're not careful."

"Where's my coke?" Barry searched the pockets of his jacket and found the stash—enough for one line.

"That's the last thing you need. You already have a head rush from the bubbly you drank at Mac's."

"Cut me some slack." He lined up the white powder and snorted it quickly. "Whoosh," he said, energized by the rush. "MacNamara, you're a fool to mess with me. I'm much smarter than you."

"Shit Barry, stop the stupid soliloquy. Control yourself!"

"I *am* in control!" His voice escalated. "I still cannot believe that videotape. That whole thing pisses me off."

"How can you sit there and talk about that stupid stuff? Why do you care? I mean, it's not like you've been exactly celibate."

"You don't understand." It was all becoming clear to Barry. Bunny's excuses for not having sex, her comments about Lucy…

"Like hell, I don't. You're jealous because you can't get off with your own wife."

"Priscilla, don't fuck with my mind tonight. I'm not in the mood."

The coke wired Barry to the point of frenzy. He needed to come down fast. Priscilla went into her bathroom and rummaged for some painkillers. She found a bottle of Lortab and took out two tablets. This should do the trick, she thought.

"Take these," she said as she returned. "Here's some water to wash them down."

He looked at the tablets in her hand. "What are they?"

"Just some pills to take the edge off. You need to mellow out and get some rest. I need your mind clear, so we can do some planning later."

Priscilla turned on the television and gave Barry the remote control. He mindlessly flicked through the channels, until he found a soft-porn movie. He gazed into the screen, fell into a stupor, and dozed off. The last thing he remembered seeing were two brunettes pleasuring each other with their tongues. Lesbians, he thought, they're everywhere.

5

Diana managed to leave MacNamara's house not long after Priscilla and Barry. Feeling distressed and in need of someone to talk to, she asked the driver to drop her off at Carl's place. Thank God he was close by, having moved only a few blocks from her apartment.

"I didn't know where else to go," she sobbed when Carl opened the door.

"Diana," he said, stunned. "Come in, you're shaking." He helped her remove her coat. "Let me get you some coffee."

"Don't leave me," she begged. Diana grabbed him, pulling him close to her body.

Carl put his arms around her, hugging her tightly. "I'm not going anywhere." He stroked her hair and felt her relax. "Do you want to tell me what's going on?"

"I think I'm in trouble."

"Okay," he said gently. "Is there something wrong with your family?"

"No, no. They're fine. It's sort of work related." She took a deep breath and started her story. "Do you remember the party we went to at the MacNamaras?"

"Yes, the outrageous Christmas party."

"Well, they taped the event. Every room was outfitted with security cameras."

Carl thought about unsuspecting partygoers who had enjoyed the excesses in the private rooms. "I bet some people are in for a shock."

"Yes, like your friend Lucy Atherton."

"What?"

"I just saw a tape of Lucy with her friend Bunny. It was quite intimate, if you know what I mean." She looked at him to see his reaction, but he remained unfazed. "You're not surprised, are you?"

"Not really. I would rather not say why." While he worked at the Atherton's, he had witnessed enough evidence of Lucy's so-called friendship to know they were more than just friends. "Are you upset because of the tape's content?"

She looked uneasy. "Personally, I'm conservative but not judgmental. The content doesn't bother me as much as what MacNamara plans to do with it."

"Start at the beginning and tell me everything."

She relayed the events of the evening, telling him who had attended, and what MacNamara planned for Lucy.

"What about MacNamara's lawyer? Wasn't he against this plan?"

"No, for some reason, MacNamara has a strange hold over his people. They're captivated—and will do anything for him."

"But *you* won't."

"No. I will not be a part of secret tapings, blackmail, and illegal business transactions. I've a bad feeling about this. Can you contact your friend Lucy? Someone has to warn her."

"I believe the Athertons are in still in Europe. I could try to get a message to them."

"Thank you, Carl."

Carl had no intention of contacting the Athertons. Let them suffer like my mother suffered, he thought. Lucy could take care of herself. She had put herself in that situation; let her get out of it. Carl was worried about Diana and her involvement with MacNamara.

"I want you to resign from Anexa. You cannot continue working there. I don't think you'll be safe there. Promise me that you'll do that. I don't even want you to step inside their buildings. Send them your resignation."

"I really screwed up my life by getting involved with Anexa. I'm afraid of what's going to happen to me."

"Nothing's going to happen to you as long as I'm here to protect you," he vowed. "Nothing."

Chapter Twelve

1

Barry tried to push away the scene of his wife having sex with another woman. The harder he tried, the more vivid the images became. It was humiliating enough just to watch her passion with Lucy. Having to watch it in front of MacNamara and Priscilla was cruel. Bunny was going to pay for this. No one made a fool of him.

When Bunny returned home, Barry was waiting for her. "You stupid cow," he hollered.

"I see you've been drinking." She avoided his gaze and scanned the mess he had left on the table. A half-empty bottle of bourbon housed stale cigarette butts. "Next time use an ashtray."

"Wha-a-at…f-for?" he asked.

"You need a shower and shave. Obviously, you're high." His disheveled appearance was disturbing. It was unlike Barry not to pay attention to his state of dress. He had a meticulous obsession with cleanliness. Her instinct told her something was very wrong.

Barry grabbed her wrist. "Chicks like it…r-rough. I'm turn-ning you…ah-na."

"Stop it Barry! I'm in no mood for your games."

He twisted her arm around her back and whispered in her ear. "Tell me…you want me."

Bunny struggled to get away. "You're hurting my arm! Let me go!"

He released her. She turned and spat at him. "Don't you ever do that," she warned. "Or else…"

He brushed the warm saliva off his chin. "Else, what?"

There was no point in arguing with him. Drugs made him high-strung and unreasonable. "Why don't you piss off and go to work. I have things to do."

"Like screwing... your...high-class bi-tch?"

"So that makes two of us. *Touché*."

"You're nothing without me. Be...grate-ful I married...you! Your parents thought...they...ne-ver...would... rid...of the loser daughter."

"You're the loser! Sure, I married you to appease my parents. Love was the furthest thing from my mind. It's just as well I never cared about you...given your taste for fucking loser whores."

"I'll show you," he snarled, lunging at her. He was so incensed he lost all sense of the rational. Barry tore at her blouse and ripped off her skirt. He shoved her on to the floor and turned her on her stomach. As he roughly entered her, he pinned her hands down.

"Get off of me, you pig!" she screamed. "Get off!"

"That's exactly...what I'm doing."

2

Carl had provided Diana with good advice. Foolishly, she did not follow it.

"What's this?" said MacNamara, reading the letter addressed 'To Whom it May Concern.' "This had better not be what I think it is."

"I'm afraid it is. I appreciate Anexa's hiring me, but I feel this is not the right company for me," said Diana.

MacNamara tore up the letter, throwing the shredded pieces over his shoulder. "I think this company is just right for you."

Diana wasn't sure what to do next. This scenario had not been covered in university coursework.

MacNamara pressed down on the intercom. "Priscilla, please come in here for a minute?"

"You'll have to accept my letter of resignation," Diana said firmly.

"No."

"Then accept my verbal resignation. I quit."

"What's up?" asked Priscilla, entering MacNamara's office. "Did I miss anything good?"

"My feelings are hurt. My new friend here wants to leave us."

"That's much to soon," Priscilla sided with MacNamara.

"I think I'll be leaving," replied Diana. She sensed an ominous mood.

"Do you see what I mean Priscilla? She wants to leave me." he said, feigning tears. "Tell her not to."

"Diana, you cannot leave Anexa. We have plans for you within the company."

"I'm sorry. This is not the company for me," repeated Diana.

"You don't have a choice," said Priscilla. "You are in this with us."

"No, I'm not."

Priscilla examined her polished nails and huffed through her nostrils. "We know that after viewing the sex tape, you went to your boyfriend's apartment. You easily could have gone to the police to tell them about the blackmail plot. You didn't so that makes you an accomplice."

"I can still go to them."

"If you do, Anexa will destroy you and your family," warned Priscilla.

MacNamara propped his elbows on the desk. He rested his chin on his fists and sadly looked up at Priscilla. "Mommy, do you think that my friend will stay with us a little longer?"

"Yes," said Diana. "It looks as though I have no choice."

3

"You look like shit!" exclaimed Priscilla when she saw Barry at the office. "You better go and clean up in the executive washroom, before Mac sees you like that."

"Yeah, maybe I should," he mumbled.

"Barry, snap out of it! You and I have a lot to discuss. We need to figure out how we can get out of Mac's latest scheme. He's really gone overboard this time."

"Do you have any of those pills…like you gave me last night?"

"What? More painkillers? No, I don't. Even if I did, I wouldn't give you any. We have to be sharp."

Barry moaned. He grabbed his head. How could he focus on anything? His mind replayed the horror of what he had done to Bunny. He had really screwed things up. Bunny would never forgive him.

"Have you been listening to anything I've said? I'm not going to risk my career for some idiotic scam. I've worked hard to get this far," she ranted.

"I think I've got the message."

"So you *can* do what Mac wants, without involving me?"

"One of us has to follow the straight and narrow path."

"But you'll tell Mac I helped out, right?"

"Sure, whatever." Barry wanted to avoid upsetting yet another woman.

She kissed him on the mouth. "See you tonight. Maybe we can do some more kinky stuff?" she giggled.

"Fine. See you later." He made a mental note to find her prescription pain pills and to steal any remaining.

4

Prison was not an option Barry wanted to consider. In the past, white-collar criminals had been lucky to serve time in separate prisons, away from the hardcore population. But, times had changed. There was no guarantee of seclusion from the dregs of society.

The words from his parole officer still haunted him. "A pretty boy like you wouldn't last a second in the real pen. Consider yourself lucky you didn't end up gang-raped or made a bitch to someone twice your size. I remember seeing one guy who ended up in the infirmary. His ass was fucked so many times he bled to death."

Barry devised a plan to satisfy MacNamara and to keep himself out of jail.

First, he would prepare legal documentation, the language carefully worded to make it appear official. Using Bunny to lure Lucy to *Windermere*, he would force Lucy to watch the ill-fated videotape. MacNamara would goad her into selling her EPIK shares in exchange for the tape's destruction, leaving MacNamara with the impression he was in possession of her shares. After doing it, Barry planned to go to the Caribbean to make it appear he was finalizing the transaction offshore. Really, Barry needed to stall MacNamara long enough to free himself from this crazy mess.

"I like your idea of using Bunny to lure Lucy," said MacNamara to Barry. "How will you get her to sign the paperwork?"

"I'll give her a party drink, laced with something nice to relax her. We can show her the tape, then you can use your powers of persuasion to help her understand her options," said Barry, hoping MacNamara would approve his plan.

"When can you arrange it?"

"Tomorrow."

"Good. Take some extra time off when you go to the Caribbean to sort out this transaction. You'll have access to our company account. Enjoy yourself while you're there." Exactly what Barry hoped MacNamara would say.

Chapter Thirteen

1

Carl slept so deeply some nights, that when he woke up he could not recall dreaming. On other nights when he did dream, he often faced the recurring nightmare from his childhood; blurry images of his stricken mother and drunken father, portrayed in terrifying scenes leading up to the horrible accident.

"I don't want to talk about this," said Martha. "You're drunk."

"Don't be ridiculous. I've just had a few with the boys," said Carl's father. His clothes reeked of stale cigarette smoke, his breath of cheap whiskey. "We'll be done with this conversation only when I say it's over."

Martha walked past him. He grabbed her by the hair and slapped her across the face. She started to cry.

"I want to know who's the father of the bastard child you're carrying. You better tell me," he roared, as he raised his hand. "I bet the other one upstairs isn't mine, either."

Carl woke up frightened by the commotion downstairs and went to find his mother. "Mommy, where are you? Mommy!"

His cries went unanswered. Martha was surprised by another vicious slap and lost her balance. She managed to pull herself up by grabbing on to a nearby chair.

"I need to lie down." She stumbled towards the stairs, disoriented by the blows.

"You're not going anywhere until I'm finished with you."

Martha headed up the stairs. One hand held her heavily pregnant stomach, the other gripped the banister. Paralyzed by fear, Carl watched his mother try to make the ascent. His father came up behind her. She tried to kick him but lost her balance. Martha tumbled to the bottom of the stairs and remained there, moaning. Carl heard the chilling sound of his own screams.

"Get up," said Carl's father, staggering towards her.

"I can't...I can't," she sobbed.

"Don't make me repeat myself, woman."

"I think something's—wrong. I'm having contractions. Oh God, the baby's coming." She gasped for breath. "Call the doctor."

"You call. I'm out of here." In his haste to leave the apartment, he didn't bother to close the door behind him. He was out of their lives, forever.

Carl didn't remember how, or when, the ambulance arrived. It all happened so fast.

"You saved my life, darling boy. You called the doctor," said Martha.

"What about the baby?" asked Carl, frightened.

A paramedic moved him away from Martha. "Son, we have to take your mom to the hospital."

Carl never had the chance to see his baby sister. Her lifeless body was born before the ambulance reached the hospital.

2

"You had the dream," said Martha, clutching the phone. "I can hear it in your voice."

"Yes, I did," said Carl. It had been months since it occurred. He was beginning to think his nightmares were over.

"Do you know what triggered it?" she asked, already knowing his new job had aggravated the situation.

"Mom, I don't know."

"Maybe you should see a doctor about this." He should have done it years ago.

"Like a shrink? No way."

"You need to talk to someone. You need to put that night behind you, once and for all."

"How can you say that when every year, on the anniversary of *her* death, you go into mourning? Mom, *you* haven't healed, either."

"When you have children you will understand," she said softly. "Besides, that's not the point. We need to stop the nightmares."

"If I could have done something to have helped you, maybe I could have saved—"

"Carl, you listen to me. It was an accident. There was nothing you could have done."

"I could have fought him, or…"

"The doctors said the accident didn't cause her death. God had other plans for baby Alice."

"Still, I hate him for the pain he caused. I even hate to think of him as my father."

"Then don't," she said sharply. "I don't."

"If it wasn't for the nightmares, I could honestly say things were going great," he said.

"Is that because of your work, or the new lady in your life?"

"A bit of both." He felt his body relax as he started to talk about Diana.

"She sounds special. You deserve happiness in your life."

"Mom, she's very special. I would like you to meet her."

"Maybe I can arrange a trip out to see you in a few weeks. I would love to see you and to meet your new friend."

"I hope she becomes more than just a friend. Mom, I think she's the one." Carl laughed, surprised by his candor.

"I'm glad you shared this with me." Martha felt a twinge of guilt. Her son was always open with her. If only she could reciprocate.

"Then it's settled. Mom, make your plans to come visit," he said excitedly. "I love you."

"I love you, Carl." Martha knew it was only a matter of time before the truth surfaced. She didn't have to be a psychologist to understand Carl needed closure. If he had overheard any of the argument from that horrible evening, it was inevitable that he would have feelings of uncertainty.

"I'm a damn fool and bad mother," she cursed under her breath. At the expense of her son, she had resisted facing the truth. He deserved better. She had to help him free the demons. Her upcoming visit would be the opportunity to do just that, to set the record straight once and for all.

3

Carl greeted Diana with a kiss on the cheek. He wanted to wait for the right moment to kiss her on her bow lips.

"Hey, you look sleepy," she said, noticing dark circles under his eyes. "Having work nightmares?"

"Something like that."

"You don't look very well." She put her hand over his. "Maybe you're coming down with the flu."

"No. I'm fine, really. I have some good news."

"What?"

"My mom is coming to visit. I would like you to meet her. We could have lunch or dinner."

"How about lunch? It's less serious."

"Okay, then dinner it is," he joked.

She started to protest but realized he was teasing her. "You're so bad."

"Speaking of bad, how did Anexa take your resignation?"

Diana shifted her eyes away from him. She bit her lip, nervously.

"Diana, looks like you're the one having the flu."

"It feels like it. They wouldn't let me resign."

His jaw dropped. "What do you mean? Of course you can resign!"

"You remember the tape story I told you?"

"Yeah, so what?" Carl was angry with Diana. She knew she was in danger, yet did nothing about it.

"Well, MacNamara threatened me with co-conspiring."

Carl waved his hand. "That's ludicrous and you know it."

"There's more. They threatened to destroy my career and…"

"And?" Had he misjudged her? Was she so hell bent on her career that she foolishly remained at Anexa despite the risks? He was seeing a new side of her, which he didn't like. He wanted the sweet and innocent Diana back.

"My family. They will go after my family if I don't stay." She looked down, ashamed and defeated.

He took a deep breath. "I see."

Diana started to cry. "I seem to have no choice in this mess. After I worked so hard to make something of myself…"

"You can't go back there. It's too dangerous!"

"It's dangerous if I don't," she protested. "Besides, I don't have anywhere to go. They know where I live."

"You can stay with me. I'll figure something out."

"But you only have one bedroom."

"Which you can have. I'm very concerned about your safety."

She hesitated. "Let me think about it."

"I would prefer you didn't. Let me look after you. I care about you."

She didn't say anything. She knew he was right.

"Are you listening to me?"

"Carl, I care about you, too," she whispered.

He brushed aside her tears and gently kissed her on the mouth. It was a tender moment.

"I think I liked that," she said.
"You think?"
"No. I do," she said, returning the kiss.

Chapter Fourteen

1

"You have some nerve coming back here!" screamed Bunny at Barry. "You're lucky I didn't call the police after what you did."

Barry shook his head. Why were women so melodramatic? She enjoyed it as much as he had.

"I could have you arrested!"

"For what? Having sex with my wife?" he said, rolling his eyes.

"You're a son of a bitch. That wasn't sex, and it certainly wasn't consensual."

"In this State, our nice old-fashioned laws protect a husband's right to make love with his wife."

"You mean rape."

"Look it up for yourself. While we're still married, I can do whatever the fuck I want with you." He was tired of bickering with her.

"Well, let me give you a newsflash. I'm getting out of this sham of a marriage."

"Whatever. Just run into the arms of your lesbian lover. At least she will be able to get you off better than I ever could."

"Idiot," she hissed.

"By the way, you might want to be careful where you have your future liaisons. You never know who might be watching."

"What's that supposed to mean?"

"From the tape I've seen, you look almost professional. MacNamara even made the suggestion to sell it on the Internet…might be a good idea."

"What in the fuck are you talking about?"

"Does 'Merry Christmas Lucy' ring any bells? I'll have to say I was surprised Mrs. Atherton took the dominant role, though. I thought you were the butch one."

Bunny put it all together—the MacNamaras' party, the private room, the moments with Lucy. "Oh my God."

Barry glared at her.

"Does Lucy know about the videotape?" asked Bunny.

"She will very soon." Barry laughed. "Unless you tell her before I do."

"You're sick!"

"And if you having any thoughts about calling the police, forget it. The same laws that protect my husbandly duties also discriminate on same sex practices. I would hate to visit you in jail. Do you get where I'm coming from?"

"Clearly," she muttered.

2

Thoughts raced through Bunny's mind. Why had it taken so long for Barry to confront her? He was not the type who could keep a secret or withhold pressing information. Maybe he had not known about it. Bunny concluded MacNamara's interest was more than one of an amused spectator. He planned to use Lucy's involvement in some sinister way. She had to warn Lucy, before it was too late.

"I'm so glad you called," squealed Lucy. "We had such a fantastic time in Europe, and I can't wait to tell you all about it."

Bunny was surprised at Lucy's ease to forget their last conversation—when Lucy had chosen Atherton over her. It made it all the more painful for Bunny. Lucy made her feel as if their relationship was—a phase, a fling, insignificant.

Lucy continued chattering. "When can you come over? We can have tea and—"

Bunny interrupted her. "Um, I'm glad you had a good time."

"Oh, yes we did and—"

"I have some bad news," blurted Bunny, ceasing Lucy's babbling.

"Oh? What is it?"

Bunny took in a deep breath. "The MacNamaras videotaped the whole Christmas party."

"So? What does that have to do with me? Let me tell you all about Greece and the…"

"Lucy, don't you get it? They filmed us! Remember what happened in the private room?"

Lucy was silent.

"Lucy!" shouted Bunny.

"Are you sure?"

"Yes."

"How did you find out?"

"Barry told me. He and MacNamara have seen it. Lucy, we have to get that tape."

Lucy felt sick to her stomach. She craved something to calm her nerves. Where had she left her Valium pills? The contents of that tape threatened the successful reconciliation she had just accomplished. She had to destroy the tape, before it poisoned her new life with James. "I hope you have a plan," said Lucy miserably.

"We're going to *Windermere*. I'll call Tamara to let her know you're back in town. We'll go there on the premise of having tea, so you can tell her about your trip. During the teatime, I'll go find the tape."

"How will you do that?"

"Trust me, I'll find it." In reality, Bunny knew it was going to be near impossible to retrieve the tape.

"We have to destroy the tape. I never want James to see it."

"Don't worry." Bunny hung up.

After a few moments, there was a second click on Bunny's line; another phone was hung up. Barry smiled, pleased his strategy was off to a good start. He picked up his cell phone and dialed MacNamara.

"Hello, Barry."

"The plan's in motion."

"Good. I'll expect them shortly."

3

It was Atherton's first day back at the office. He spent most of the day in meetings, hearing reports from his legal and financial teams.

"There certainly seems to be a buzz around here," Atherton said to Murray. Murray agreed. "Nervous energy. People don't quite know what to expect."

"I should address those issues at the next Town Hall meeting."

"Do you think MacNamara will want to say anything?" asked Murray.

"I would rather he didn't. Who knows what he might say?"

"True. I haven't had the chance to ask you how things went on your trip. You certainly look refreshed."

"After today's series of back-to-back meetings, I feel like I never left."

"That's not what I meant."

"I know. We worked things out." Atherton remained evasive, revealing just enough information to satisfy Murray's curiosity.

"Really?" Murray arched his eyebrow.

"Yeah."

"I'm glad." Murray hoped Atherton's marriage worked out. He knew, from experience, the wounds a divorce would bring.

"Speaking of Lucy, I'd better call home."

"Back on the leash so soon." teased Murray, waving goodbye.

After several attempts at trying to reach Lucy at home, he dialed her cell phone. She answered.

"It's been a zoo around here."

"I believe you." The line crackled and her voice faded in and out.

"We must have a bad connection or you're leaving the network range. Where are you?"

"Oh, Bunny and I are going to see Tamara to catch up on…"

"I thought we discussed that. I don't want you near the MacNamaras, or anyone associated with Anexa, without me."

"What did you say? I missed that."

He grew frustrated. "I said I don't want you to go to the MacNamaras!"

"James, this is a bad connection. I can't hear you."

"Is Bunny with you?" he shouted.

"No, she's driving separately. Why?"

"Lucy? Repeat that!"

"I can't hear you. I'll see you when you get home. Love you so much …"

Atherton cursed.

Carl was coming into see his boss when he saw Atherton's distress. "Something wrong? We could reschedule our meeting."

Atherton stared into the receiver. "It's probably nothing—"

"Well you look refreshed," said Carl. "Welcome back."

"Sorry, let's get started. Bring me up to date on your reports."

4

When Bunny and Lucy met up at *Windermere*, they were escorted into the library by the butler. They were told Mrs. MacNamara would join them in a few minutes.

"Ladies, how nice to see you," said MacNamara, shortly thereafter, surprising them both. "I'm so glad you came to visit."

Bunny looked confused. "I'm sorry," she apologized. "We really came to see Tamara."

"That's funny because I sent her off to the city on a shopping spree. You know how excited women get over clothes."

"We must have got the days mixed up," said Lucy warily. "Please tell Tamara that we'll call her to reschedule our tea." She made a move for the door.

"You can't leave yet. I've planned something special for you."

"Pardon? I don't think—"

"No protests, please. I insist you both have a seat and make yourselves comfortable."

Lucy and Bunny exchanged worried glances.

MacNamara muttered to himself. "Where did my number one go? Barry, where are you? Come out, come out, wherever you are."

Barry stepped into the room.

"What the—" said Bunny. "What are *you* doing here?"

"Hello dear. It was good of you to come. You're so predictable. I knew you would run over here as soon as you heard about the tape."

"Bunny, let's get out of here," said Lucy, tugging at her friend's arm. "I've heard enough."

"Sit down!" MacNamara commanded. The severity in his voice caused them to freeze. Having their attention, he quickly changed his tone, to appear more pleasant. "Ladies, please. I've arranged a private showing for you. Let me see your appreciation. Please watch it."

"You're really going to like it." Barry smirked. "Maybe, afterwards, you could give us a live performance."

"Oh, you're teasing me. Barry, stop that," bantered MacNamara.

"You two deserve each other. You're both sick and twisted," mumbled Bunny. She searched around in her purse and found an old crushed cigarette packet. It was ages since she had last succumbed to a nicotine craving. Now did seem a perfect moment to light up.

Barry, I hope you enjoy having the upper hand because it won't last long. I'll bury you for this! vowed Bunny.

"Without further ado. Lights, camera, action," mocked MacNamara, dimming the lights and starting the show.

The naked images of Bunny and Lucy were projected onto the oversized movie screen. The film captured an intimate portrait of the women sharing their innermost emotions. There was no mistaking the identity of the intertwined lovers.

Bunny turned to look at her friend. So what if MacNamara had this tape? No one could take away the precious moments they had shared together. Unfortunately, Lucy did not share Bunny's perspective of the situation. Lucy sat frozen, her lurid image moving across the screen.

"Please turn it off. I've seen enough," whimpered Lucy. She thought her humiliation would kill her.

MacNamara ignored her. "We're coming up to my favorite part. You tell Bunny how much you love her ... some juicy kissing, all over. Quite intimate."

She lit up her second cigarette and offered it to Lucy, who accepted it. Show them how tough you are, thought Bunny. Beat them at their own game.

"I'm so pleased you're enjoying this," said Bunny.

"Shhhh! No chattering," said MacNamara. "Just look at you two, writhing about on the floor. Naughty, naughty ladies."

The tape finished. MacNamara and Barry both clapped and hollered.

"Encore," cried Barry.

"Don't be so barbaric," laughed MacNamara. "Show some manners. Fix these lovely ladies a drink." It was Barry's cue to prepare Lucy's relaxing tonic.

"Yes, of course. Coming right up." He prepared two glasses of cognac, one for Bunny, one for Lucy. To Lucy's drink, he added several crushed Lortab tablets before handing it to her.

Lucy finished her drink in a single gulp. She did not have time to detect the bitter taste of the drug. "I could definitely use another one," she said, handing her glass back to Barry. Her hand trembled. He grabbed the glass before she dropped it.

"I don't know if that's a good idea," said MacNamara, eyeing Barry, who in turn shrugged his shoulders. They had not anticipated giving her another drink. MacNamara understood the dangers of mixing too much alcohol with the relaxer they had slipped her. The last thing he wanted to do was inadvertently kill her.

"A lady of your pedigree should enjoy her drink. Cowboys gulp their drinks. Besides, aged cognac should be savored," said MacNamara.

"Come on, don't be cheap MacNamara. Give her another one. It's the least you could do…after making her watch that tape," said Bunny.

MacNamara's head started to hurt. Why couldn't she keep quiet? Keep focused, he commanded himself. Don't fall for prey to the bitch! He rubbed his temples until the pressure dissipated, as quickly as it started.

"It's interesting that *you* didn't seem to mind watching the tape. Why is that? Is it because you are in love with the married Mrs. Atherton?" MacNamara quizzed Bunny.

"I've nothing to be ashamed of," said Bunny.

"Be quiet," said Lucy. "Don't say anything else. This has been embarrassing."

Embarrassing? She was the one who had instigated the passion, thought Bunny. Lucy deserved to face whatever MacNamara had in store for her.

"What do you want from us?" asked Lucy.

"I want nothing from Bunny," replied MacNamara.

"There's a surprise," said Bunny.

"What do you want from me, then?"

"I'm a simple businessman, with simple needs," he sang.

"Lucy, don't be a fool," warned Bunny.

"Shut up, bitch," said Barry, slapping his wife across the face. "Keep quiet."

Bunny touched her cheek, which tingled from the slap. It had sounded much worse than it felt. Barry was such a loser—he could not even fake a good slap. Why was he pretending to scare Lucy with this phony cruelty? Let's see where this is going, she thought. Go on, humor me, badass Barry.

The theatrics were working. Barry threatened to slap Bunny, again. Lucy looked terrified. "Leave her alone," cried Lucy.

"Hey, it's just a little spat," said MacNamara. "Marital problems, you know? Do you and Mr. Atherton have marital problems?"

"That's none of your business," snapped Lucy.

"But it is my business when a married lady is caught in my house doing some hanky panky, especially when it involves another woman. I think the husband has the right to know what kind of woman he married. I certainly would want to know if it were my wife."

"Don't tell me you're doing this out of male brotherly love?" asked Lucy.

"Well, not exactly. I thought we could do an exchange. The tape for your EPIK shares."

"You must be crazy. Never!" said Lucy.

"Don't do it," warned Bunny.

"I thought I told you to shut up!" said Barry.

Bunny offered little resistance as he grabbed her and pushed her out into the hallway, locking the door behind her.

She placed her ear against the closed door.

"I think Mrs. Atherton needs to watch the video one more time," said MacNamara. "Obviously, she didn't get the impact of her performance first time through." He rewound the tape and played it.

Lucy began to feel lightheaded. The alcohol and painkiller concoction kicked in. It was impossible to focus on the screen. Instead, she imagined Atherton's reaction. "You deceived me! I thought we shared all our private secrets when we were in Europe. I told you everything. Purposely, you neglected to tell me about this. I will never be able to trust you. I want out."

Lucy's head swayed from side to side. Her eyes looked glassy, her pupils dilated.

"Is anyone in there?" asked Barry. "Hello?"

"Hello, the soon to be ex-Mrs. Atherton. Wakey, wakey." echoed MacNamara.

She barely heard them. "I don't feel well." she said.

"It's understandable that you're upset. I don't want your husband to find out about this tape anymore than you do. Let's just swap what we both want. The EPIK shares for the tape," said MacNamara.

"I don't know..." said Lucy, drifting off slightly. "May-be he'd... understand."

"Your husband will never forgive you. You know that. Do the right thing!"

"But if...I sold my...sh-ar-es to you...he'll be...furious."

"It's in our interests to protect both the buyer and seller. The stock's sale will be buried in a pyramid of offshore accounts, so deep no one will ever know you sold to Anexa," interjected Barry.

Don't screw up your marriage, she thought. If the merger was going through anyway, then there was no harm in selling her shares. "F-fine, I'll...d-do it."

"You're a smart woman," said MacNamara. Barry produced the documents he had prepared and helped Lucy sign the fake transaction papers.

"I n-need...one...dr-ink."

"How about your tape instead?" MacNamara held it up. He had obtained what he wanted. He unlocked the door to the hallway and waited for her to leave.

Lucy swayed toward MacNamara. She snatched the tape from his hand and staggered into the hallway, where Bunny was standing.

"What have you done?" Bunny eyed the tape in Lucy's hand.

"De-al...with...t-the...d-de-vil."

"Let me drive you home. You're in no state to drive." Bunny put her arm around Lucy's shoulders.

"Get…ha-nds…off…me," spat Lucy. "Your f-fa-fault."

"Please Lucy, let me drive you home. I won't even talk to you," pleaded Bunny.

Lucy glared at Bunny. "I…said…no!" There was an edge of steel to her voice.

"Fine. Do as you please. Just don't kill anyone on the way home."

5

It was a miracle Lucy made it home without having an accident. She stumbled into the basement and stuffed the tape into a sack full of trash.

"H-a-h…b-by-e." She fastened the bag, ready to be taken out the next day, and tried to remember how many drinks she had consumed. One? Three?

She went into her bedroom and looked at herself in the mirror. Bloodshot eyes stared back at her. Mascara streaks stained her dull complexion. Her crying had left her face bloated and marked with blotches. She ran her fingers through her hair and examined the locks damaged by excessive coloring. "You're certainly not the international debutante you once were," she mouthed at the gruesome reflection. "You're lucky to keep that handsome husband."

Lucy fixed herself another few drinks, helped herself to several Valiums, and took a long, hot shower. Clean yourself up, she thought. You don't want your husband to see you in this condition. Be proud of the way you handled MacNamara. With the tape fiasco behind you, you can focus on your continued reconciliation with James.

Unfortunately, those thoughts were not to be acted upon. Lucy's housekeeper found her naked body slumped over in the shower. By the time the paramedics arrived, it was too late. She had been dead several hours.

Chapter Fifteen

1

Reports of Lucy's death were well publicized in the press, but the true nature of her demise was withheld. There was no need to reveal publicly that Lucy had overdosed on booze and prescription medication.

Over six hundred mourners filled the Church of the Resurrection in Manhattan, where Lucy had occasionally attended Christmas and Easter services. The crowd included friends from Europe, business leaders, two senators, and several celebrities. Many came out of respect for Atherton.

Atherton respected his wife's wishes by holding a brief service. Her will requested a simple service, which was to conclude with Holst's "I Vow to Thee My Country," her favorite hymn from boarding school. Lucy hated to attend what she termed 'staged funerals', over-the-top weeping, open caskets, gothic-veiled mourners, morbid gossip, and slow funeral processions.

Murray accompanied Atherton, in the black limousine, back to *Ma Maison*. "I don't know how much more of this I can take," Atherton's hoarse voice whispered to Murray. "If one more person tells me how sorry they are…"

"You've done well this far," replied Murray. "Keep it together, friend."

2

Atherton received a flurry of visitors paying their respects, then retreated into his study, accompanied by Murray. They listened to the sound of the rain hitting the roof. Dark clouds had brought rain, without threat of thunder or lightening. The wind picked up; it splashed water, violently, against the windowpanes. Atherton was mesmerized, watching the water trickle from the beautiful roses. Vibrant yellows and reds stood proudly, seeming to defy the storm. Perfect hybrid tea roses absorbed the moisture to intensify their delicate shades of pink. He cursed not noticing this splendid sight, before.

"Lucy was quite a gardener," said Murray, interrupting Atherton's reverie. He patted his friend's shoulder. He felt uncertain as to what to say or do. No amount of consolation would relieve Atherton's emotional pain. The situation was tragic. Only weeks before, he had been in Europe, reconciling with Lucy. Poor soul, thought Murray.

"All these years, I listened halfheartedly to her gardening stories. I missed the point entirely. She composed a living painting for us to enjoy. She tried to create a bit of heaven for me to enjoy. I laughed at her efforts."

"I'm sure she knows you cared," said Murray.

"I can't believe this is happening. I feel like I'm in someone else's nightmare." Atherton buried his face in his hands.

"James, you probably need time on your own. You've been through a hell of a day."

"Yeah, I wouldn't mind some solitude. Thanks for being here for me."

"Think nothing of it. Can I get you anything before I go?"

"Tell the staff I want privacy. I don't want to be disturbed."

3

"You're a pitiful sight," said Senior.

Atherton wiped away his tears and blew his runny nose. Trust his father to show up at a time like this.

"What do you want?" mumbled Atherton.

Senior crossed his arms. "I want to know why you're crying."

"Why do you think?" spat Atherton. "I just buried my wife, Lucy, remember her?"

"Nice performance. I almost believed you for a moment." Senior clapped his hands.

"Get out of here," hissed Atherton.

"Stop the façade, boy! Drop the act. Tell me how you really feel—happy the old shrew is gone, thrilled about your financial position, guilt-free to play around with Gillian." *Greed is good.*

"I didn't want it to end like this," said Atherton miserably.

"No one does," replied Senior. "Hey, do you think she will pay me a visit? No doubt, she will be in the market for a new plaything."

"Senior, even by your standards, that's twisted and disgusting."

"I just thought—I would inquire. How about a drink?" asked Senior.

"I thought you didn't drink."

Senior snickered. "It's worth a little sip to propose a toast. To my son, the ever-ruthless and conniving bastard—may I wish you continued success in orchestrating events, leading to more money and body bags."

4

Atherton dismissed Senior. He thought about all the kind people who had extended sympathies to him. Many had come to his house bringing food or had expressed sentiments in a personal note.

At the service, Atherton had spotted Gillian, discreetly sitting towards the back of the church. She was dressed in a navy suit and matching hat. He felt comforted by her presence. Carl had attended with a young woman, who looked as though she had been crying. The person he did not see at the church, or at the house afterwards, was Bunny. He had expected to see her. Was she so grief stricken that she had been unable to attend? He had anticipated a telephone call from her; she was Lucy's best friend.

Atherton tried to distract his thoughts from Lucy by flipping through past issues of *Business Week*. That failed, so he turned on the television—also, an ineffective distraction. He grew increasingly agitated. There was a knock on the study door.

"Damn it. Didn't you hear? I want to be left alone," his voice boomed.

A soft but gentle voice apologized and said that she would come back, later. That voice! It sounded familiar. "No wait!" he commanded, rising from his chair. "Come back."

He opened the door. His eyes rested on the soft features of a petite woman. "Martha! What are you doing here?"

She was even smaller than he remembered. Her face remained unlined, gently framed by rich brown curls. She looked up at him and smiled sadly. "I was visiting Carl when I heard the news. I wasn't sure whether to come, or not. I thought that, maybe, I could offer you a friendly ear…if you needed it."

"I'm glad you're here," he said, hugging her. "I can't relax."

"That's understandable."

"Is Carl with you?"

"No. He doesn't know I'm here."

"I saw him earlier, at the service. I believe he was sitting with one of Lucy's friends. She looked quite distraught."

"That must have been Diana Roberts, Carl's girlfriend. I don't know if she knew Lucy, or not. I haven't met her yet."

"So you're in town to see Carl?"

"Something like that," she said evasively. "This must be a terrible shock for you."

Atherton nodded and said nothing. What was he going to say? That in part, it was a relief she was gone? That he resented her blackmail attempts to keep him married to her?

"The paper said she had a heart attack. Was she in poor health?"

"Not exactly," sighed Atherton. He had to tell someone the truth. Atherton knew Martha was trustworthy, so he decided to reveal the vices responsible for Lucy's death. "There's more to it. Lucy's heart gave out…the stress of alcohol and pills."

"Pills? What do you mean?"

"She took so many different medications, antidepressants, sedatives, and painkillers—prescribed for various ailments. The problem was she abused them—combined with booze."

"I'm so sorry."

"I wanted to keep it out of the press. I could barely read the coroner's report. I knew Lucy drank and took meds, but I never realized she mixed them. I should have foreseen it."

"Don't blame yourself. It was an accident."

"I just can't understand why she did it. We had just come back from a wonderful vacation."

"It was an accident," repeated Martha.

"But I could have put her in rehab, or…"

"Stop! Playing the what-if game doesn't do any good."

"I'm sorry, you're probably right. Too bad that we have to be reunited under these circumstances…"

"Mmmm. Could I cheer you up with stories from the old days?"

He smiled. "That would be nice. I could use some laughter."

5

"You bastards killed her!" Bunny accused Barry. "You and MacNamara are responsible for her death. I know it!"

"Don't be ridiculous! I saw the press reports. She died of natural causes," replied Barry. When he had seen initial reports of her death, he had been alarmed that the drugs or alcohol in her system could have been a problem for him—he had mixed up the relaxing tonic. Still, it should not have been enough to kill her. She must have done something back at her house to cause the fatality.

"A heart attack? You call that natural? I don't think so! You drugged her drink at *Windermere*."

Barry spun around to face her. His face was red.

She could see that she had touched a raw nerve. "You served us both what appeared to be the same drink. From the way she was stumbling around, I would say we had different potions."

"Geez! Some detective you would make," he laughed cruelly.

"Don't push me Barry. I could go to the police."

"And report what? Lucy Atherton was drunk? That's hardly fresh news."

"Before she left the house, she told me she made a deal with the devil. I bet you coerced her into selling her shares. If that's the case, you will never get away with it. You tricked her while she was drugged!"

"I don't hear alarm bells going off. Atherton must have seen the coronary report. If anything out of the ordinary had been found, I'm sure the police would've been involved. Just face the facts Bunny, your lover was a druggie."

"That's rich, coming from you. Okay then, what about her EPIK shares?"

MacNamara had been foolish to discuss the proposed share transaction in front of Bunny. Who knows what she might do with that kind of information? She could tell Atherton, the SEC, or the police. MacNamara did not know Bunny the way he did.

"Answer me! I know you tricked her," said Bunny.

"You're wrong. The only one who has been conned is Mac."

Her jaw dropped. "What do you mean?" Something was up. Bunny remembered how Barry had faked hitting her in front of Mac. Barry had a plan!

"It means he's been fucked. He thinks the deal's done, but it didn't even happen."

"I don't understand."

"Look, MacNamara wanted Lucy's shares. God knows why, but he did. I tried to talk him out of it. He wouldn't listen. He didn't care about the SEC's regulations or anything else," he blurted.

Bunny stared.

Make her think I'm the good guy, thought Barry. Make it personal. Say something about her dead lover. Barry added quickly, "I prepared fake transaction documents for Lucy to sign, so I could have time to figure out how to get *her* out of the mess."

Bunny was suspicious but confused. Did he really do it to protect Lucy? "Are you crazy? What do you think MacNamara's going to do when he finds out?"

Barry shrugged. "He's not gonna."

"Mac *will* find out. If he doesn't kill you, Atherton will, after I tell him about your sinister plotting."

"Listen to me, bitch! Breathe one word of this to anyone and you'll be the one to go," said Barry. He grabbed her by the shoulders, shaking her like a rag doll. "Don't fuck with me! I've lost my patience, dealing with women like you."

Something inside Bunny snapped. "Fine, go ahead and kill me. My death will be worth the cost of you rotting away in prison for the rest of your life."

Barry released her. Prison was not an option. He had to make a choice. Whose wrath was worse? MacNamara's or Atherton's?

6

Gillian sighed with relief as she returned from the funeral service to the comfort of her home. Her body shivered from the damp, chilly air. She decided to have a hot bath to soothe her nerves. She inhaled the fragrant steam and turned on the Jacuzzi. Gillian was in a deep trance, when she was startled by voice.

"That looks like fun," said MacNamara. "Maybe I should join you."

"How in the hell did you get in here?" He must have been hiding in the closet.

"I see we still haven't improved our greeting?"

Gillian shielded her breasts. "How did you get in?" she repeated, irritated.

"Money can buy many things." He unfolded a bath towel, spread it on the marble tile, and sat down. "What's with the sudden modesty?"

She sank down into the bath, allowing the bubbles to cover up her body. "You could have had the courtesy to call."

"No doubt you would have had the courtesy to answer my call."

She remained silent.

"That's what I thought. What's got you in such a foul mood?"

"I just came from Lucy Atherton's funeral." She had attended strictly out of morbid curiosity. She had wanted to observe Atherton's grief. If she had not known him as intimately as she did, she would have concluded that he was overcome by grief—the red eyes, the drawn complexion, the somber mood. He had put on quite a show.

MacNamara clapped his hands with delight, laughing heartily. "That's truly marvelous! How inappropriate! Did you cheer and whistle throughout the service?"

"Hardly."

"Don't tell me you and honey buns spent the service winking and exchanging lingering looks?"

"For your information, I snuck into the service and seated myself in the back row."

"So you didn't see him?" He feigned disappointment.

"I wouldn't go that far."

"Aha! That's my trollop!"

"For God's sake, just shut up."

"While you're here in a heavenly state, celebrating your lover's freedom, old what's-her-name must be rolling over in her grave."

"I certainly don't see it like that."

"Don't tell me you wouldn't give your left tit to become the next Mrs. James Atherton."

"Must you always act crudely?" Gillian shook her head at his barrage of disparaging remarks. The thought of marrying Atherton had crossed her mind several times. His present, vulnerable state facilitated the perfect opportunity to replace Lucy and to become his new wife.

"I expect better reports from your trysts with lover boy, especially now that he's able to spend more time with you."

"Aye, aye sir," she said, saluting him. "If you don't mind please respect my privacy, so I can finish my bath in peace."

"Women don't deserve respect. Didn't you read Plato's theory on reincarnation?"

"What? Just leave!" she said, exasperated.

"Pay attention, you'll appreciate the lesson," he said, patronizing her. "Plato's reincarnation worked like this. If you owed something to another person, then you would be reincarnated as a dog in the afterlife to serve that person."

"I'm not a dog."

"That's correct." He continued, "The worst possible punishment, for really horrible humans, was to be reincarnated as a woman. So you see Gillian, according to Plato, I'm treating you like the criminal which you are."

"You mean were," she corrected him. "My womanly form exonerates me from previous sins."

"Hah! Aren't you the clever one?"

"Leave."

"Not so fast. I came here for two reasons. Since our business is taken care of…I'm feeling tense…which leads us to the second reason for my visit." He reached into the bath and found her breasts. Her nipples hardened in response. Embarrassed by her body's desire, she pushed his hand away.

"Take your tension elsewhere," she said.

"Why should I? My favorite whore is freshly bathed. Dry off, while I make myself comfortable among your Pratesi sheets."

"Forget it. I would rather make love with the devil himself."

He laughed. "Like I said, I'll see you in a few minutes. Be ready."

Chapter Sixteen

1

MacNamara was surprised to see Barry in the office. "Hey, I thought you were incommunicado. I expected you to be sunning yourself somewhere offshore, taking care of business."

"I need to talk to you about a potential problem."

"What?"

"Bunny knows too much. The tape, the coerced stock sale, the suspect drink—"

"So deal with her."

"I'm worried she might go to the police or to Atherton."

"Let her blab. Lucy's death has nothing to do with us. You read the newspapers. The old cow died of a heart attack."

"Mac, come on. Stop and think! As you well know, there's a holding period before the stock transaction can go through. The minute the information gets out about Lucy's request to sell her EPIK shares, questions are going to start flying in our direction, and connections made. If she were still alive, it would be another story. She's not, and we could get busted."

"You're the one who gave her the spiked drink."

"And you're the one who made her watch the tape and forced her to sell her EPIK shares," Barry shot back. "Besides, too many people know about the tape—Bunny, Diana, Priscilla, and whoever they might have told."

"You're the cleaner. Do your job!"

"Hang on a minute. I'm the company counsel, not some sort of hit man."

"Once a criminal, always a criminal," said MacNamara.

"I've changed."

MacNamara snorted. "Look on the bright side, if things went sour for you, at least you'd know what to expect in prison. I, on the other hand, have not experienced—"

"White-collar crime hardly compares with murder. You're out of your mind if you think I'd even consider such a vile act."

"I thought I could trust you to handle the situation. Looks like I was wrong. Priscilla said you were weak and pathetic."

"I know what you're trying to do. You can count me out. You're crazy to pursue this line of thinking. I'm going to destroy the paperwork we had Lucy sign before this goes any further."

"Don't do that. I will handle everything, myself, from this point on."

"I don't know exactly what that means but I'm telling you, stay away from my wife. Leave her out of your game." Barry cursed himself for involving MacNamara. It was a foolish thing to have done.

"You forget, you're already in the game. It was *you* that brought this problem to my attention."

2

It had become increasingly difficult for Barry to read MacNamara. In the beginning, he had dismissed his boss's behavior. As it became more erratic and unpredictable, it was clear to see that something was seriously wrong with MacNamara. The MacNamara he knew would not toy with murder.

Barry decided to drive over to see Priscilla. He had to warn her about Mac's latest comments. As he pulled up to her townhouse, he froze. MacNamara's black Mercedes was parked out front.

Barry rang the doorbell several times, before resorting to pounding on her door. "Priscilla, open the damn door. I'm not leaving until you let me in."

He heard her voice from behind it. "This is not a good time. Come back later."

"Open the fucking door!"

Priscilla opened the door, scantily covered with a small towel. "Are you quite satisfied?"

He pushed past her. "Where the fuck is Mac?" screamed Barry. "I saw his license plate, ANEX E9. How many other people have abbreviated Anexa one billion in scientific notation on their license plate?"

Her face, neck, and chest were flushed.

It took him a few seconds before he realized his worst fear. "I interrupted you fucking him. You whore!"

"Duh," she responded dryly.

"You slut! I can't believe this!"

"Well, believe it, because it was real nice," she purred. Priscilla touched her neck and grinned.

Barry took a closer look at her neck. He noticed the skin was more reddened than flushed. "I see you're back to your old deviant behavior."

MacNamara emerged from the bedroom, wearing boxer shorts. "Oh hello, Barry," he said casually. "I was wondering when you would show up."

"I take it that this is not your first visit here."

"I'm a free woman. I can do whatever I like," interjected Priscilla.

"I can see that."

"Hey, old sport, don't look so glum." MacNamara stretched his arms and yawned. "That's what sharing is all about."

Priscilla ignored MacNamara's cavalier remark. He had given her the career move she wanted so desperately. She was on her way to becoming one of America's most formidable businesswomen. If she played her cards right, she could be on the cover of all the industry magazines.

"Barry, would you mind dropping by another time?" asked Priscilla, wanting to get rid of him. His moods could be as unpredictable as MacNamara's.

"I'm not going anywhere." He wanted to make her feel uncomfortable.

"You're quite right to want to stay put," said MacNamara. "Barry, how about a drink?"

"Stiff scotch," he replied, evenly. He felt uncertain as to how he should handle this encounter. How could Priscilla replace him? And with MacNamara?

"Sounds good," said MacNamara. He turned to Priscilla. "Fix me one, too."

She huffed and retreated to the kitchen. Priscilla understood her new position came with conditions.

MacNamara chuckled. "I'm taming the beast."

"My hat's off to you," replied Barry, annoyed at MacNamara's insensitivity.

"Has Priscilla told you the good news?"

Barry shook his head.

"She's my new Chief Operating Officer."

Barry, unconsciously, dropped his jaw. He had coveted the COO position. It had not crossed his mind MacNamara would offer it to anyone else. "What about the Board's approval process?"

"I can promote people without their approval."

Priscilla returned, handing each man his drink. She moved behind MacNamara and draped her arms around his neck. "Did I miss anything good?" she asked, nibbling on his ear, looking at Barry.

Barry glared at Priscilla. She was a two-timing bitch, who had used him all along. "This must be a joke. You? The new COO?"

She stood upright. "It's no joke! You're looking at Anexa's new COO." *Greed is good.*

"Well, enjoy the title while you can."

"Ditto. That goes for you too," she spat back. "At least, I have the support of Mac—"

MacNamara threw up his hands in protest. "Priscilla, take it easy. Why don't you go and have a shower, while we do some man talk."

"Good idea." She gave him a peck on the cheek. "Don't take too long. I want to continue thanking you for my promotion," she called out as she left.

MacNamara made a choking gesture at his throat. "That piece of information you told me really came in handy," he whispered to Barry. "I can't thank you enough, if you know what I mean."

"I can't believe you promoted her to COO in exchange for some ass. I'm sure you could sleep with her without giving her a promotion she doesn't deserve."

"You're understandably bitter. You probably would have liked that job."

"Damn right."

"I have to disagree with your assessment of Priscilla, though. She's extremely well qualified for the position."

"What about me? I've busted my balls for you."

"I know. View this as payback. I'm helping you out."

"Huh? I don't understand."

"I only gave her the title to shut her up about the tape." He smiled broadly. "Get it?"

Barry nodded.

"You know Priscilla's ambitions. If she could, she would eliminate us both, to become Anexa's new CEO."

"That's what I'm afraid of. You're playing with fire, Mac. Priscilla will fight like crazy to keep her career aspirations on track."

"'He who knows the art of the direct and the indirect approach will be victorious. Such is the art of maneuvering.'"

Barry hated it when MacNamara resorted to quoting Sun Tzu. "In plain English, if you don't mind."

"Priscilla will be so focused on her new rank, and maintaining it in the new hierarchy, she will lose sight of peripheral threats."

"So, her position's only temporary?"

"What's that Biblical line I find amusing?"

"'God giveth and taketh away.'"

"Yes, that's it. Barry, soon it will be back to the way things were—you and me, having fun."

Barry was pleased with the way MacNamara was handling it. Previous references to MacNamara's thoughts of violence seemed to have been forgotten. Barry concluded that he had overreacted to their previous conversations and had judged MacNamara unfairly.

"Speaking of you and me, do you want to join her in the shower? She's already worn me out. I could really use a nap," said MacNamara.

"You're more outrageous than ever. I appreciate the offer, but I'll pass. She's garbage to me."

"Gotta like that white trash." MacNamara waved goodbye, before heading off to the bedroom for a siesta.

Chapter Seventeen

1

The progression of MacNamara's headaches reached the point where he carried multiple bottles of ibuprofen or acetaminophen in his trouser pockets. As his attacks became more frequent and intense, he found himself doubling and tripling the recommended dosage.

"You really should see our doctor," Tamara told her husband, seeing him empty another bottle.

"I don't need a quack. I'm fine."

"When was the last time you accompanied me to an event in the city? Either you're too tired or experiencing another migraine—it's repetitive. You've become rather boring."

"Nice to see your compassionate side," he said, avoiding her glare.

"Mac, we have a responsibility to our community. If you continue to avoid the circuit, people will talk."

"I don't give a shit."

"You used to," she commented.

"No, I never did. Actually, my hiatus away from your stretched-face *amigos* has done wonders for my disposition. I'm sick and tired of your emaciated, phony, and banal entourage."

"Fine, have it your way. Keep on taking those pills and have your stomach bleed."

She passed Harvey on her way out. "He's in a foul mood," she huffed.

"Oh, ignore the female antique," said MacNamara. "She's having her period or starting menopause."

Harvey laughed at MacNamara's joke, pleased he worked in an environment offering plenty of spectacle. "In either case, I wanna stay clear of your missus."

"Wish my life offered that luxury," said MacNamara. He rubbed his forehead and took out another pill. He tilted his head and swallowed the pill without water.

"You can arrange anything for money," offered Harvey. "That's what it's there for, right?"

MacNamara moved his head in circular motion. The pain seemed to subside. "Damn headaches. Nothing seems to relieve them."

"Boss, I could get you something stronger. Over the counter stuff never gave me much relief, either."

"Nah, I think it's just about gone. What were you saying about arranging anything for money?"

"I was just joking about removing the annoying stick woman." Harvey immediately regretted the derogatory comment concerning Tamara, so he began to apologize. "Sir, I didn't mean anything by…"

"Quiet down. You've just given me a wonderful idea."

"Huh?"

"Well, I've a slight problem I need attending to—I think you've pointed to a way of solving it."

Harvey gulped hard. He anticipated MacNamara's resolution. "Tell me your dilemma, sir."

"I'm afraid the infamous Christmas tape you provided, caused a backlash. Without exposing you, too much, let's just say two women plan to use the contents of the tape against me."

"I don't understand. The tape had nothing to do with you."

"I'm glad you see it that way but others would stop at nothing to try to take me down—accuse me of blackmail attempts, even murder."

MacNamara knew Bunny would not keep her mouth shut for long about what she had seen and heard that night. As for Priscilla, she was capable of anything in her quest for power. It was only a matter of time before Priscilla started her blackmail attempts. Only Diana Roberts had managed to escape the grouping of MacNamara's imagined consortium threat. He liked the sincere innocence the red-haired beauty projected. She was someone who could be useful, later, he thought. She might even make a good replacement for Tamara.

"You're in need of some assistance, then…to help alleviate your headache troubles."

"Yes, my headache troubles. Do you have any contacts capable of eliminating my pain?"

Harvey grunted. "You bet. Do your headaches have names?"

"Bunny Moore and Priscilla Meyers."

2

From his days spent in security, Harvey had amassed an address book of contacts available for any service imaginable, both legal and illegal. He thought about MacNamara's request. The person he targeted for the job was Simon Le Mort.

Harvey had met Le Mort while they both served time in a Texas prison, Harvey for fraud, Le Mort for an armed robbery attempt. Simon was unlike the other prisoners. He kept to himself, distant from the inmates. When he was not smoking French cigarettes in the yard, he would be in his cell reading. One would have thought his boyish good looks, together with his soft-spoken manner, should have made him a target as some man's bitch. This was not the case.

"What's the story on the pretty boy?" Harvey asked his cellmate, pointing to the lone, diminutive figure blowing smoke rings outside in the yard.

"Shit. Stay away from him. One of the cooks told me he killed three men in here who tried to make him their fag boy. Apparently, one man was found with his penis stuffed in his mouth and a broom handle stuck up his ass. No one knows what happened to the others. I bet it wasn't pretty. Someone else told me he'd been a professional killer, on the outside."

One day, Harvey approached Simon to ask him for a light. Simon was smoking one of his gold-wrapped filter cigarettes. He exhaled the chocolate-scented smoke, and Harvey wished he could share the experience.

"Those cigarettes you smoke smell real good, not like the crappy tobacco I've been inhaling."

Simon's clear blue eyes flashed. He smiled. His freckles ran together as he crinkled his small nose. He looked more like a boy scout than a killer.

"Shit man, *those* don't even stain your teeth," said Harvey, amazed by Simon's dazzling whites.

"I wouldn't go that far. Would you like to try one?" Simon opened up the flat box, displaying pastel-colored cigarettes enveloped in a ribbon-wrapped interior. "Each color's a different flavor—cherry, vanilla, mint, or chocolate." Le Mort fancied himself as a connoisseur. In reality, he was more a dilettante.

"Very flashy! I want to take a cherry one—I'd better stick with the chocolate," said Harvey, scanning the elegant box. "Can you imagine the trouble if I took a pink one? My ass would never be the same. Sick faggots…"

Simon extended his hand to Harvey, well-aware that the other prisoners were watching. "I'm Simon Le Mort." His voice reflected a trace of a New Orleans accent.

"Le Mort. Sounds foreign to me."

Simon giggled. "A family name—my ancestors can be traced back to the French Revolution."

"Hmmm. Does it mean anything important?" asked Harvey. He knew the prisoners called him 'Mister Death.'

"Interesting question. When I was a kid, I looked up both words in a French dictionary, and they translated to, "the dead." I played around with the notion of calling myself, the dead, the death, but in the end, I settled on a combination of French and English. I prefer to use the name *Monsieur* Death but for the benefit of the populace, I'm forced to use the name Mister Death."

"I see," agreed Harvey. "People don't appreciate good taste."

"Indeed."

3

After his stint in Huntsville Prison, Simon relocated to his roots in New Orleans, to focus on freelance opportunities. He vowed to work solo, especially after the last operation, headed by a friend, had failed and landed him in jail. His reputation as a liquidator spread throughout the city's underworld, providing him with steady work.

"Brother, I had one hell of a time trying to track you down," Harvey told Simon on the telephone. "I must have gone through ten numbers before getting you on this one."

Harvey heard his friend's familiar giggle and envisioned him dragging on one of his French cigarettes.

"Been a long time. You well?" Simon asked.

"Yeah. Things are pretty good for me. I'm up on the East coast. I have a sweet deal, working for quite a character. You'd like him. He's just up your alley—clever, charismatic, and moneyed."

"Sounds like a character from a Harold Robbins book."

"Hmmm. Don't know. Don't read much. Anyway, he's the reason I'm calling. My employer needs some assistance cleaning up. He needs a real pro, if you know what I mean."

"Clearly."

"Would you be interested?"

"Depends. I've changed my business model recently, so I can afford to be selective on which jobs I perform."

"You sound like the fucking *Harvard Business Review*." Harvey asked, "How much?"

"I only get out of bed for two million." *Greed is good*.

"How about three? One mil for each head plus a bonus mil when the job's done."

"I'm just putting on my monogrammed velvet slippers and robe, now."

"Good," said Harvey. "I'll call you with further input, later. It was great talking to you, buddy."

"Likewise," said Simon, stubbing out his cigarette.

4

MacNamara asked Barry to accompany him on a short drive. "I've been doing some thinking," said MacNamara. "I think we should abort the Lucy Atherton transaction…us taking control of her shares."

Barry could not believe his ears. It came as a big relief, as there was no way he was going to be able to pull it off, anyway. "Wise decision. What changed your mind?"

"Nothing, specifically. I'm sure your constant pecking at my conscience contributed, slightly."

Barry grinned. "I see."

"You look happy. If I didn't know better, I would think you had no intention of executing the stock sale."

"Always trying to test my loyalty …" said Barry, trying to avoid another confrontation.

"How about another test then? What's our stock price?" MacNamara loved to quiz his people on company business. Barry understood the importance of this game. He kept current on the stock price, monthly sales, forecast information, and business plan objectives.

"When I checked half and hour ago, it was up two points to one hundred and one," recited Barry. He took out his EPIK phone to view the current quote. "For the United States, monthly sales are eighty percent of forecast, for the United Kingdom—"

"Enough," interrupted MacNamara. "I just have to check every now and then." Reality was it was more of a daily occurrence.

MacNamara turned off the main highway and pulled up at a rundown bar. In the window, was a neon sign flashing the word BEER. The R flickered, so the sign read BEE.

"Don't tell me. It's your latest find," said Barry.

"Wait here for a few minutes. I just need to drop something off." MacNamara grabbed a large envelope.

"I'm not going to sit out here and get shot by some redneck. I'm coming in with you."

"Suit yourself."

Barry followed MacNamara through the screen door and saw MacNamara wave to a heavyset figure, sitting at the bar. "Hi there. Barry, you remember my security guy, Ron Harvey?"

"Sure," Barry said, firmly gripping Harvey's hand.

Harvey flagged the bartender. "A round for my guests."

"Sorry, we can't stay. Duty calls us back to the office. I just wanted to drop off the items you requested." MacNamara passed him the envelope. A stack of hundred dollar bills peaked out of the unsealed opening.

"Great," said Harvey, quickly sealing the packet. "See you back at *Windermere*."

The money did not go unnoticed. Barry wanted to know what was going on. "What the fuck was that all about?"

"Harvey likes to be paid in cash."

"I can see that," said Barry.

"For his wages at *Windermere*."

"Oh?" The bulky envelope seemed to hold more than just a couple of week's pay. Why drive out here to give it to him?

MacNamara laughed at Barry's nervousness. "What did you think the money was for?"

"I never know what to expect. You're two steps in front of me, at all times."

While they drove back to Anexa, Harvey, meanwhile, was sharing the contents of the envelope with his friend, who had been sitting in a nearby booth.

"The deposit and the photographs are in there," said Harvey. The first photograph he removed was Priscilla's. He kissed her mouth before rubbing it crudely against his crotch. "A waste of fine pussy."

"Let me see it. Just throw it here," said Simon, pointing to the space in front of him. "I don't want to touch it after you defiled it." The hard blonde in the photograph stared back at him, defiantly. "She looks like a stripper, only better dressed."

"Okay, let's see if the next one does anything for you." Harvey pulled out Bunny's picture and handed it to Simon. "The short guy who was just here with MacNamara...she's his wife."

Simon studied Bunny's picture. She was an attractive woman, without excesses of makeup or over-styled hair. He sensed sadness in her eyes.

"Can't imagine those two, together. I would have thought that he would've gone for the other broad. His wife is so butch-looking," said Harvey.

"I disagree. She possesses natural beauty." Simon blew a thin stream of the aromatic smoke from his lungs.

"Man—to each his own. I would not have picked *that one* for you."

Simon flashed a broad smile, crinkling his nose and corners of his eyes. "I know."

Chapter Eighteen

1

At EPIK headquarters, Atherton barely had time to review his calendar when Murray arrived to debrief him. Murray launched into the latest issues list, without so much as a formal greeting. There were many matters to resolve.

"I don't think we need a new building to combine organizations. It's something we'll need to look into. Some of Anexa's players have joined Diana Roberts to start up the integration team. We need to formalize the integration team...which leads me into the next issue, the new org structure. Obviously, we don't intend to run both companies separately," opened Murray.

He frowned when he saw Atherton's eyes glaze over. It was frustrating to have to coddle him. When was he going to snap out of it? Murray raised his voice. "Hey friend, are you with me?"

"I'm sorry. You probably noticed, my mind keeps wandering."

Was that all he had to offer? What was his problem? It was only a matter of weeks before MacNamara would gain enough support from the new Board to oust them both.

"Listen, you'd better get it together before it's too late. MacNamara can't wait to get rid of his enemies. Don't give him the chance! I know you're still suffering about Lucy, but you have to move on, for the sake of your people. They need you. I need you. Show me the Atherton I know best."

Senior broke in. "He doesn't need you. He wants to get rid of you, so he can take your place."

"That's not true. Murray's not like that," said Atherton.

"James?" asked Murray.

Atherton didn't hear Murray's question. He only heard Senior's creaky voice.

"Oh, he's just fine," said Senior, sarcastically.

"You don't give a shit about me. You never have! My people care for me, and I plan to protect them!" shouted Atherton.

Murray grabbed Atherton by the shoulders. "Hey, what's gotten into you? I had no doubt of your loyalty to us."

Atherton looked tired, the strain displayed across his face.

"Ah, James I'm sorry. I didn't mean to dig into you. I should have been more sensitive to your circumstances."

"You're absolutely right to get on to me. Anexa's management will look for any sign of weakness from the EPIK camp. It's my duty to lead a strong, united team. As far as making decisions on subjects affecting the new organization, such as new buildings, implementation teams, etcetera, let's discuss them and decide on our positions. We can address them with the Anexa members of the Board at our next meeting."

"Fine."

2

Priscilla was still reveling in the new status MacNamara had granted her. About time too, she thought. She typically maneuvered her promotions to occur every three years; this latest move came dangerously close to missing her timeline. While some women planned for marriage and children, Priscilla rebelled against adopting the traditional female role. She relished the power and the thrill the corporate world provided. It was a natural high.

Dumping Barry in favor of MacNamara was an excellent move. MacNamara was the one who could help her fulfill her ambitions. It pleased her that he understood and supported her need to excel and to move upward. While Barry was a distraction, MacNamara was a real partner. His COO offering proved his commitment to her. She, in turn, cemented her dedication to him by becoming his new lover.

"I want you to go over to EPIK's headquarters. See how our integration team is getting on. While you're over there, find yourself an office. One which suitably reflects your COO position," said MacNamara.

"Oh," she sounded, surprised. "I thought I would stay in the Anexa towers."

"I don't mind you keeping one at Anexa, but I need you over at EPIK to keep an eye on things—be my eyes and ears. You can also check up on your recruit, Diana Roberts."

3

It did not take long for Priscilla to find an office at EPIK which suited her space and taste requirements. Though she would have liked to have moved into Atherton's spacious office, she decided to settle for the quiet corner office, currently housing EPIK's Chief Financial Officer.

"I've found the perfect office," she told MacNamara over the telephone. "One problem though. Its present tenant is EPIK's CFO."

"What's the problem? You outrank him. Move the bean counter out," said MacNamara.

With her boss's blessing, Priscilla did just that. While Montgomery was on his two-hour lunch break, Priscilla organized the building services crew to pack his stuff up and move her belongings in. She even went as far as removing Montgomery's brass nameplate from the door. Priscilla was about to order her personalized nameplate when Montgomery's secretary returned from her lunch. She found her boss's office ransacked and occupied by a tough-looking broad.

Priscilla looked at her watch and glared at the confused secretary. "I'm afraid these long lunches will have to stop. That is, if you want to continue to work here."

"I beg your pardon?"

"I believe you heard me the first time. There's no need to repeat myself. Your name?"

"Oh, it's...it's Sari," she stammered.

"Fine Miss Sarah, let's get a couple of things straight. I expect professionalism from my people in terms of work quality, timeliness, and appearance. So far, you've failed on two categories. I hope you can impress me with your secretarial services."

Sari smoothed her wrinkled skirt and looked at her black discount shoes.

"Yes, that's right, I can see you get the message. Neatly pressed clothes create the *right* image. Avoid polyester blouses and pleated skirts. They make you look more matronly. Shoes must be immaculate—no scuffs, worn heels, or dirt. Also, I would encourage you to wear pantyhose. A woman your age can't hide varicose veins any other way."

Sari was speechless, if not frightened by this new woman. Where was Mr. Montgomery? Was he fired?

Priscilla spoke. "Does all this make sense to you?"

Sari nodded.

"Good. I'm glad we've had this little chat. Now for the introduction—I'm Priscilla Meyers, Anexa's COO and, lucky for you, your new boss." Priscilla smiled.

Sari smiled back, not wanting to upset her new mistress. "Ma'am, is Mr. Montgomery coming back?"

"You mean the bean counter?" laughed Priscilla. "When he returns, tell him to go see his boss. Let them sort out a new place for Monty to sit and numerate."

As Sari was leaving Priscilla's office, Montgomery returned. He found his family photographs, company awards, and office materials all bundled together; crudely packed in cardboard boxes and dumped out in the corridor.

"What the hell's going on here?" he screamed at Priscilla.

Sari returned to her desk in silence, not wanting to interfere.

Montgomery looked around his office. His pictures, previously hanging on the walls, had been replaced with beaming pictures of Priscilla—some with MacNamara, some with her team, some accepting awards. The only things in the room which looked remotely familiar were the company plants and furniture.

"You're in my office," he hissed. "And who gave you authority to pack my things?"

Priscilla ignored his outburst and proceeded to order her new nameplate. "I'm busy," she said, covering the mouthpiece with her hand. "Make an appointment with my assistant, outside."

Her assistant? Montgomery was bewildered. He turned around to look at his secretary, who in turn refused to look up from her station. Who did this blonde think she was, moving into his office and stealing his staff?

She continued her telephone conversation. "I would prefer it if you had my nameplate ready by close of business. Yes, that's the correct spelling, M-E-Y-E-R-S. Don't forget the title, Chief Operations Officer," she told the caller, before hanging up the phone. She sighed at Montgomery. "How you get anything done around here is amazing. Your building services crew is inept."

"Madam, I will be heard! Who gave you permission to move my things?"

Priscilla grew tired of his whining. "Like I said, I'm too busy to see you. Make an appointment with my assistant, Sarah."

"Her name is Sari."

"Sarah, Sari, whatever." Priscilla waved at him, signaling his dismissal. As she picked up the phone to place another call, he leapt forward, grabbing the receiver from her hand. How dare she ignore him? He hated female managers. They were so aggressive. Why did they feel the need to prove something?

"One last time. What are you doing in my office?"

She raised her index finger and tapped the desk with her long red talon. The sound further separated the silence between them. Tap, tap, tap…

"Sari, call security," he called out to his assistant.

"Ignore that," said Priscilla. She addressed Montgomery using her best icy tone. "I think *Sarah* will prefer working for a woman. Men can be so emotional."

Montgomery had not had a woman treat him like this. He wasn't sure what to do. "Who are you?" he asked in defeat.

"Rewind. I *am* your COO," she said, exasperated by his reluctance to accept his fate and leave. "You must be the accountant guy."

"CFO," he proudly corrected her. "Chief Financial Officer."

Patronizing little shit, she thought. Men always felt compelled to explain the obvious. "I see," said Priscilla. "Then you understand that the Chief Operating Officer outranks the Chief Financial Officer."

Montgomery swallowed hard.

Priscilla continued her speech. "We've cleared up the introductions…run along, little man. I have work to do. I'm sure you have some profit and loss statements to review, or standard cost updates to apply."

That was all it took to get him to leave. Without wasting another word, he went to find Atherton or Murray to help him evict his new foe.

4

Carl went to find Diana in the war room that Anexa had set up at EPIK to house the integration project team. The walls were covered with timelines, sketches of business processes, team assignments, and to-do lists—all filled with key business jargon. Computer terminals were linked to the test database, which held Anexa's and EPIK's customer and product master files, and various business programs. The room smelled of stale cigarettes and old coffee.

"So, this is where you've been hiding." Carl approached Diana.

"Yup," said Diana, not wanting to appear too friendly in front of the Anexa team. They looked him over and returned their attentions to their computer screens.

He mouthed the word, "Coffee." She turned off her terminal, got up, and slipped out of the room.

In the company's cafeteria, Carl spotted a remote table in the corner. "I like seeing you all dressed up in your work attire. You look so professional," he complimented. "I take it Anexa's not into business casual attire?"

"No, they do things quite differently. Did you hear about our run in with Jack Murray?"

"Yeah, he was pretty annoyed the Anexa mob was smoking, all day, in the war room. After all, this building is supposed to maintain a smoke-free environment."

"It's bad enough that we're virtually squatting, to set up shop. I told our guys to obey the EPIK rules, but they refused to listen. I suspect they need the nicotine and caffeine buzz to keep up the pace our leader has set."

"Speaking of Mr. MacNamara, anymore run-ins to report?"

"None so far."

"I really wish you'd reconsider moving in with me. That way, I can keep an eye on you, both here and at home."

Diana checked to make sure no one was nearby. "I think things have fizzled out."

"How so?"

"The tape no longer poses a threat now that Mrs. Atherton has passed away."

Carl thought Lucy's sudden heart attack had been suspicious. She had not mentioned anything to him about her having heart problems. And he would have been the first to have known, based on their bedroom antics.

"I'm not convinced you're out of danger. I still think you need to leave the company."

"You wouldn't understand," she said miserably. The truth was, she needed the money to pay for her exorbitant living.

"Try me."

"If I left, my family would be disappointed. They think I've achieved so much, first with my education...with this job."

"Did you tell them Anexa lied about the job description, and they threatened you?"

"There's no point in getting them mixed up in my work problems. I'm old enough to take care of myself without getting my parents involved." Diana's father habitually stressed the importance of her becoming independent from the family unit as quickly as possible, both financially and emotionally.

"What's so attractive and captivating about this particular job?" he asked loudly in frustration.

"Three things. Money, power, and prestige," announced Priscilla in answer to Carl's question.

Diana groaned as her superior sauntered over to them.

Priscilla focused her attention on Carl. "We haven't been properly introduced. I'm Priscilla Meyers, Anexa's COO." She loved repeating her new title.

Diana raised her eyebrow. Priscilla anticipated her question. "Mac gave me the promotion I deserved."

"Ms. Meyers, I'm Carl Swan, assistant to Mr. Atherton," he said, mimicking her introduction style.

"Good contact to have," she approved. "Diana, where have you been stashing away this handsome exec? Is this your boyfriend?"

Diana turned away. Priscilla ignored her brooding subordinate. She ran her hand through her over-highlighted hair and softened her scarlet lips into a smile. "Well, if you're available, I sure would like to get to know you," she cooed. It was about time she found herself a younger man, without marital ties. She could keep MacNamara for his business offerings, Carl for her seedier passions.

While Carl was flattered by this attention, he felt the importance of projecting a clear message that he was not available. It was impossible to decipher a woman like Priscilla. The combination of insecurity, ambition, and beauty seemed to breed unpredictability; Priscilla possessed that composite. Let her down gently without antagonizing her, he thought.

"Beauty, brains, and company status." He whistled. "You're too good for *me*."

"Are you trying to turn me down?" she giggled. Priscilla playfully touched his arm. She flicked her hair. "Think it over."

Diana rolled her eyes at Priscilla's adolescent performance. She coughed, hoping to put an end to the nauseating flirtation.

Priscilla got the hint. She turned to face Diana. "I want to see you in my office, in one hour. You can update me on the group's progress."

"Back at Anexa?"

"No. I've taken an office here. You can find me in the CFO's former residence. He's quite the Napoleon," she said, before making her exit.

"I bet Montgomery loved that," said Carl. His eyes followed Priscilla's departing figure. "She's a piece of work."

"I'd better get back to work to prepare my report for your new admirer, the she-dragon."

"You're jealous," he teased her.

"Please don't tell me you fell for her charming act."

5

Atherton and Murray had finished their discussions, when Montgomery burst into Atherton's office.

"I have a real problem."

Atherton waved. "Hello Michael. Great timing. We can review the issues list we just—"

"In a minute." Montgomery's face was red and flustered.

"What's got you so fired up?" asked Murray.

"That COO bitch, Priscilla Meyers, from Anexa. Who gave her permission to move into my office?" He was acting like a spoiled child.

Atherton smiled. What did he think was going to happen when EPIK merged with Anexa? This was only a hint of things to come.

"You approved it," Montgomery unfairly accused Atherton. "I can see it in your face. Someone could have had the courtesy to let me know. She moved her stuff in while I was at lunch."

Atherton and Murray exchanged looks, before bursting out laughing.

"Both of you were in on this!" Montgomery announced.

Murray was first to regain his composure. "Stop with the conspiracy theory, will you? We had nothing to do with it."

"You must see that it's kind of funny," said Atherton.

"For whom? You still have your office," said Montgomery. "What are you going to do about it?"

"What do you want me to do about it?" asked Atherton. There were many other pressing matters to address.

"Get her out!" he demanded.

"I can't do that," said Atherton.

"Why the hell not?"

"Because she outranks you. Granted, the way she handled the situation was not appropriate but that doesn't change the hierarchy," replied Atherton.

"But she works for Anexa, and I work for EPIK," whined Montgomery.

"No, we work for the same entity," corrected Murray. Did that prospect slip your mind when you cast your approval vote to merge with Anexa?"

"So that's what this is all about, payback?" asked Montgomery. "You could have found another way to say 'I told you so.'"

"Get a grip, Montgomery," scolded Atherton. "We have important things to focus on. Your office space is not one of them. You can share an office with another employee."

"But…"

"Stop your whining. The subject is closed," stated Atherton. He handed Montgomery a ten-paged document. "I would like you to review the issues list we have put together. Go into my meeting room and look it over. You may want to add items we haven't considered."

"Looks like I have my marching orders." Montgomery settled in the next room to review the document.

"There's something strange going on." Murray spoke quietly so that Montgomery could not overhear the discussion. I thought Priscilla Meyers's title was Chief Strategist?"

"You're right. On the employee list Anexa sent over, that's how she was labeled."

"I wonder what this COO stuff is all about. MacNamara knows he can't promote anyone to executive level without approval from both camps."

"MacNamara likes to play solo…doesn't mean he can continue to get away with it."

"What do you mean?"

"Let's join him in his own game by bringing a player of our own to the party. What was the name of that guy you visited while I was in Europe? The one who got fired from Anexa?"

"Who? You mean Cam Phillips?"

"Yeah, that's the one. Bring him in to work with our technology group and implementation team. We could use an amicable resource with Anexa experience. He would be useful to us, and his presence would piss off MacNamara."

"I'll get him on board ASAP," replied Murray.

Chapter Nineteen

1

Through their respective secretaries, Atherton and MacNamara settled on a date for the next meeting of the new Board. Atherton was surprised to hear how affable and agreeable MacNamara had been to having the ANEXA/EPIK players work through the steadily growing issues list as rapidly as possible.

Atherton looked at the clock. It was close to nine-thirty p.m. He was tired and knew he should drive home to get some rest. When Lucy was alive, he had dreaded going home to *Ma Maison* because she was there. Now, he dreaded going home because of *Ma Maison's* reminders—the emptiness, the lies, the children which never were, the arguments, the pain of bad times and death.

"Hello James." Atherton heard the sexy voice of Gillian.

He looked up from his desk. She was posed in his doorway, dressed in a pale green dress and stiletto heels. Gillian's skin glowed. She was ready for action.

"Gillian." He stood up.

She moved slowly toward him. Atherton watched the outline of her shapely legs dance through the transparent sheath. He felt himself grow hard.

"I've missed you, so much. I can't stand it, the last time we were together was back in Paris. My body aches for you." Gillian pressed her body up against him.

As she moved closer, he breathed in the familiar vanilla fragrance of her perfume. "Shalimar," he said, mesmerized by her presence.

"Mmmm."

He hesitated. "I don't think this is such a good idea."

"Hush. Let me work my magic."

"It's not right. The timing's inappropriate."

She rested her cheek against his and gently bit his earlobe. *Greed is good.*

He moaned. She ran her tongue over the grooves of his ear. He grabbed her firm behind, pushing her body against his.

"You feel so good." Gillian grabbed his hand and slipped it into her silky panties. She was moist with anticipation.

He moved his fingers expertly along her folds and unzipped his pants with his free hand. He shuffled her up against the wall. Gillian removed her panties. He entered her roughly, thrusting deep inside her. She met his demanding movements, pushing her body down on him.

"Keep going! Do it harder!" she cried out.

It did not take long for Atherton to release his passions. It had been quite some time since he had had sex. His pent up desire could not be contained. "I guess I'm out of practice." Embarrassed, he started to dress.

"Hey, don't do that. We have all the time in the world." Gillian dropped to her knees. She licked the tip of his penis, tasting salty remnants of his passion, while tickling his balls with her fingertips. Gillian took him into her mouth and expertly moved up and down the shaft, until he started to harden.

"I like that," he said. "Do it deeper." Atherton grabbed the back of her head and pushed himself into her throat. The sound of her greedy slurping made him moan louder. She felt his balls tighten. She placed a finger between his cheeks and probed his small opening.

"You're gonna make me come."

She sucked harder and faster. Atherton groaned as he held her tightly, shooting the juices down the back of her throat. When he finished, he withdrew himself from her lips and inspected himself. His used member was decorated with red lipstick smudges. Gillian saw them and took a linen handkerchief from her purse.

"Let me clean you up, my darling."

Atherton sat back in his black leather chair, letting her finish her duties. He looked satisfied. Gillian certainly hoped so! If she was going to set a trap, now was the time to do it.

"You know, you could have this treatment every day, if you wanted—breakfast, lunch, and dinner," she offered.

Atherton pulled up his trousers. It was unlike Gillian to make such a suggestion. She understood their arrangement; permanency was not part of it. He had just buried his emotionally demanding wife and did not need to replace her with another. What was Gillian up to?

"Gillian, I'm happy with our relationship, the way it is."

"But I thought with Lucy out of the picture, we could start our lives afresh," she blurted out. "Move into *Ma Maison*—become your new…"

"No! Marriage is out of the question." She was foolish to consider he would marry her. She was the mistress, nothing more!

"But James, powerful men often marry their mistresses."

Senior arrived in time to watch Atherton debating Gillian. "She does have a point there. Powerful men do marry their mistresses. History shows us James Goldsmith, Averell Harriman, etcetera, but the difference is that you're not a powerful figure."

"Shut up, Senior," snapped Atherton.

"Who are you calling Senior?" asked Gillian.

"Look, I don't give a fuck about other men," said Atherton, addressing both Senior and Gillian. "This is not a subject I will entertain any longer."

"Go on, marry the whore," said Senior. He started to hum the tune to Wagner's "Bridal March."

"We could have a private wedding. No one would even have to know," she pleaded.

"'All dressed in white,'" sang Senior.

"James, please know that I really care for you. I would do anything for you," Gillian continued.

"Give her a chance," said Senior.

Atherton finally spoke up. "You're a great woman. You deserve someone who will treat you right. Unfortunately, that's not me."

"If you can't marry me, then our *arrangement* is off," said Gillian.

Atherton ignored her bluff. "Then we will need to part ways."

With her threat falling on deaf ears, she regretted pushing him. "Don't speak in haste. I can wait for you, no matter how long it takes." Gillian started to cry.

Senior pretended to cry alongside her. "Take me back, please," Senior cried out.

"Go," said Atherton. He picked up her small purse and handed it to her.

"Please James, I—"

"Just go, both of you, before it before it gets any worse."

Gillian left. Senior stopped crying. "Hey boy, did I tell you, juicy Lucy and I met up recently? She was really good."

"Leave," hissed Atherton.

2

Gillian was not the only one wanting to see Atherton that evening. Martha had mustered enough courage to face him, to resolve unfinished business. As she made her way down the long corridor to see Atherton, she passed Gillian. Initially, Gillian kept on walking. But something told her to take a second glance at the woman. Gillian slipped into an open office. She watched Martha knock on Atherton's door. The turn of events that followed took her by surprise. Atherton opened his door, embraced Martha, and kissed her on the mouth. Atherton had replaced her with this plain *haus frau*! How could he do this to her? From the look of things, he was going to continue his passion where they had left off.

"If I can't participate, I might as well watch," said Gillian. She wanted to find out about her new competition.

3

"Martha! Well, hello there!" Without thinking, Atherton hugged her and kissed her innocently on the lips. He backed away but remained affable. "To what do I owe this pleasure?" The evening certainly was providing unexpected visitors.

"I was heading over to Carl's apartment and thought I'd drop in to see how you were getting on. We haven't seen each other since the funeral."

"I'm doing fine. Actually, I'm doing better than I thought I would. It was a bit of a shaky start, but I think I'm back into the swing of things. I can't afford not to be with all the politics going on. The EPIK crew will have to watch their backs."

"I don't miss corporate ducking and diving." She punched the air pretending to throw punches like a fighter.

He enjoyed her jovial attitude. "I suppose things were simpler in sanitation?"

"I wouldn't go that far," she laughed.

"Martha, it seems a lifetime ago when we first met. We would discuss life, politics, and love, after you finished your cleaning rounds."

"If I remember correctly, you wouldn't talk to me unless I finished dusting your office, first."

"Me? Did I do that?"

"Yes, you did. I can't believe you have such a selective memory!"

"Have you had dinner, yet? We could get a bite somewhere. You pick the cuisine, I'll pick up the tab." His interlude with Gillian had left him famished.

"Thanks for the offer. I've already had dinner."

"How about a coffee or an after-dinner drink?"

"No thanks." Martha fidgeted with her purse strap.

"Something tells me you didn't just drop by for a casual visit."

He still could read her. There was no use pretending this was an informal visit. It was her personal mission to face up to the past.

"Tell me about Carl's work at EPIK," she said.

"We're putting his hard-earned education to use. He prepares reports for the team, after analyzing various pools of information like sales, market trends, customer requirements, and competitor data. I'll have to say he's doing a great job. "

"I'm impressed and glad to hear he's getting along. Carl doesn't like to share much about his work. He probably thinks I wouldn't understand anything," she said.

"You've done rather well for yourself, too, you know. I'm proud of the way you put yourself through school and carved out that sales career. You didn't have it easy, did you? Why you stayed with that alcoholic husband is beyond me?"

"Don't forget abusive."

"Exactly. Why didn't you let me help you? I could have saved you, a long time back."

"Things were complicated…"

"Martha, I'll always disagree with your perception of what was so complicated."

"You were my superior. I was just the lowly cleaner who shared an unlikely camaraderie with you after hours. I was uneducated and married." Martha felt her cheeks burn. "Should I continue the list?"

"Those are not reasons. They're excuses. I respected your work ethic, your mind, and your drive. For your ex, as far as I'm concerned, that despicable man was responsible for nothing good, only for being the father of your son."

"Don't go that far. Carl did not know what it meant to have a real father. Actually, I'm to blame for that."

"Don't blame yourself for your ex's lack of interest. He was a sick man."

"It's not that. Carl never knew his biological father, until…"

They stared at each other.

"What's that supposed to mean?"

Martha nodded her head in silence. She did not have to say anything else.

Atherton understood the revelation.

"But how?" He was astounded. Thoughts raced through his mind. He tried to comprehend the magnitude of this blinding news. He had a son! Why had he not thought of it before? They had shared the same alma mater, studied similar coursework, and even possessed the same piercing blue eyes. "My God Martha, why didn't you tell me? And why now? Is that why Carl came to work for Lucy at *Ma Maison*?

"I think I'll take you up on your dinner offer. I can tell you everything while you eat, starting from at the beginning. I hope you'll understand my reasons for not approaching you sooner, even if it takes time for you to accept them."

"Fine, but I want to hear the whole story. You owe me the truth." he said, reeling, trying to comprehend the news. "I'm sure you can appreciate my shock."

"I don't expect you to say anything until I tell you everything."

Atherton was not the only one stunned by Martha's news. Gillian stood in the adjoining office, dazed. As she watched them leave, she cursed her former lover who was comforting the small woman with a protective arm around her waist. Their body language spoke. Gillian was infuriated to realize she had been dumped for this simple-looking woman. Two can play at your game, Atherton, she thought. Just wait till MacNamara finds out about the love child. My humiliation tonight doesn't compare with the one you'll face through your archenemy.

4

"I'm ready. Start from the beginning." said Atherton. "I can't believe Carl's mine. We were only together once."

"Then, there's your answer."

"Why didn't you tell me?"

"Like I said before, things were complicated. Remember that night you saw my swollen face, after my husband had beaten me?"

How could he forget? The fragile skin around her eyes had been bruised, purple and blue. Above one eye, there had been a gash which needed stitches. Her injured lips had swollen.

Martha continued. "As you know, I still went to work, despite my condition. When you saw me, I was embarrassed and ashamed. At that time, I blamed myself for the beatings. I respected you and cared about what you thought. I didn't want you to see me like that, disfigured and ugly. Anyway, that night you showed me compassion and helped me to understand it wasn't my fault. You said *he* was the problem, not me."

"Yes, I remember."

"Well, after that horrible incident, you and I began to have our discussions which led to a friendship, something I had not had before. You respected my thoughts, encouraged me to go to school, even offered to give me a higher paying job so I could quit the others. How I wished that I'd been born into a different class, someone suitable for your standards. I dreamed of having the love and friendship of a man like you."

Atherton reached across the table and held her hand. Her touch was soft and warm. "I'm so sorry. I wish I had known—"

"One night, my dreams came true. We shared a passionate kiss, which led to an intimate moment between us. That was the night Carl was conceived…in tenderness and love. By the time I found out I was pregnant, you were beginning to become involved with Lucy. I was out of my league in thinking that you might have wanted me, never mind the complication that I was already married."

"So, you decided for me. You never gave me the chance to make up my own mind."

"I didn't want to use the baby as bait for your affections."

"If I remember correctly, you told me we couldn't make love again. *You* made the decision to end our affair. Was I supposed to guess that you secretly wanted to be with me?" He felt angry and betrayed. "What about the baby? I had a right to know."

"If I had to do it all over, I would have made different choices. Unfortunately, circumstances prevented them. You got engaged. I had to move on."

"And you allowed a violent and abusive alcoholic to raise my son."

"No. He was hardly around the boy. I raised Carl alone."

"Don't you see I could have helped?"

"I can't change the past, but I can alter the future."

"What does that mean?" he asked in exasperation. "Carl doesn't know about me, does he?"

She shook her head. "No, but the time has come for us to help him. He needs to know the truth."

"Why now?"

"For years, he has been plagued by violent nightmares, playing out a scene where my ex-husband calls Carl a bastard and accuses me of lying about my baby girl's parentage. Because Carl is working alongside you, I fear something bad might happen if I don't tell him the truth."

"Your lies seem to have worked so far," he said bitterly.

"Please try to understand the difficult position I was forced into," she pleaded.

"Like you said earlier, this will take time for me to accept and to adjust to. I want your promise on one thing, we both tell Carl together."

"You have my word."

5

Gillian relayed the story she had overheard. MacNamara rubbed his hands together with glee. "That was the most delicious thing I've heard all day."

"I'm glad you enjoyed it." It annoyed her to think how Atherton had used her. He was ruthless and selfish.

"I forgot this part though," she said. "He had the nerve to call me a senior citizen, after I finished sucking his cock."

"You're angry. I've never heard you say *cock*, before."

"Angry? I'm furious! He told me to 'shut up senior.'"

MacNamara hooted, grasping her misunderstanding. No doubt, Atherton had been talking to his father.

"Gillian, the only thing you left off is why you are so mad. Whores are not supposed to get emotionally involved."

"Why do you care?"

"Are you upset that lover boy has replaced you? Or are you jealous that he has taken up with his former mistress?"

"I wouldn't call her the mistress type."

"You can't believe that he would dump the lovely and voluptuous Gillian du Monde?" MacNamara rubbed her shoulders.

Gillian pulled away. "He needs time to decide what he wants."

"Like hell he does. Face it, you're history my dear." MacNamara felt the pressure return and rubbed his forehead. He took two white pills from his pocket and swallowed them. "That should do the trick."

"Another bad headache?"

"Mmmm. Over-the-counter analgesics have stopped working. Barry gave me those little sweethearts. Hopefully, they won't kill me like they did Lucy Atherton."

Gillian had learned to ignore most of his commentary. It was hard to establish what was real and what was fiction. In this case, she suspected that he was joking.

"It looks like our dealings are over, now that I have been dumped."

"New deal," he said. "With Atherton gone from your pocket, I anticipate you're in need of a new buyer."

MacNamara made a valid point. She needed another patron to support her. They were an odd pairing, but suited to one another. Gillian hated to admit it, but she had begun to enjoy his visits—the verbal jousting, the bedroom antics. MacNamara kept her on her toes.

"Oh, what the hell! You amuse me," she said.

"Super, then it's a done deal. You probably want to know what I plan to do with the information you generously provided."

"I might be a tad curious."

"Let's just say I will avenge my paramour's hurt feelings. Atherton will be sorry he messed with you, my poor little 'Senior.'"

Gillian smiled. Here was a man who could teach her a trick or two about life's lessons.

Chapter Twenty

1

With Barry banished to the guest suite, Bunny spent most of her time in seclusion within her master bedroom. She missed everything about Lucy—her smile, her outgoing nature. Bunny felt a void within, burning with sorrow.

"You can't hibernate in there, forever," Barry yelled at the door. "At least let me know you're alive. Say something."

She wished she had died with Lucy. It would have been better than trying to fight tears and overwhelming sadness.

"Open up the door, Bunny. I'll break it down if you don't."

"Go away," she said weakly. "Leave me alone. Haven't you done enough destruction?"

He was relieved to hear her voice. There had been a few signs of her presence around the house. She had left unwashed dishes in the kitchen, and she had eaten food he had left for her in the refrigerator.

"Do you want Chinese or Mexican for dinner?

There was no reply from the bedroom. "I know you sneak out of your hole when I'm gone. Bunny, please open the door. We need to talk."

"No!"

"Suit yourself. I'm off to work. You can reach me at EPIK, should you need to contact me." He heard her grumble something. Even if she did not want to see him, he was pleased she spoke to him through the door. It was a start. Bunny would eventually resurface and snap out of it.

He pulled out of the driveway and accidentally ran over the morning newspaper. "Shit. Why do they always leave it in the middle of the driveway?"

Barry climbed out of his car to retrieve the paper and threw it up against the house. He noticed a faint vanilla and chocolate aroma in the air, almost masked by tobacco smoke. There was something familiar about the smell. It will come to me, he thought.

Hidden behind a tree on the property, Simon watched Barry drive off in his Mercedes. He smoked down to the gold filter before extinguishing it against the tree's bark. He glanced down at his watch. In five minutes, Bunny would come out of the house to pick up the paper. This job was going to be easier than he had thought. Her strict routine made it simple for him to decide when to perform his task.

Out she came. She paused, stared in his direction, and retreated into the house. She had conveyed a message to him! Beautiful, silent, and mysterious Bunny, you know that I have come for you. I will eliminate your sadness in time, but I intend to save the best for last.

2

Board participants made their way into EPIK's conference room. The few token players left from EPIK's previous Board sat together; Anexa's representation outnumbered them 2-1.

Atherton looked at his watch. It was 8:15 a.m. Where was MacNamara?

"Do you think he's coming?" asked Murray quietly.

"He'd better. Unfortunately, we can't start without him."

Priscilla, tired of waiting, decided to open the meeting. She addressed Atherton. "While we wait for Mac, why don't you list the items you want *us* to review?"

"Let's wait for MacNamara," he cut her off abruptly.

Priscilla blinked behind a Botox expression, crossed her long legs, and shifted in her seat. "There's no need to feel threatened. We're all *friends* here," she responded, examining the sleeve of her bright yellow power suit.

"Cut it out, Priscilla," said Barry.

She smiled and looked over at him.

MacNamara casually entered the meeting room. He went straight to the refreshment table, helped himself to fruit and pastries, and poured a coffee. "I don't have all day to play around so make this meeting quick," he announced.

Barry and Priscilla glanced at each other confused at their boss's statement. This was supposed to be an all-day meeting. Murray and Atherton exchanged confused looks, too.

"We have important business to attend to back at Anexa," said MacNamara, picking up an iced pastry and taking a large bite.

Priscilla jumped in. "We can't afford to dwell on topics. Since the agenda is open-ended, why don't we aim to finish by 7 p.m.?"

"We need to stay as long as it takes," said Montgomery. "Even if it means an all-nighter."

Priscilla pressed her lips together and curled up the corners of her mouth. Her menacing smile communicated, "Die Montgomery." He was so transparent. She knew he was still bitter that she had evicted him from his office.

"Our aim is to cover only relevant issues today. Time is important for everyone," said Atherton, addressing the group. "The first topic we need to tackle is communication. We are one company, and it is essential we communicate as if we are one entity. Only joint decisions should be communicated out to the employees."

"You have my support," said MacNamara. "Next item, please." He picked at the watermelon seeds on his fruit slice.

"There's more to it. Specifically, we need to address communication between our management teams. For example, both groups can't simultaneously create implementation teams, strategic plans, etcetera."

"Well, someone had to take the initiative," said Priscilla. "Diana Roberts's group was instrumental in getting our implementation teams lined up."

"That's what we are talking about," interjected Murray. "Let's create a proper implementation team, utilizing skill sets from both organizations. Also, we need an experienced project leader and someone who is neutral. Diana Roberts is not an appropriate choice."

"So, we hire someone from one of the big six consulting firms to lead the way," said Barry. "Roberts can work alongside this person."

"Fine," said Atherton. "She's not the only one who will benefit from learning from an experienced project leader. A number of our employees haven't been through a merger before, so it'll be a real eye-opener for them."

Barry watched MacNamara continue to eat, seemingly obvious to the discussion. "Sounds like a good plan. Anexa wants this project to go smoothly. I can think of several names to submit for this role," said Barry.

"Great. Schedule candidate interviews in the upcoming week," said Atherton. "Murray, I believe you also have some names to put forward?" It was important to find a candidate acceptable to both teams. Even more imperative was the need for this person to possess skills flexible enough to accommodate Anexa's methodical and mechanical approach together with EPIK's creative flair.

"Let's discuss the topic of eviction," said Montgomery.

"I was wondering when you were going to bring that up," said Priscilla. "Yes, I agree, let's talk about rank and order."

"I move for a motion to freeze headcount and promotions in both organizations until both companies are fully integrated," said Murray.

"I agree," seconded Barry. MacNamara's promotion of Priscilla over him was still a sore point.

MacNamara smugly looked over at Priscilla. "We got your promotion in, just in the nick of time."

Not to appear outwitted, Atherton spoke up. "We are pleased about Priscilla's promotion and hope you will support our rehiring of Cam Phillips."

"In what capacity? He's useless," said MacNamara. He dropped his plate. It crashed by his foot. Mac hopped away from the debis.

"Yeah. Why would you want him back," asked Barry, staring at the mess left on the floor.

"His services on the R&D front are valuable for our technology team," added Atherton.

MacNamara winced. It wasn't worth the effort to fight about Phillips. Sooner or later he would eliminate both of them, anyway. "Whatever, just keep him out of my sight."

MacNamara's subdued reaction surprised Priscilla. "Cam Phillips was a traitor. I hardly think rehiring him shows good judgment or morality."

"Good judgment was neglected when the COO position was granted," said Montgomery. He enjoyed watching her squirm as her every statement was squashed or ignored.

"Is there anything else?" asked MacNamara impatiently. He rubbed his head. The pounding pressure was going to make it impossible for him to sit through the entire meeting.

Barry noticed his discomfort and called for a ten-minute break. MacNamara went into the men's room. He splashed cold water on his drawn, ashen face. He wiped the moisture from his forehead and found his bottle of painkillers.

"You look like shit," said Barry.

"I've got to stop bonking all those whores," replied MacNamara. "Between Gillian the pro and Priscilla the ice princess, I'm shagged out. I don't how you manage to survive *your* active sexcapades."

"Viagra and cocaine," joked Barry. "It'll work magic on your chopper. Let's get serious for a minute, Mac. You need to go home, get some rest, and call the doctor."

MacNamara agreed. His pain was excruciating, if not unbearable. "I need to lie down and sleep this bitch off. Man, I'm grateful for those pills you gave me. They seem to help out."

"Let me drive you home," offered Barry.

"No, I can manage. I want you and Priscilla to finish the meeting for me. I trust you to handle things. Watch out for that bastard Murray. He could spell trouble for us. One more thing, make sure they keep next week's Town Hall meeting on the calendar."

Barry suspected MacNamara's headaches were the symptom of something serious. Their increased intensity and frequency were warnings. If the headaches were the cause of his crazed behavior, it was essential to get him medical help. From the look of things, even the painkillers seemed ineffective in relieving his searing pain.

"Where's Mac?" asked Priscilla when Barry rejoined the meeting.

"I'm afraid he's taken ill and has gone home."

"Bad timing," said Atherton. "We needed his input to resolve several matters."

"I have his power of attorney to do just that," said Barry. "Gentlemen, shall we continue?"

Priscilla coughed. Barry ignored her.

"There have been rumors circulating referring to the relocation of the companies and possible headcount reduction plans," said Murray.

"That's stupid. I wonder where they came from?" asked Priscilla.

"From the Anexa camp, no doubt. Everyone knows MacNamara's history on streamlining the headcount," retorted Montgomery.

"Come on you two. Let's work together," said Atherton. He was pleased Montgomery understood, finally, what he had been saying all along, that this merger was not going to be as easy as it looked on paper.

"There's no reason to look into buying other buildings for the company. I believe we can use the existing premises," said Barry.

"I like that," said Atherton. "And about the headcount rumors, I want to quash those immediately. I have the perfect forum to do just that—EPIK's next Town Hall meeting."

"Okay. We would like MacNamara to participate in that session. He could answer any questions regarding Anexa. Also, I know he's keen to say a few words. You know, to introduce himself," said Barry.

"An introduction is fine, anything else I would prefer to handle," said Atherton.

"I'll have to check with him if that's acceptable," said Priscilla. She looked at Atherton. "You did say that we were one company. Shouldn't we act like one and give Mac the opportunity to speak?" asked Priscilla. She was beginning to annoy everyone in the meeting.

"Priscilla, Atherton's idea is fine. We need the Anexa folks to back down. Our cultures are too distinct, at this time, to force our ideals on them," said Barry. He ignored the dirty look coming from her.

The more Barry spoke, the more Atherton liked his approach. It was too bad he had to deal exclusively with MacNamara. "We are making excellent progress gentlemen."

Priscilla was furious that she had been left out of the decision-making process. Just wait until Mac heard about her unfair treatment. He wouldn't like that at all, she thought.

3

After the meeting concluded, Barry called MacNamara at home. Tamara told him that he was not there.

"Strange," said Barry. "He was really sick when he left the EPIK offices. I was sure that he would be at home in bed."

"Let me guess, another headache?"

"Yeah. I don't have to tell you that he's not very well."

"*You* try to get him to see a doctor. He refuses to seek any medical attention I've recommended."

"I've tried."

"Get his new mistress to suggest a medical visit. Let her look after him," she said bitterly, ending the conversation.

Barry laughed. Which one?

4

MacNamara spent his day off enjoying himself. He deserved to have some free time. His first stop was at Gillian's place for a quick nap and brunch. She knew how to take care of him and fulfilled his every whim.

"You need another head and neck massage," she suggested, the minute he walked into her apartment.

"You *are* a worthwhile investment." He collapsed on her couch. "Fix me up, baby."

After she finished manipulating his pressure points, she ran a hot mineral bath for him, and let him relax in it for thirty minutes.

He emerged feeling relieved. "I feel wonderful!" he announced. "Let me do something for you. Hand me the phone." He dialed EPIK and asked to speak to Carl Swan.

Carl answered. "This is Carl."

"I know something about your daddy," said MacNamara.

"Who's this?"

MacNamara continued his charade. "Your momma lied to you. Go on, ask her about her lies. As they say in Greek, *eisai bastardos*, you're a bastard."

"What's this all about?" Carl demanded, but the line was already dead.

Gillian appeared satisfied. "Nice work...all the elements of a Greek tragedy."

"I'm glad you liked it. Consider it the harbinger of things to come. Listen to this," he said, dialing another number. "Oh yippee! It's ringing!"

"Who are you calling?"

"The bastard's mother." He danced around the room holding the receiver up to his cheek, swaying his body from side to side. Gillian, immune to his bursts of madness, sat back, thoroughly amused. He stopped his euphoric routine, abruptly, when Martha answered the phone.

"Hello."

"Hello, Mumsie. How are you today?" MacNamara played on.

"Excuse me? Who *is* this?"

"How amusing. That's the same thing your son said. Well actually, he said, 'Who's this? What's this all about?' I stand corrected."

Martha thought about hanging up the phone but hesitated when the caller mentioned Carl. "Is there a point to this call?" she asked.

"Questions, questions. What is it with you people? A man deserves simple, straightforward conversation."

"I don't understand what you mean. I'm hanging up. Don't bother calling back, because I won't answer it." Martha was confused and irritated by the caller. Crank callers were getting weirder and weirder.

"Carl had a dream last night. He spoke the words, *to haima nero den ginetai*."

Martha froze. What did this person know about Carl's dreams? "I'm listening," she said.

MacNamara was pleased with the reaction he had stirred up. "*To haima nero den ginetai*," he said. "Blood is thicker than water."

She swallowed hard. "What do you know?"

"Everything," said the caller, before disconnecting.

Gillian burst into peals of laughter. "Oh my God, that was so naughty! So evil of you!"

"That was nothing. The real fireworks commence, when I host EPIK's Town Hall meeting. Free up your calendar, because I want you there to witness the whole thing."

"I wouldn't miss it for the world."

5

MacNamara's next appointment was to meet Harvey.

"How's my three mil investment?" asked MacNamara.

"Dividends are due out in a few days," replied Harvey.

"Great. When this is all behind us, I want to take you to California for a Harley weekend. Just you, Barry, and me."

Harvey looked puzzled. MacNamara was planning to eliminate Barry's wife, yet he wanted to include him on a boys' weekend away. "Is Barry in on it?"

"Nah. I'm doing him a favor like any good buddy would do. You could say he reaps the benefits without harboring any associated guilt."

"I see." MacNamara was really nuts, but it didn't matter. He liked his boss for his money, not his personality. "Friends like you are a rare breed nowadays."

"Yes, they are!" said MacNamara, giving Harvey a slap across his back.

Chapter Twenty-one

1

Back at Central Park West, Priscilla continued to scream at Barry, as he tried to explain his actions at the Board meeting.

"You trashed me in front of everyone. Not once did you support me!" Her arms flailed wildly around her head.

"You're blowing this way out of proportion," said Barry.

"If Mac was in his right mind, he would not have stood for any of that shit."

Barry agreed with her. "The point is Mac is not in his right mind, and we both know it. You knew that when you finagled your way into the COO position."

"Oh, what the fuck!" The way she bit down on her lower lip, to pronounce the f sound, exacerbated her overbite. "We all use each other, from time to time."

"You're certainly the master at that game. I hate to think how many people you screwed to get where you are today. I was foolish to get involved with you."

"Grow up, you big baby. What was I going to do with a married man? We both got what we wanted out of the arrangement."

"Look Priscilla, I didn't come here to upset you or to argue. My intention was to discuss Mac's declining mental state."

"Liar," she said bitterly. "You came here to gloat. You fucked me over in the meeting! I saw the way everyone was receptive to your ideas. You hid behind your thin backbone very well!"

"Shut up, bitch," he said angrily, before grabbing her by the throat. "I've heard enough. You're like a rabid Rottweiler who latches on and won't let go."

She had pushed him too far. That was it. Barry was tired of trying to appease her. He held her around the neck, only releasing her when he realized she was enjoying it. "You're one sick woman." He picked up his coat and reached the door before she stopped him.

"How about one for old times' sake," she said, rubbing her neck. "That's the least you could do for me after today's meeting."

"Would you shut up about the goddamn meeting? I've had enough of your ranting."

"Barry, don't make me beg for it."

"You want some fucking? Fine. I'll give you some action you'll never forget." As he ripped open her silk blouse exposing her braless breasts, she threw her head back and moaned. He squeezed her nipples roughly, bit her shoulder, and grabbed her long hair in one hand.

"Promise that you'll do, *the thing*," she pleaded. "You know, the neck thing—right as I come."

Barry carried her back to her bedroom and threw her across the bed. He took off his tie and wrapped it around her eyes, creating a blindfold. "Don't move," he commanded, wrapping his belt around her wrists. Barry was ready. "If you're good, Daddy will choke you until you come."

2

There was something perverse about watching two people having sex. Worse was becoming aroused as a voyeur. Simon scolded himself for putting himself in a situation where he fell into this category. Abstinence was a religion to him. The more he denied himself sexual gratification, the more powerful and invincible he felt. Witnessing their morbid pleasure was a problem to him in his uncontaminated world. There was only one way out of this, to allow him to reserve his energies and powers. Eliminate the problem, he told himself. It would absolve his peccadillo while fulfilling his contractual agreement.

3

"Did you hear something outside?" asked Priscilla, coming out of her pleasured state.

"No," said Barry, "my phone just buzzed." He reached for it and saw his home number flash on the display. "That's weird." Bunny was still avoiding him, so it was strange she would call.

"What's weird?"

ACQUISITION OF POWER

"Oh, nothing," he lied. "Let me take this call while I freshen up. When I return, I'll release your hands." He retreated into the bathroom, closed the door, and ran the water. He did not want Priscilla listening to his conversation. "Hey, I thought you were still incommunicado," he told Bunny.

"Someone was lurking around the house, earlier" said Bunny. "I need you to come home tonight. I'm scared."

"You're probably seeing things, Bunny. I would be, too, if I had locked myself away in the bedroom. Keep the house alarm set. It will put your mind at ease."

"I know what I saw. You have to come home." Her voice sounded strained. It was unlike Bunny to fear anything or anyone.

"Okay, I'm on my way," he said reassuringly.

Barry crept back into the bedroom and looked at Priscilla's naked body. No matter how many times he saw her nude, the sight of her manufactured body aroused him. Save the replay for another time, he thought, reprioritizing his needs. Bunny required him more than he needed another session with Priscilla. In his haste to dress, he forgot to pick up his wallet, which had fallen to the floor during their activities.

"Aren't you forgetting something?" she asked. "Release me, you pig."

"Oh yeah," he said suddenly distracted by her harsh tone. As he freed her hands, she stirred slightly. He left her blindfold in place. "I have to go. You can return my tie another time."

"I think I'll just keep it on a little longer. To savor the moment…"

"Suit yourself," he said in haste, letting himself out of her townhouse. Behind him, the door's latch caught against the ill-fitting frame, leaving the door ajar.

Sitting on top of Priscilla's back garden wall, Simon viewed Barry through her shutterless bedroom window. When Barry had dressed and left the bedroom, Simon jumped off the wall. He waited in the alley for Barry to drive off.

"Naughty Mr. Moore, the company you keep will bring you down," he whispered, approaching the front door. Simon extinguished his cigarette against the door and was surprised when it pushed open. How about that, thought Simon, what an easy job! He entered Priscilla's bedroom. She started to moan.

"Oooo, back for more, huh?" she teased. "It's a good thing I kept my blindfold on."

"Mmmm," replied Simon, straddling her naked body. He choked her and watched her exultant expression. He had not killed anyone who had looked as happy as they reached death. Priscilla had passed out so often from her dangerous pleasures that she never considered her passion fatal. This time, Simon was only too happy to oblige her in reaching a new, ultimate high.

4

"Ah, shit," mumbled Barry, realizing his wallet was missing. He turned the car around and dialed Priscilla's number. "Come on, pick up the phone cunt." The answering machine switched on. "Priscilla, I'm on my way back over. Find my wallet, will you? I'll be there in about twenty minutes."

Simon gazed upon Priscilla lifeless body. He finished another cigarette. She looked peaceful. "You were a bad girl today," he told her. "You almost got me into trouble with your sordid activities. My psyche is not allowed to witness such depravity."

He cocked his head to one side, waiting for an answer. After a few moments, Simon got up and finished his work. He removed the answering machine's tape and pocketed it with Barry's wallet. They might come in handy, he thought.

5

"Did you find it?" inquired Barry as he entered Priscilla's bedroom. "Hey, didn't you hear my message?"

Her body remained motionless, resting in the same position it had been before he had left her house. He smelled the scent of vanilla candles. She must have lit one after their session, then fallen asleep. No wonder she had not answered the phone. Such a sound siesta! He left her alone, to sleep in peace, while he searched for his wallet.

After checking under the bed, in the bathroom, and on her bedside table, he decided to wake Priscilla for assistance. "Priscilla, I need your help." He poked her arm, repeating his request. "Come on, get up."

When she did not move, he noticed she was not breathing. "Oh my God, what have I done?" He frantically felt at her neck for a pulse. "Priscilla, wake up! Come on, wake up!"

Oh, dear God, he thought. Was she dead? She was alive when I left. Damn her and her sick sex games. It was all her fault! He was in real trouble, this time. If he called the police, they would arrest him for murder. There was no way he was going back to prison. What was he going to do? He had to call someone but whom could he trust?

"I fucked up," Barry told MacNamara over his cell phone.

"I know," he replied, ominously. "Did anyone see you come in?"

"I don't know. My car is right outside, and I can't find my wallet anywhere." Barry was frantic. He stared at Priscilla's corpse. "Mac she's dead!"

"*Kalo ksefortoma*," said MacNamara in Greek. "Good riddance."

"What? How can you say that at a time like this?"

"What's done is done," said MacNamara evenly.

"But I didn't do it!"

"Of course, you didn't." MacNamara sounded very matter-of-fact. "Listen to me, calm down."

"Jesus, I'm looking at her fucking dead body! How can I calm down?"

"Barry, don't look at her. Look away! I want you to wipe any surface you might have touched and drive over to my house, immediately."

"What about my wallet?" he said desperately.

"Not to worry, friends look after friends."

That was just what worried Barry. Friends look after friends. What did Mac know about Priscilla's death? Was he trying to set him up? MacNamara's behavior was peculiar. Surely it did not extend to committing acts of murder.

On the way out, Barry neglected to notice Priscilla's faulty door catch. Only this time, her front door did not remain partly closed, it swung wide open.

6

To Harvey, smoking was more a social habit than a physical one. On the odd occasion, when he needed a cigarette, he bummed one from a companion. Simon was generous to him with his expensive treats but would have been appalled to have known Harvey had amassed a large collection from him, stashing them away in cheap, plastic sandwich bags.

"Would you like a smoke?" Harvey asked MacNamara. Harvey opened the plastic zipper, carefully examining his collected loot, before choosing a vanilla cigarette.

"No thank you. I don't indulge in addictive behaviors. But please, don't let me prevent you from enjoying your moment."

"Thank you, sir. Would you like an update on our progress?"

"Yes, please. Barry just called from Priscilla's. He's in quite a state."

"That's unfortunate."

"Indeed. More unfortunate was his misplacement of his wallet. I hope your guy picked it up."

Harvey had planned to keep quiet about the wallet and answering machine tape. Simon's finds would have provided excellent blackmail material against Barry. Harvey rethought, when he reconsidered how fond MacNamara was of Barry.

"Fortunately for your friend, my guy picked up both his wallet and an answering machine tape recording of his voice. Both items would have placed him at the crime scene, if we hadn't recovered them," said Harvey.

MacNamara was pleased. "Good. I want the tape and wallet as soon as you get them. What's the status of our second lady problem?"

"It's arranged for tomorrow. His wife follows a set routine, so it won't be a problem to complete the task."

"I see. Barry will accompany me to an important meeting at EPIK tomorrow afternoon. Pass that along to your *amigo*."

"Okay."

"Disappear before my friend Barry gets here."

7

When Barry arrived at *Windermere*, a smell lingered in MacNamara's study. It was the second time that the odor triggered something. Think, Barry think! It was so familiar. Damn, where was it from?

"I've saved your ass," said MacNamara casually.

"Come again? Explain that to me."

"Thanks to me, you'll have your wallet back not to mention an answering machine tape. It was foolish of you to forget your wallet at Priscilla's. As for the message you left on her answering machine…what bad timing!"

MacNamara had been there, thought Barry. Mac must have finished her off as soon as he had left.

"You bastard, how could you do this to me? You killed her and let me believe that I did it!"

"Come, come now," said MacNamara. "I did not say you killed her, and I certainly didn't."

"All right, well what's all this *good riddance* talk about? And how did you get my wallet?"

"I can't exactly say."

"I knew it. Do you realize that you will rot in jail for the rest of your life? You have to call the police and confess."

"Nope. That's not part of my agenda."

"What fucking agenda? There's a dead woman strangled in her bed, and you don't seem to care about it."

"I know how she was killed, and I'm sure you can figure it out."

"Stop the bullshit, MacNamara."

"All of this screaming is going to give me another migraine. Barry we're in this together. Be grateful, I cleaned up after you."

"You're fucking crazy," said Barry.

"So that's the thanks I get?"

"If you don't call the cops, then I will."

"And tell them what? That you tied up your former girlfriend, blindfolded her with your tie, got carried away fucking her, and strangled her to death? Yeah, that charming scene will play out real well for you."

"I forgot about the tie," said Barry somberly. "I'm really screwed." He watched MacNamara closely. "Why didn't *you* get it, at the same time you picked up my wallet and the tape?"

MacNamara stared blankly at Barry. "I'll arrange for someone to get it before anyone discovers the body."

"And why would you do that for me?" asked Barry. MacNamara must have something to gain from this cover up, concluded Barry.

"Because I love you like a brother. You're my family. It's my responsibility to take care you." It was the least MacNamara could do for him. He felt a tad guilty about arranging to terminate Bunny, even if it was best for both of them. Barry could do better than her. As for Priscilla, she was not right for him, either. What he needed was a real woman, someone like his Gillian.

"I'm not buying any of that family rubbish. You want something."

"The only thing I want from you is to accompany me to EPIK tomorrow, for the Town Hall meeting. I have a surprise planned for the folks."

MacNamara was not prepared to divulge his true plan. It was up to Barry to follow him closely.

"What about Priscilla?" asked Barry.

"What about her? It's not like she's cold or anything. The old trout will be fine just where she is."

"Show some emotion or respect, Mac. You slept with her!"

"If you think she cared for either of us, then think again! Her type was devoid of compassion."

Chapter Twenty-two

1

By a strange twist of fate, the news of Priscilla's death resurrected Bunny's interest in her husband's life. "I'm sorry about your friend," she offered, knowing Barry and Priscilla had had an affair.

Barry nodded.

Bunny scanned the story for a second time and pointed to the section detailing the murder.

"The newspaper reports that a neighbor was concerned seeing the front door open at night—there was no sign of a struggle—and she was strangled to death with a tie."

"Let me see that!" MacNamara obviously had not retrieved the tie.

"Here, read it for yourself." She pushed the newspaper towards Barry.

He felt sick looking at the black-and-white photograph of Priscilla, which had accompanied the article. The caption under the picture read: Anexa COO murdered.

Even in death, her eyes taunted him: you're a loser, Barry.

He pushed the article away.

"It's all very strange, if you ask me," said Bunny. "My guess is that she was killed by her lover."

"No one is asking you for your theories."

"It wasn't too long ago you shared her bed."

He was pissed at her insinuation. "She was fucking Mac, if you really want to know."

"Interesting—you sure you didn't share a *ménage à trois* with them? It wouldn't surprise me."

"If you're implying something, you're wrong. Don't forget I was here, looking out for your boogieman. Remember your frantic call?"

"Yes, but you did take a long time to get here."

"So I fucked Priscilla, strangled her, drove around, and came home. Is that what you want to hear?" He looked emotionally drained. She knew Barry was incapable of murder, he was too weak, but she did not grant MacNamara that same amnesty. His involvement in Lucy's death was proof enough that he was capable of anything.

Bunny reached for the coffee and poured herself another cup. "More caffeine, dear? I suspect you're in for another long day."

2

Montgomery, Murray, and Carl gathered around Atherton's meeting table to read the report of Priscilla's death in the newspaper.

"Horrible," said Murray. "Poor lady."

"She probably got what she deserved," said Montgomery. "And I can get my office back."

Atherton looked up from his computer terminal to express his disgust at Montgomery's callousness. "She may have been difficult. Is that reason enough for someone to kill her? Priscilla Meyers was part of our company."

"It says that she practiced something called autoerotic asphyxiation and was found blindfolded with a Hermès tie," said Carl. He looked at Atherton. "Hey boss, you're a Hermès man."

Everyone, except Atherton, laughed. "Funny," he said. Atherton hoped his sarcasm told them that he had had enough of their childish discussion. "I called you guys here to discuss the email MacNamara sent to the employees, not to speculate on, or dissect, the Priscilla Meyers tragedy."

"What email?" asked Montgomery.

"You twit, where have you been? The one discussing this afternoon's Town Hall meeting. He copied everyone on the email distribution list," said Murray.

Carl handed out copies of the email to the group. Montgomery read it for the first time.

To: *Distribution list 1—all EPIK employees;*
              Distribution list 2—all Anexa employees;
From: *Dean MacNamara*
Subject: *Town Hall Meeting*

I have accepted the kind invitation of James Atherton to address the EPIK employees at this afternoon's Town Hall meeting. Employees will have the opportunity to hear the new company vision, objectives, and to voice any concerns or questions to me.

Anexa employees will have their own meeting next Monday, where we will repeat the same meeting format.

Join me today at 2 p.m. in Meeting Room six. Goodies provided.

Atherton pressed down on the intercom. "Candice, please get Barry Moore.

"I'll buzz you as soon as I have him on the line," she responded.

"We've been hoodwinked," said Montgomery.

"Looks like we need to put some damage control in place, right away," said Carl.

"Yeah, that's what I meant to say," said Montgomery.

"Sure," said Murray. Montgomery's worthless attempt to contribute something meaningful to the conversation really pissed him off. How he had lasted this long in the company was incomprehensible. The only reason he was still around was because he was one of Atherton's university buddies. He hoped the new Board would offer Montgomery *the package*, the sooner the better.

Candice buzzed. "Mr. Moore is on line one."

"Hello there," said Barry. "You caught me on my mobile phone. I'm stuck in traffic. I hope the connection remains clear. One never knows when the service will cut out—damn Anexa technology."

"Barry, we agreed MacNamara was only going to have an introduction at the Town Hall meeting," said Atherton. "Not run it."

"That's true," replied Barry.

"Then what do you make of his latest email?" asked Murray. "You haven't seen it yet?"

"No, like I said, I'm stuck in traffic. Read it to me." Work issues were the last thing on his mind.

As Atherton read the email message, Barry winced. MacNamara appeared to have been in full agreement when they had discussed details of the last Board meeting. Now anything seemed possible.

"Mac has been under the weather recently," offered Barry. "He probably forgot you were supposed to address your staff."

"Bullshit," said Montgomery. "This stinks of a setup."

"Atherton, give him his fifteen minutes of glory. What harm can he do by answering some questions from the audience anyway? It will appear that you support his attempts to reach out to the employees. Otherwise, if you pull the plug, the reaction could be unfavorable. The ANEXA employees will view it as a snub, while the EPIK people will not understand your lack of hospitality. We should show some togetherness," said Barry.

"In theory, I would agree with you. However, Mac's history of unpredictability makes it something of a risk," said Atherton. "Let me confer with my team. I'll call you back."

"Fine. I'm not going anywhere."

"It's a trap," said Montgomery. "Don't even consider it. Look what that Meyers cunt did to me."

"Are you still going on about your office? Shut up about that! I'm sick of hearing about it!" shouted Murray.

Carl joined into the conversation. "Barry has some valid points. It will not hurt you to allow him to introduce himself to the EPIK employees. Most of them are a little curious, anyway."

"If you can control the meeting's format, I don't think it's such a bad idea," said Murray.

"The problem will be controlling MacNamara," said Atherton.

"If you don't think you can handle him, then don't do it," said Montgomery.

"I didn't say I couldn't," said Atherton, dryly. MacNamara had orchestrated this whole thing. MacNamara had cornered him and expected him to back down from the challenge. "Okay, I'll call MacNamara and let him know that we agree to his participation, with some added conditions."

"You mean restraints," said Murray.

"I hope it doesn't come to that," said Atherton.

3

In the war room, Carl found Diana sitting behind her terminal. She was alone. Her staff had been instructed to go back to their prior duties at Anexa.

She looked up from her email, shaking her head as she finished reading MacNamara's blanket-email. "I still can't believe the madman has been given a freeform forum." Didn't EPIK management know he was a loose cannon, capable of anything? His appearance was likely to cause a commotion.

"MacNamara didn't give EPIK much of a choice. His email went out to everyone, without approval from the guys upstairs," said Carl. "They were forced to allow it, otherwise it would look like they were opposing the Anexa management."

"Surprise," she said. "Whoever gave him access to EPIK's email distribution list is in for some trouble, huh?"

"I doubt it. Besides, I would have thought your war room crew would have handled security procedures, computer access, and whatnot." Carl liked teasing her and watching her turn serious.

"The war room antics are frozen until further notice. My rank as project leader caused some upset. I've been reassigned. I think they're going to hire a consultant type, with experience in mergers and systems implementations, to fill my position."

"Speaking of vacancies, what did you think about Priscilla Meyers's death?"

"I would rather not think about it. It's just awful."

"Did she have many enemies or lovers?" asked Carl, intrigued by the lurid sex accounts described in the newspapers.

"How would I know? I was just a flunky to her," she said bitterly. Priscilla had used her. It was likely Diana had not been the only victim of Priscilla's manipulation. Perhaps, Priscilla had finally met her match when she had met her end.

Carl sensed he had touched a raw nerve. "Sorry sweetie, I got carried away. I know you've had a hard time with the Anexa bunch. I won't ask anything more."

"Just remember to save me a seat this afternoon. I plan to watch the fireworks, sitting down."

4

Typical EPIK attendance for a Town Hall meeting was less than 40 percent of the total employee population. Meetings were not mandatory, and few employees showed up. Town Hall meetings were boring. Atherton and his staff talked about sales figures, stock prices, and new developments. The only interesting part of the session was when Atherton would answer employee questions—submitted in advance. Will the company sponsor a daycare center? How can someone qualify for stock options? Why are there so few women in management positions? Response to questions, like these, was the reason many employees went to Town Hall meetings.

MacNamara's email invitation provoked the EPIK staff into an overwhelming turnout. They wanted to hear what the charismatic and enigmatic leader from Anexa had to say.

"Next time I will promise free food to get this kind of turn out," Atherton told MacNamara, envious of the attention he had achieved.

"It's not the buffet that brings the masses. It's the interest in the *new man."*

"Just remember what we discussed. Stick to the agenda, or I'll pull the plug on you."

"Of course, you have my word."

"That's what I'm afraid of."

MacNamara responded in Greek, *"Pas na me trellaneis*—you're driving me crazy."

Atherton sighed. The games had begun. *"Eisai theotrellos,"* he whispered. "As the Greeks would say, you're totally insane."

"You don't have to translate it for me. I understand what you're saying, perfectly." Just wait and see what's in store for you, he thought. You'll be sorry you tried to compete with me.

Atherton emerged at the podium to greet the awaiting crowd.

MacNamara spotted Barry at the back of the room. A few people further down stood Gillian, wearing a pale pink dress. MacNamara waved, signaling both of them to join him at the front.

"Barry, this is my friend, Gillian du Monde. Gillian, this is my number one guy, Barry Moore."

Atherton's voice sounded from the stage. "I'm pleased so many of you were able to join us today. As you know, Anexa's CEO, Dean MacNamara, is here to provide an overview of Anexa's company and its technology. He will then respond to questions you've submitted in advance."

Carl circumspectly squeezed Diana's hand. MacNamara took command of the podium.

"It's show time," she said. The audience's applause died down.

MacNamara extended his hands theatrically to the crowd. "Thank you for the warm welcome. All of you share something in common with me— you love money!" The audience broke into applause for a second time.

MacNamara singled out a man towards the front of the crowd. "You, in the green shirt and jeans, what's the ANEXA share price?"

The young man shrugged his shoulders. MacNamara continued the momentum. "Can anyone tell me the Anexa share price?"

Someone in the back of the crowd shouted out an answer.

MacNamara grinned. "Yes! Give that man a raise! As of one hour ago that was the correct price, but it has changed for the better. Everyone should carry the handheld phones which made EPIK famous. You're the reason I can check my stock prices every second. You made me rich, EPIK, thank you!" He threw his EPIK phone to the green-shirted man, who had shrugged off the correct answer, moments before. "Tell me the correct price."

The young man looked embarrassed by the sudden attention but provided the new quote using the device.

"That's more like it. I hope you hold Anexa shares. Our stock will keep going up as long as we have motivated players in the companies." MacNamara refocused his address to the crowd. He visually separated the masses into thirds; speaking to each one, from left to right, then back. His oratory skills were impressive, if not mesmerizing.

"We can all use a reminder of what's important to us. Be proud of your creative product. Advertise it! Scream about it from the rooftops, if you have to. Never forget, *you* were part of this wonderful science, not your management. *You*, the people! Take pride in your appearance. The guy wearing the sloppy green clothes could not answer my question, because he did not want to get rich or succeed. This new company is about excelling and succeeding by staying alert, motivated."

It was time for Atherton to interrupt MacNamara's lecture. "Let's move on to the questions, as we usually do." The men locked eyes.

"It's things like that which hold you back—staying in the past, doing the same routines over and over. Has EPIK lost its creative edge? Change, my people...change is what it's all about! I will address only one pre-submitted question, then open up the forum for your questions. Let's get to know each other."

Atherton placed his hand over the microphone. "Your time is up, Mac."

MacNamara ignored the attempted interruption. "Atherton, or are you Senior, today...why don't we ask the audience for their opinion?" Without waiting for Atherton's response, MacNamara shouted, "My people from EPIK take control! Voice your opinion. Do you want to continue?"

The crowd, overwhelmingly, responded positively to MacNamara's encouragement.

"See? They want to hear me," said MacNamara, taking back the microphone. "Let's answer the submitted question. It asks: 'Will there be a layoff?' Simple. Those of you who have read about companies which I've acquired, know that streamlining is an inevitable process. It's not just in terms of people but removal of old-fashioned rules and procedures. I like efficient, profitable companies, operated by excellent personnel. Only dregs will be streamlined out, such as the deadbeat in the green shirt and jeans, who doesn't seem to care about making money. Remember, *greed is good*."

Atherton and Murray exchanged worried glances. This meeting was headed in the wrong direction.

"I want the next question to come from the audience."

A young woman raised her hand. "What's your feeling about women's leadership programs?"

"I promote and reward people based on performance. Race, religion, or sex don't receive special attention. If you compare the number of women in executive positions at Anexa, versus EPIK, then you will see that our numbers are higher because of mentoring programs and an aggressive recruiting department."

"He's on a roll," said Diana. "An impressive speech."

Carl confirmed her statement. "I've got to hand it to him, some things make sense."

Diana nudged him. "Don't be naïve. None of this is real."

"Anyone else?" asked MacNamara. "I have time for two more questions."

"I have a question," said Montgomery. He was standing to the right of the podium, resting against the wall.

MacNamara turned to face him. "A question from the *old* management team. Ask away."

"By what means will you merge and control both companies' distinctive cultures?" asked Murray.

"Great question. It's not something I can answer in less than a minute. Let me just say that, although our company styles are very different, I believe they will complement each other in the end."

"He's pretty slick," Murray whispered to Atherton.

"Folks, time for one last question," boomed MacNamara, enjoying his moment.

"What about nepotism?" An anonymous male's voice sounded through the room.

"Oh God," said Murray. "He's been planted in the audience. He's not from EPIK."

"Are you sure?" asked Atherton.

"Yes," said Murray.

MacNamara nodded in response to the question. "The answer I just provided covers that question, but I would add that at Anexa you wouldn't have the CEO hiring his son as his assistant."

Carl heard a voice mutter behind him. "So that's why he got the job. No wonder it wasn't posted up on the job notice board."

Diana looked at Carl's expression. His stunned face stared at Atherton who in turn stared back. Could it be true? Was Carl really Atherton's son?

"Carl?" she asked. He remained silent. She looked around her. The surprised crowd was murmuring. Her attention was drawn to MacNamara's escorts. His legal sidekick appeared startled, but the redheaded woman smiled broadly.

Gillian was pleased. MacNamara had put on an excellent show. He had given Atherton exactly what he deserved, public humiliation. She hoped Atherton would see her with Mac, so she could wave and smile.

MacNamara finished his address. "Thank you for your participation and attendance, today. I look forward to working with you. Now, back to the other guy. He'll officially, close the meeting." MacNamara walked to his entourage, avoiding eye contact with Atherton.

"How about that, my sweet?" MacNamara asked Gillian.

"I loved it," she replied, satisfied.

"What about you, Barry?" he asked, seeking the same approval.

Barry started to reply. MacNamara gasped strangely. His eyes rolled back. His body collapsed to the floor and twitched.

Gillian screamed. "Someone call an ambulance! He's having a seizure."

"Everyone back away," ordered Barry. "Give him room." He bent over MacNamara to perform CPR but needed help to remove MacNamara's jacket. "Gillian, help me get this thing off."

As they opened up his jacket, two pictures fell out. One was of Priscilla, which had been defaced by a black **X** across it. The other photograph displayed a mousy woman, with the words "You're Next" written across her face.

"Bastard!" said Barry, recognizing Bunny's sad face. He snatched the photograph, jumped up, pushed people from his path, and ran to the exit. He had to find her before it was too late.

5

When Barry fled, Atherton took over CPR on MacNamara's unconscious body. He tore away at MacNamara's dress shirt. He pumped furiously on MacNamara chest, trying to bring life back to the dormant body.

"Breathe, Mac, breathe," pleaded Atherton. He gasped heavily, as he worked on MacNamara's chest. "Don't die like this, you bastard," he muttered, oblivious to the gathering crowd.

The gawkers had to be dispersed to allow Atherton room to work. "Everyone out! This is a medical emergency!" shouted Murray. "Return to your offices immediately!"

"Save him!" Gillian cried out.

What was she doing here? Did she know MacNamara? Atherton knew if he took away one precious minute from his work on MacNamara to ask her the answers, MacNamara could die. This was not the time or place for questions.

"Where is that goddamn ambulance?" Atherton heard the desperation in his own voice. "Come on Mac! You can make it!"

Murray reassured Atherton that the ambulance was only minutes away. It felt like hours to Atherton before help did arrive.

"Sir, step aside," said the paramedic. "We can take it from here." They strapped MacNamara on to a stretcher.

Atherton wiped the sweat from his face. "Will he be okay?"

"Can't say," stated the medic. "But you probably helped save his life."

They transported him to the waiting ambulance. Gillian pushed her way past Atherton. "I need to ride in the ambulance with him."

"Are you family?" asked the paramedic.

"Yes," lied Gillian. "I am."

Atherton said nothing. She climbed into the ambulance. The doors closed. The sirens howled as the car drove away.

"Who was that?" Murray asked Atherton.

"I'm not quite sure, myself," he replied. The truth was he did not know the real Gillian, appearing from behind the mask.

Murray studied Atherton a moment. He was proud to work for a man like him. He knew that he would not have helped a man who had tried to destroy him. "James, you did something really important today. I don't think I could've done it, myself."

"What choice did I have? I couldn't watch him die."

Murray wondered if MacNamara would have done the same thing for Atherton, had the positions been reversed. He was tired. It was a hell of a long day and a hell of an end to it. He wanted to go home.

"I'm going to the hospital," said Atherton.

Murray was amazed by his boss's sincerity. It was an honor to work for him. "Let me go with you."

Chapter Twenty-three

1

"911 operator. Is this an emergency?"

"Yes! This is Barry Moore again. I want to know if the officers have arrived at my house. Is my wife safe?" Barry panted between sentences. He had been frantic since finding Bunny's picture.

"What is your wife's address?"

"I've gone through all that! This is the fourth call I've made to you!" he cried. "Sir, please try to remain calm…"

"Oh fuck it, I'm almost there." He threw the phone on the empty passenger seat and shifted into third gear. "Hurry up, car." Barry pulled into his driveway, running over the curb, narrowly missing his mailbox. "So much for the cops showing up," he spat.

Barry saw the side door wide open. He made his way into the kitchen. Barry inhaled the familiar smell he had noticed outside his house a few days before. It was the same smoke as at Priscilla's! Whoever had killed Priscilla was here, in his house. It certainly wasn't MacNamara. He had been left in a heap back at EPIK's headquarters.

Barry felt a sharp blow to the back of his head, then another. He blacked out.

2

Barry woke with a searing pain shooting through his head. He rubbed his eyes, trying to clear blurry images surrounding him.

"How do you feel?" asked a male voice. Barry made out a white coat and name tag. He was in the hospital.

"My fucking head throbs." Barry sat up abruptly. He remembered going into his house to find Bunny. "Where's my wife?"

Another voice spoke. "You're lucky to be alive. We arrived just in time."

"Don't keep him talking for too long. He needs rest to recuperate from his concussion." The doctor spoke softly to the other man. Barry struggled to overhear.

"What concussion? Where's Bunny?"

"Mr. Moore, I'm detective Matthews." A man came into view. He was young and wore street clothes.

"Is my wife okay?"

"Yes, she's fine, a bit shaken up, but that's to be expected. If you hadn't interrupted the hit man, she would be dead. I still don't understand why he spared your life, though. Maybe you could shed some light on that, and your involvement with Priscilla Meyers."

He was a hero! Bunny would owe her life to him. The price of his concussion was worth having her everlasting gratitude.

"Should I repeat myself?" said the officer.

"Nah, I heard you the first time. Why don't you ask Dean MacNamara about his involvement? He hired someone to kill Priscilla—and my wife."

The detective raised his eyebrows, startled by Barry's zealous statement. "Interesting."

"If you don't believe me—go and ask him!"

"I can't. He's in a coma. Following his seizure, he was taken to the hospital and diagnosed with acoustic neurinoma."

"What's that?"

"The surgeons removed an intracranial tumor. He hasn't woken up from the surgery."

How convenient of MacNamara, thought Barry. There wasn't anyone to corroborate his story. If MacNamara ever woke up, he could be a vegetable. "Is that why he began to act like a fucking lunatic?"

"Excuse me?"

"The tumor. Was it responsible for his behavior?"

"A jury will have to make that decision." The cop paused. "About the tie…the one we found on Priscilla Meyers."

"Yeah, it's mine," said Barry. "Priscilla and I had one last dance—before she was killed." He closed his eyes…prison. "I didn't kill her."

"I know."

Barry's eyes flew open. "What?"

"Mr. Le Mort confirmed your story. We arrested him at your house, just as he was about to kill your wife. He confessed to the killing, once we offered immunity for his testimony. He implicated your boss and someone called Ronnie Harvey."

"Harvey, Mac's security guy? Who's this Le Mort character? Oh, don't tell me, he was the one smoking the girlie cigarettes." Barry rubbed his head. He was off the hook! He buzzed the nurse's station, "Could someone bring me some prescription narcotics? I'm a man with a concussion. Make it quick."

"I won't keep you much longer. Why did MacNamara want to kill Priscilla and your wife?"

"God only knows—ask the coma victim."

"Rest up, Mr. Moore. You are in the clear, for now. Don't be surprised if you have to face some charges for failing to contact the police about Miss Meyers." The detective left Barry's room to find a doctor who could shed some light on MacNamara's prognosis.

A nurse brought Barry the medication he had requested. He swallowed it quickly, without drinking the water she offered.

"Mac, I hope you never wake up."

3

It was time for Atherton and Martha to pay a visit to their son. They needed to explain the revelation Carl had heard at the Town Hall meeting. Arm-in-arm they strolled through the Upper East Side and stopped in front of Carl's building. Atherton rang Carl's apartment.

"I'm scared," said Martha.

Atherton pressed his lips together. He nodded.

Through the intercom, Carl answered, "You two are the last people I want to see."

"Please, Carl," said Martha. "Let us in. I need to explain."

The door buzzed, and they went upstairs. Carl's door was open. He was sitting in a chair, arms folded across his chest. He glared at them.

"I didn't want you to find out like this," said Martha, taking off her coat.

"You knew all along, and you didn't say anything!"

Martha clutched her coat. She could see she was not welcome.

"Why?" asked Carl.

Martha struggled to find the right words.

"How could you do it to me?" Carl pointed to Atherton. "I hate that man! How can you stand there with him? He killed my sister! Your baby!"

Atherton looked confused. "I don't understand."

"Tell him mother. Tell him he's the father of Alice, too."

Martha shook her head. "James is not the father of Alice. Sadly, your stepfather was."

"More lies! Mother, I've seen Alice's birth certificate. You listed James Atherton as the father."

"Martha?" asked Atherton. "Did you do that?"

She faced Atherton. "I wanted *you* to be the father. I hated myself for conceiving a baby with a wife-beater. I put your name down when they asked me for the father's name. I was distraught. Alice was dead, so I figured, what difference did it make if I used your name instead—"

"You deserve each other. This is sick," said Carl. He stood up and turned his back to them.

"Carl, you were conceived out of pure love. Yes, James Atherton is your father."

"That makes you a whore and me a bastard."

"Carl, don't say that," said Atherton.

Carl moved over to the wall and put his head up against it. "Atherton, stay out of this. Haven't you done enough, already?"

"He didn't know he was your father, until recently," she said.

"What do you mean?" asked Carl. He spun around, intrigued.

"By the time I found out I was pregnant, James was involved with his future wife. He had every right to find someone else. I was married…I rejected James…I didn't want to burden him with my problems."

"Mo-ther," he hissed. Do you realize I slept with his wife to get back at him? Lucy Atherton was my stepmother! Oh God, this is so twisted. I don't want to hear anything else from either of you."

"Carl, please…" she said.

"Not another word!" shouted Carl. "Get out!"

They obeyed. They left without saying another word. Carl slammed the door behind them.

"I've lost my son," said Martha. Tears ran down her face. Atherton held her until she stopped crying. He helped her put her coat back on.

"Give him time, Martha. He will come around, eventually. I can't say I'm happy about the way things have turned out. At least, he knows the truth and can put some of his demons behind him."

She sniffed. "I was staying with Carl…"

"Come and stay with me. You can stay at the guesthouse until you resolve things with Carl. It's the least I can do for you. You are the mother of my son."

Martha hesitated.

"It's settled. I insist."

4

Diana paid Carl a visit; an hour after Atherton and Martha had left.

"Carl, please talk to me." pleaded Diana. "I promise it will help."

He covered his ears. "I doubt it," he responded, angrily. "Just leave me alone. I need time to think." His whole life was turned upside down. His belief system had been shattered by his mother's lie. How could he trust anyone?

Diana understood his need for support and time alone. She took his hands and held them. "Carl, know I'm here for you." She tried to hug him, but he pushed her away.

"Don't do that!" He felt confused and angry.

"I'm going to go home. Call me, if you need anything." Diana sensed his pain and anger. It was best to leave him alone, so he could work through his feelings.

"No, don't go. I need you here."

She offered a smile.

Carl returned it. He knew she was doing her best to cheer him up. None of this was her fault. It was unfair for her to receive the brunt of his anger. Carl offered an apology.

"Diana, thanks for being here. I'm sorry it has to be under these circumstances, though."

He was acting like someone had just died. Why wasn't he happy that he had a real-life father? Atherton was decent, hardworking, and successful, not to mention incredibly wealthy. Carl had it made.

"Carl, you're so lucky to have found your real father."

"I wasn't looking. I don't want him, or *anyone*, for that matter."

Diana had heard enough. He wasn't capable of listening to reason. "I'm going to give you some space. Call me, if you *need* me."

He heard the door close behind her. She was one more person he had shut out. Unfortunately, she was the most important person in his life. He knew it, the minute she left his apartment. She was right. Carl ran to the door and chased after her.

"Diana, please wait," he panted. "I've been a fool."

She stared at him not knowing what might come next—more harsh remarks, or an apology.

"You're right. I should be grateful for circumstances," he said.
"What do you mean?"
"It's time I moved on and accepted my new beginning."
"You'll make amends with Atherton?"
Didn't she understand what he was trying to say? "Diana, you're the most important thing in my life. I want to be with you, for the rest of my life." He embraced her. He was happy, for the first time in his life.

5

The aftermath following MacNamara's speech was minimal. Most EPIK employees were impressed by the ideas and concepts presented by the Anexa CEO but were taking a wait-and-see approach to what would really happen within the new company.

"I spoke to Barry. He'll be back in a month," said Murray.

This was good news. Barry was willing to work *with* the EPIK team. With luck, MacNamara's health condition would keep him away long enough for them to continue to create the new company, free from animosity.

"We have the chance to build a dynasty here," said Atherton.

"I'm sure that's what MacNamara had in mind but only for himself."

"This time, it will be done with all players involved by honest and fair means."

"What an adventure this has been," sighed Murray.

"And, it's only the beginning," replied Atherton.

6

As a wealthy patron of the hospital, Tamara MacNamara used her influence to have her comatose husband assigned to a private suite. She rearranged the room to provide Mac with the comforts of home. Pictures from his office covered the bare walls. Two overstuffed cream cotton armchairs and matching sofa, provided comfortable seating for visitors. Fluffy beige pillows were positioned carefully, on the seating. Classical music played softly in the background. She instructed the nurses to play only Bach and Vivaldi, MacNamara's favorite composers. Tamara went as far as eliminating gaudy flower arrangements, which arrived for her husband, replacing them with orchids. Only when she attempted to bring in an Oriental rug, to cover up the hard tiling, was she met with resistance. MacNamara's physician objected to the possibility of it disrupting the sterile environment, not to mention the difficulty in rolling the medical equipment over it.

Overall, Tamara was pleased by the new look. If it were not for the armed police guard outside the door, everything would have seemed perfect. She settled into one of her chairs and flipped through a fashion magazine.

Gillian walked in. "How is he doing? The doctors won't tell me anything."

Tamara, irritated by the interruption, looked up and eyed her rival. "That's because you're not family," she said coolly. "He had some sort of mass pressing on his brain. The doctors said his headaches and crazed behavior could be attributed to pressure from the growth. They operated successfully. Shortly after coming out of intensive care, he slipped into a coma."

"Any idea when he'll wake up?" Gillian missed him and hoped he would recover without any ill effects.

"The doctors don't know. As far as our lawyers are concerned, the longer he stays in the coma, the better chance they have of getting him out of the legal mess he's in." She paused for a moment. "Perhaps, the detective should talk to you about the Meyers murder and the attempt on Bunny Moore's life. You probably know more than I do about my husband's underhanded dealings."

Murder? Gillian was shocked to hear MacNamara was involved in any plot which involved killing. She had no idea he was capable of such atrocities. "I would be happy to talk to him. This is all news to me. MacNamara and I had, or should I say have, an intimate relationship. I don't know anything about his business dealings."

"You're just another one of my husband's whores. Well, I'm not paying you, so you can leave."

Gillian's body stiffened. She hated it when someone called her a paid companion, a whore. She knew she was so much more than those words implied. "I believe that the illness was responsible for Mac's actions, nothing else."

"Yes, that's what my legal team will try to prove," Tamara said, going back to her magazine.

MacNamara's lungs inhaled and exhaled so deeply that his nostrils made a wheezing sound. Gillian whipped her head around to see if he were waking up.

"He does that. Poor bastard. He probably can't hear a thing or enjoy this nice setup I've arranged," said Tamara, without looking up.

No wonder MacNamara came to me, thought Gillian. The poor guy lived with such a cold-hearted woman.

7

Vivaldi's Four Seasons filled the room.

"Gillian, I can hear you. We made such a splash at the Town Hall meeting, didn't we? I saw you smiling when I broke the news about Carl. It was *so* funny! Say something to me! Ignore the bag lady sitting in the chair! Hey, where are you going? I'm talking to you. Don't leave! Come back, Gillian, come back!"

Epilogue

At *Ma Maison*, Atherton went into his study. He closed his eyes and pictured Lucy, at the start of their marriage. She was smiling and giggling, through a sunny haze. Everything had seemed so simple back then. Lucy, did we really love each other? Lucy, did you really love me? Lucy, would you still love me if I didn't have the money, the power, or the success?

Greed is good. Greed is good. Greed is good.

"Hey old boy, why bring up the past?" asked Senior. "What's done is done. Leave it at that."

"What a surprise! I thought you only dredged up the past when it suited you."

"Me-ow," sounded Senior. "Aren't we a little touchy, tonight?"

"Senior, just this once, let me relax in peace." Atherton waited for the reply. There was none. "Good, I'm glad you left," he told his father. "Now I can collect my thoughts, in silence."

But Atherton was mistaken. Senior was still there. "I made you," said the crotchety voice.

"Made you," repeated Atherton. "Maybe—but you don't own me."

Senior snickered. "In a way, that's quite true. I certainly would have left MacNamara to die, to wither away on the floor. No heroics from me. No sir."

"That's the difference, old man. You're evil to the core. I'm not."

"Well, goody-goody gumdrops for you. Just keep patting yourself on the back. I won't do it! I think you really screwed up this time!"

"How do you figure?" asked Atherton in amazement.

"You went soft on me boy. MacNamara will be back to haunt you. Remember, *greed is good. Greed is good. Greed is good.*"

Atherton spoke up to defend his actions but realized Senior had vanished.

I did the right thing, thought Atherton. He felt so much stronger, surer of himself. Atherton had taken control.

*****

Printed in the United States
6348